MYTHS
OF OUR HUMANITY
TALES FROM FOREVER FOR TODAY

CARLOS J. RANGEL

MYTHS OF OUR HUMANITY:
TALES FROM FOREVER FOR TODAY

Rangel, Carlos J.

ISBN: 9798991567718
U.S. Library of Congress Control Number: 2024920493

Production and book design by **JumpAngel Studio** (*jumpangel.com*).

Cover design by Magdalena T. Rangel. Edition **Relatos de Tierra Firme** (*relatosdetierrafirme.com*).

All illustrations and art used with permission by their respective copyright owners. All permissions and authorizations by Museums and Galleries are fully credited on page 119.

Shield of Medusa on pages 23, 26, 27; Wreath of Victory on page 24; Serpent of the Deluge on page 27; Owl of Wisdom on page 28; Triskelion on page 29, and Zeus in his carriage, on page 97, used as permission-free images from the catalog *Magic and Mystical Symbols*, Dover Publications, Inc, Mineola, New York, 1969. Some of these same images and illustrations are also used as part of the cover art for this book. Acknowledging their usage in this page complies with the terms of usage. Sword of Vengeance on page 26 by M.T.Rangel after the Fournier Spanish cards.

OTHER BOOKS BY CARLOS J. RANGEL:

Campaign Journal 2008: A Chronicle of Vision, Hope, and Glory (2009) Transaction Publishers, New Brunswick.

La Venezuela imposible: Crónicas y reflexiones sobre democracia y libertad (2017) Alexandria Library, Miami.

Printed and distributed by Ingram/Spark.

For

Bárbara, artist,

and

Carlos, thinker.

MYTHS OF OUR HUMANITY:
TALES FROM FOREVER FOR TODAY

*"A reimagining of the longing for liberty
in our myths, tales, fables, and traditions."*

CJR

MYTHS OF OUR HUMANITY:
TALES FROM FOREVER FOR TODAY

Reviews for *MYTHS OF OUR HUMANITY*

Every culture has myths, stories passed down throughout history to make sense of the world. For the author, a Venezuelan businessman, writer, and political analyst, myths are also crucial to how a population conceives and protects democracy...

...Rangel eagerly plays with form: A Zeus vignette takes the form of a news article; another reads as a scene in a screenplay with Sandro Botticelli; a third uses an internal memo within a conservative political party... One of the most arresting sections is a gruesome comic, with an epigraph by former Venezuelan president Hugo Chavez, that uses a zombie apocalypse as metaphor for how citizens pay the price for political apathy and extremism...

The ease with which Rangel weaves ideas and struggles from centuries and millennia past into the present political landscape, both in the United States and the world beyond, has a chilling effect. But like hope, left at the bottom of Pandora's box, there is still the feeling that we can move forward, if only we heed our past.

[This book is] A vibrant play of visual art and the written word that attacks apathy and implores us to act.

The book was selected by Kirkus as one of the 100 best independent titles of 2024.

Kirkus Reviews

"*Myths Of Our Humanity*" is a wildly original literary novel that is not only exciting and fun to read but has something important to say on a crucial topic — mankind's search for freedom. Rangel has masterfully woven beautiful illustrations with myths of our shared past, from the ancient Greek Gods to the modern-day myth of Dracula, all in order to create an insightful and thought-provoking novel. No one can read this book without admiring the extraordinary talent of this author. "*Myths Of Our Humanity*" is a literary treasure.

Anne Jordan
President, Northern California Writers

VIII I

FOREWORD

"The sleep of reason produces monsters."

FRANCISCO DE GOYA Y LUCIENTES

(1799)

Francisco De Goya y Lucientes: *The Sleep Of Reason Produces Monsters, (Caprichos #43)* (1797-1799) Etching, aquatint on laid paper, 12.05 x 7.91 in. (Cat. #G002131). © Photo Archive of Museo Nacional del Prado, Madrid.

FOREWORD

A COMPLEX IDEA FORGED FROM SIMPLE ELEMENTS CONCEIVED AS AN EASY READ OF HARD PILLS TO SWALLOW.

That is how *MYTHS OF OUR HUMANITY: Tales From Forever For Today* might be described. The texts in the book rewrite old recognizable stories in contemporary form to illustrate, in a familiar manner, modern ideas focused on the underpinnings of liberal democracy. The book thus becomes an exploration of humanity's longing for liberty as embedded in our myths, tales, fables, and traditions. A hybrid creature begat from political essays intertwined with political fiction.

The book's sequential segments, its "vignettes," are accompanied by a collection of illustrations complementing the ideas in the written text. Just like the art, which is presented in multiple styles and forms, the vignettes are written in diverse styles and formats. Finally, the book was simultaneously written in English and Spanish, including both texts in the same volume, with the intention of serving both audiences of this multiverse which I straddle daily.

I owe many thanks to all those who collaborated in this project, especially the artists who contributed the accompanying artwork, the institutions which generously granted permission to reproduce masterpieces from their collections, and to Dr. Carlos Di Bonifacio, for guiding me in securing the rights to use an image from the Uffizi Galleries, in Florence. Special thanks go to my sister, Magdalena Rangel, for using her unique talents not only to contribute with two vignette illustrations but also to design the book's layout and cover, as well as assisting me in detecting typos and other such proofreading errors to which I was blind. I also owe thanks to Gemma Pineda and Mark Comstock, who also spent time reading the texts typo hunting, and snared some more. Any strays left are my fault. It would be an unforgivable dereliction not to thank Beatrice Rangel, my kin in spirit, whose constant insistence in making me part of her multiple projects and interests reinspired me to retake this one, which for various reasons I had abandoned in the past.

I also thank my artist friends who tapped their own networks to widen the net of contributors, and my agent Maria Elena Lavaud for always asking questions. I must particularly acknowledge an editor I will not name from my previous publishing house who took up the project to the editorial committee but was told it was "too creative; we are academics." I was thus sent down into the rabbit's hole to explore its potential, find the enigmatic cat—and into self-publishing.

My toughest critic is Dr. Esmeralda Garbi, my wife. When she finished reading an advanced draft of the book and told me "it's good," I knew that indeed it was. Her sharp eye, quick commentary, and keen editorial corrections make this book better many times over than the early draft she had read. Her quiet support as I dedicated countless nights to writing the text and to the project's carpentry, was priceless. Unfortunately, sometimes you have an impossible-to-tame urge to write, absorbing body and soul; she allowed me to satisfy it. Without her, I accomplish nothing. I know she sacrificed much in doing so; my gratitude and love run deep. Her love is manifest in many ways.

CJR

Francisco De Goya y Lucientes: *The Sleep Of Reason Produces Monsters, (Caprichos # 43) (detail)* (1797-1799) Etching, aquatint on laid paper, 12.05 x 7.91 in. (Cat. #G002131). © Photo Archive of Museo Nacional del Prado, Madrid.

TABLE OF CONTENTS

XIV I

RENEWED

"It is a sickness which somehow comes with
every tyranny, to place no trust in friends."

AESCHYLUS
Prometheus Bound (c. 450 B.C.)

KRONOS DEVOURS HIS CHILDREN (*Deity Post* Exclusive)

Art by
Itamar Martínez: *Untitled* (2022)
Charcoal, Watercolor on paper. 15 x 10 in.

RENEWED

The Deity Post

THE UNIVERSE OLYMPUS STYLE & PLEASURE HIGH SOCIETY THOSE BELOW

MAJOR SHAKEUP: Ruler of Universe is Overthrown by Son, Ending Ten-Year War.

Begun by a Succession Conspiracy, Gods of Man Subjugate Gods of Nature, Bringing the Gods' War to an End.

by **Pheme**.

OLYMPUS: – *Universal date, antiquity (Deity Post Exclusive).*

Old prophecies can come true. When Kronos learned of his predicted fate, that one of his sons would depose him as ruler of the universe, he did what any rational being with eternal entitlement to power would do: he devoured his children. After all, he himself had deposed his own father in a violent *Coup d'État*. Kronos did not want the order of the universe to be renewed once again. The Golden Age of the Universe upon which he reigned as supreme leader should last forever.

Anonymous sources report that Kronos' wife (and sister), Rhea (a.k.a Mother Nature) was not happy at this turn of events. Rhea would bear his immortal sons and daughters only to see them disappear for all eternity down Kronos' gullet. In conspiracy with Gaia, her mother-in-law (and mother), she tricked Kronos by switching their sixth baby for a large stone, which he promptly devoured. At that celestial moment, Kronos' clock began its relentless tick-tock towards the god's prophesized final destiny.

Rhea named the baby Zeus and reared him hidden in a remote island. When the time was right, Zeus and his rescued immortal siblings (forcibly regurgitated from his father's insides by a potion prepared by Rhea), unleashed the War of the Gods, the Titanomachy. This war ends with the unquestionable victory by the Olympians over the Titans. Kronos is banished and his Commanding General, the Titan Atlas, is condemned to bear the world upon his shoulders. All other Titans, except Prometheus and Thetis, who sided with the Olympians, are now locked up in the notorious nowhere of Tartarus. Kronos' last words before his final banishment were: *"Natural order will always prevail over unnatural disorder."*

Zeus tasked Prometheus to create man, a feeble earthly creature whose purpose was to serve the gods and from whom the strength of the Olympians will grow. Yet, rumor has it that Zeus is not pleased with Prometheus' special gifts to humans: initiative, imagination, craft, trickery, reason, and wiles. Especially since it is rumored that Prometheus also gave them fire, stolen by his raptor, the kite, from the Olympus' sacred hearth. This incident has displeased Zeus and does not bode well for Prometheus.

4 I

Prometheus' creatures have firmly settled the Olympians' presence and created new gods. Humanity's devotion and servitude has made Zeus into the god of *Power*, his wife, Hera, that of *Family*. Their sons, the gods Ares and Hephaestus, of *War* (and blood), and of *Work* (and fire), have arisen from human conflict and toil. Other new gods manifested by humanity are Athena for *Wisdom* and Dionysius, god of *Revelry*. Aphrodite, an aloof Titan born from that violence by Kronos against his father Uranus and neutral during the fray of the recently ended war, has syncretized *Beauty* with *Love* — a godly mixture of nature and humanity. With the end of the Titanomachy, a humanity centered divinity ascends to rule the universe.

ZEUS, SON OF KRONOS AND RHEA
(Deity Post Exclusive)*

UPDATE 1 –

An exclusive dispatch to the Post from our reporter Hermes confirms that Prometheus has incited the divine wrath of Zeus and been banished to an isolated mountain where, bound in the heights, he will endure eternal torture. Our sources, requesting anonymity for their own protection, claim that as Zeus' strength increases by mankind's devotion to *Power*, the god has unleashed a reign of tyrannical abuse, including transforming himself into bulls, swans, golden rain or mist to engage in sexual acts with women he desires, and striking down with thunderbolts anyone who displeases him.

UPDATE 2 –

The Post has learned that a city of **Those Below** named Athens, after the goddess of *Wisdom*, is attempting a system to rotate power between its citizens to renew, innovate and perfect its institutions. The humans attempt, with a rationality based renewal system, to minimize the blood spilt by a succession of tyrants seeking to remain in power. Interviewed about this idea of institutional periodic renewal, Zeus declared: *"These men claim that—what they call it, 'democracy'? — they say it's a rule by all the people, but don't be fooled: it's just for their own few chosen ones, their so called 'peers.' They will never want to be renewed; they'll just rotate amongst their lackeys the power to rule. That's why it's an experiment doomed to failure. Weak!"*

Art by
Itamar Martínez: **Untitled** (2022)
Charcoal, Watercolor on paper. 15 x 10 in.

RENEWED

However, this reporter could see signs of worry in his majesty's face, as he carefully peered back over his shoulder, wondering if this idea will come to Olympus. Concluding the interview, he declared: *"I have a democracy too. I ask everyone here all the time what they're thinking."*

Pheme is lead reporter and editorial director of The Deity Post.

© ***The Deity Post***–Universal date, antiquity.

UPDATE 3 –
From the city of Athens, a source who does not want his name revealed or to write anything down for fear of being struck by lightning or forced to drink hemlock, believes history is not a model to emulate or celebrate; that it should not be used to project a filtered view of past glory.

Mr. Source thinks that we must use the history of our elders to learn about ourselves today; to move forward, renewing leaders and governments; that renewal is necessary to avoid remaining stuck, attempting to emulate a poor replica of a happy past; an ideal devotedly preserving our toxic social ballast on a glass shelf, or as an idol on a pedestal.

UPDATE 4 –
The powers that be have forced us to reveal our source for the previous update. His name is (was) Socrates.

Art by
Itamar Martínez: **Untitled** (2022)
Charcoal, Watercolor on paper. 15 x 10 in.

BOTTOM OF THE BARREL

"One does not become enlightened by imagining figures of light, but by making the darkness conscious."

CARL G. JUNG
The Philosophical Tree (1945)

Art by
Magdalena Rangel: *Pandora's Gift #3-Color-04* (2022)
iPad Pro Digital painting. 7 x 10 in.

BOTTOM OF THE BARREL

Pandora's Gift

She struggles helplessly to close the lid. Dark feelings, sadness and fear overpower her will, weakening her spirit. The relentless forces overcome her feeble attempts to subdue them as they unleash upon the world hate, pain, sickness, famine, war, division, strife...

All ills are let loose upon humankind by a cruel god that uses curiosity to destroy innocence and happiness in this world. But it is she who will be known to have delivered the bitter tasting fruit of unwelcomed wisdom to mankind: suffer and bear the harshness, pain, and evils of life; the unwelcomed wisdom of knowing that after all our sufferings only death awaits; the harsh reckoning that each day we live is a day closer to the day we shall die.

At long last she shuts the lid of the box. Her world has changed, her heart is heavy with grief. Despair, that almost irrational belief that everything will go wrong, sets in as she looks around, seeing what she has done. Dark clouds gather in her soul, and she wonders if the box contains yet her final deliverance. She holds it lightly. She feels a powerful stirring inside. She could open it one more time, her final act. Is it bravery? Is it cowardice? She cannot tell. She doesn't care.

She slowly lifts the lid, looks inside, and finds that not all is lost. She can overcome the moment, this darkness. Her will to live returns, her will to act is restored, her will to be herself and take a stand for what she believes is back, to face the daily challenge of life. She knows now that every day will always have a tomorrow and is lifted by that almost irrational belief that everything will be alright: Hope.

III

IO RUMINATES

"We're not going to stand for it anymore."

ALYSSA MILANO

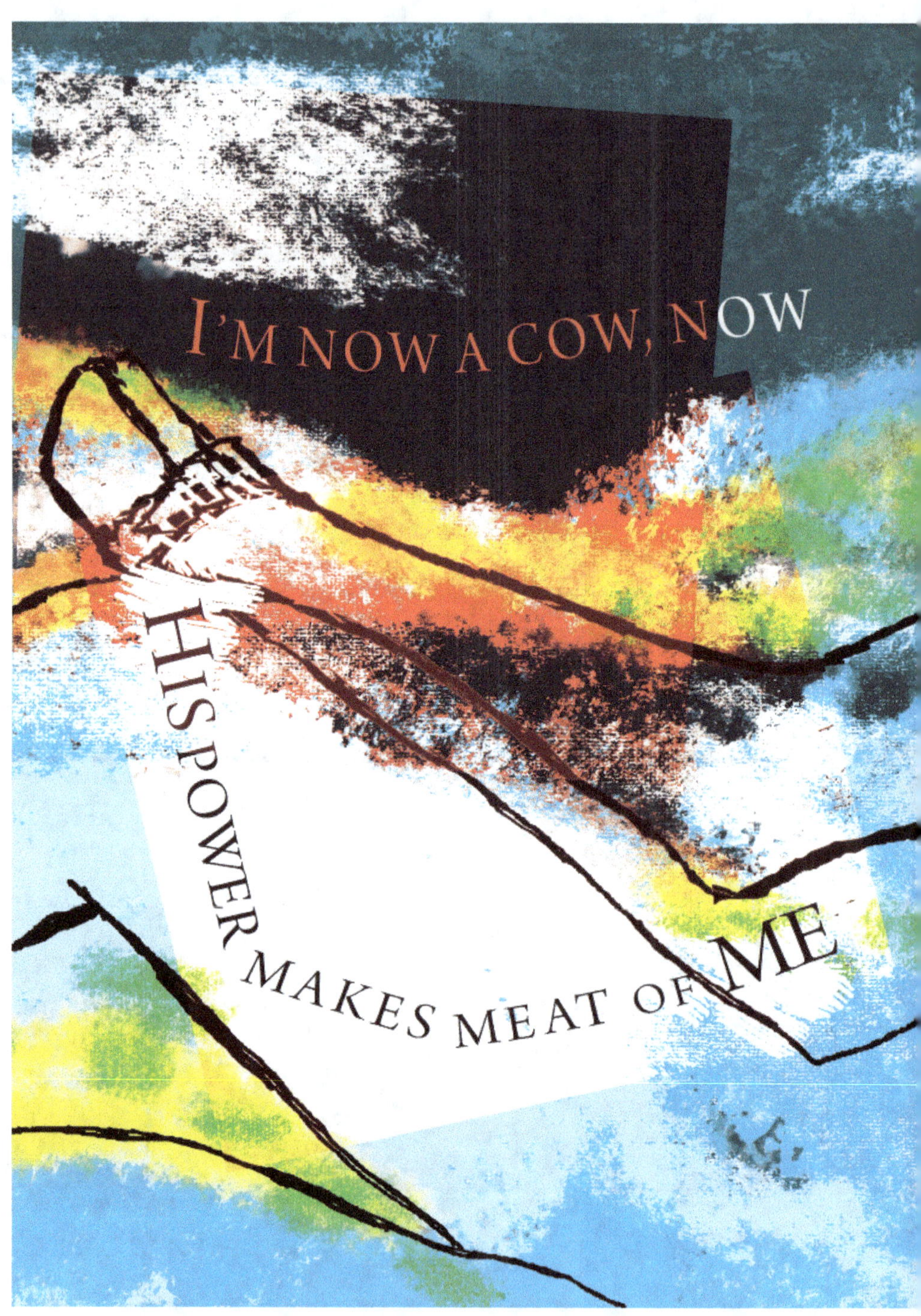

Art by
Magdalena Rangel: *Io Ruminates, Me Too? #48* (2023)
iPad Pro Digital Painting. 7 × 14 in.

IO RUMINATES

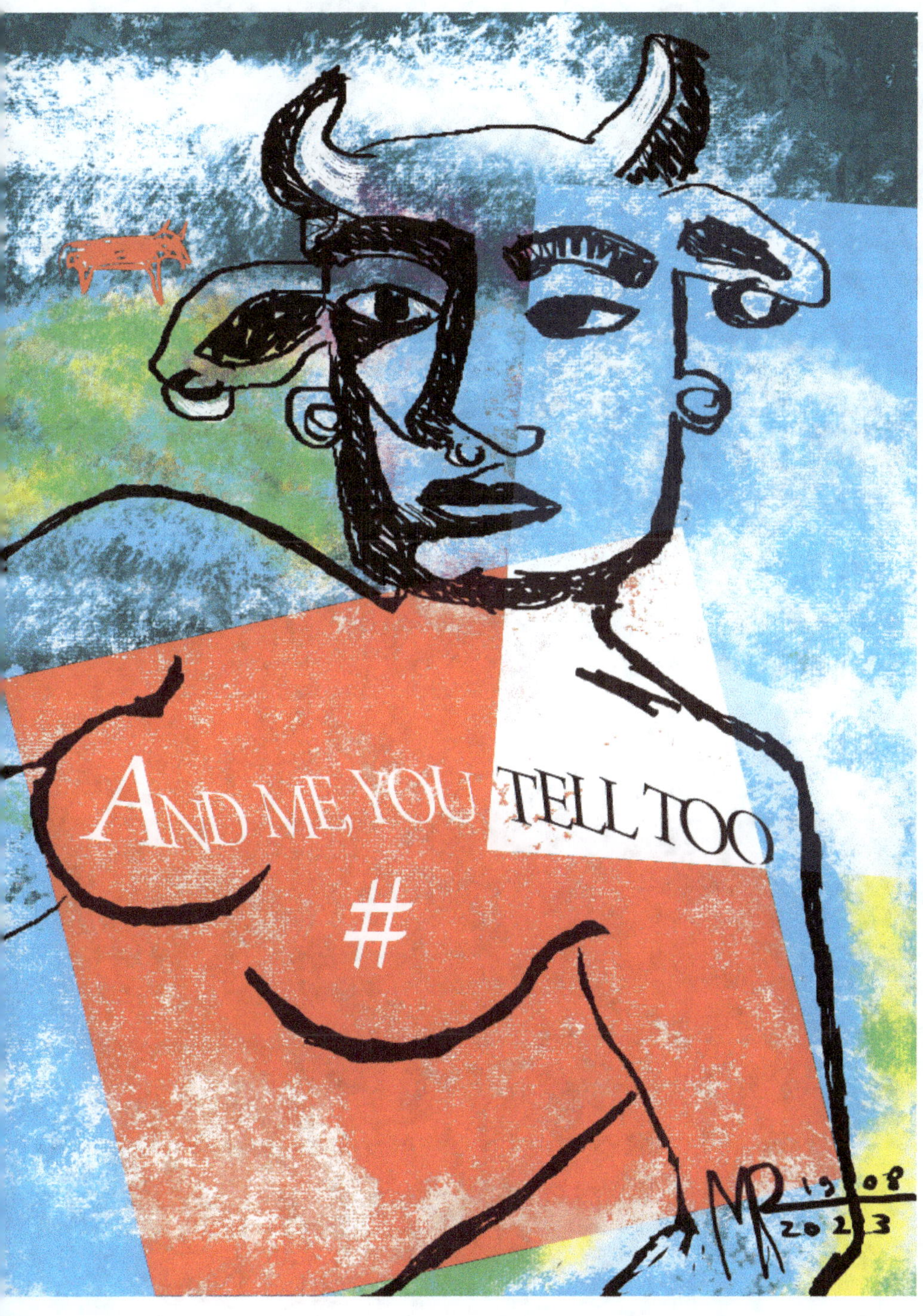

IV

TYRANNY

"My God, my God, why hast thou forsaken me?"

JESUS CHRIST
(Matthew, 27:46)

Art by
Peter Paul Rubens And Frans Snyders: ***Prometheus Bound*** (1611-1612,1618)
Oil on canvas. 7 ft, 11.5 in. x 6 ft, 10.5 in. (With permission by the Philadelphia Art Museum).

TYRANNY

It Lasts Not Forever

Under the yellowish dawn, the few lights still shining below slowly dim as the stars above fade. Another day awakens after his own sleepless night whipped by the icy wind, screaming, howling. Each day blurs into the next, but nights always bring to him the sight of progress. An endless number of nights ago, the deep valley was immersed in black darkness; but at first with a few flickers, and now with thousands of them, the imprint of his creation grows and thrives unquestionably.

He has almost forgotten when it was that he breathed life into that clay. Mankind has surely forgotten about him, chained here by the Tyrant's shackles to a barren cliff beyond Meteora, sharp rocks pressed against his bare flesh; his only companion that old ally, now a winged hound with sharp talons and a poisonous beak, come to fulfill its mandated task of daily tearing his flesh and feasting on his entrails. The beast had not forgotten him. Not a day. The beast was faithful. After a thousand years, he named the kite: Milvós.

Milvós once sat next to him, as if weary of its gruesome task, before proceeding to tear his skin, rip his meat, gush his blood, pierce his bones, agony once again, his incarnate nature tortured once more. Clearly etched in his mind, is that first time, nearly 1,700 years ago, when the beast did not rip his liver out, perhaps the Tyrant's task a heavy burden for the beast too. It sky-dove, screeching loud as usual, to its perch on that jutting rock next to him. Then... it just... flew away... Over hundreds of years, that first reluctance became more frequent. Perhaps the Tyrant had taken his eye off him, or his power was diminished. Perhaps Milvós' task was not that important anymore.

What had been his sin? What had condemned him to this tortured oblivion? To immortal eternal torture? Was it really breathing transitory life into those ambulatory clay forms? Giving them reason and fire? After all, it was mankind itself that empowered those lesser gods which toppled the old order, his own old order; the order in which he, Heaven, Earth, Time, Nature, and his other Titan brethren created and ruled the universe for thousands upon thousands of years. Until man, his creation.

Art by
Peter Paul Rubens And Frans Snyders: *Prometheus Bound (detail)* (1611-1612, 1618)
Oil on canvas. 7 ft, 11.5 in. x 6 ft, 10.5 in. (With permission by the Philadelphia Art Museum).

TYRANNY

Mankind granted divinity to Power, Wisdom, Love and Beauty; to War, Work, and all that mundane daily kind. He believes these lesser gods, left on their own will debase mankind; that his creatures, astray from their true place in the universe, trusting their own gods and leaving behind the gods of nature, will destroy themselves.

Power is the worst of all of them, flashing fear, anger, and revenge to rule over the others; brute strength to force himself upon the unsuspecting; sometimes surreptitiously as a beast, sometimes as himself, brazenly. It was against Power's abuse that he rebelled — and the reason why he gave mankind its own source of power: fire. Fire, which can warm up a soup in a hearth or reduce a majestic forest to ashes. The power of fire makes mankind closer to gods and, at the same time, more distant from them. Unforgivable for the Tyrant. As a twisted irony, the Tyrant sent a kite to torture him, the same creature he used to spread the fire of the gods to mankind.

The struggle against tyranny is not one with comfort. These are his thoughts as he suffers the spiked rocks, the hot sun. Fighting against that tyrant god cast him down, immortal yet incarnate, to this eternal torture by the elements and the winged butcher. Mankind would prefer to believe his mortal body died, hung high in scorn, rather than to believe he lives immortal, chained to the scraggly cliff of an unknown mountain in a distant land. But, when he sees the valley below, he knows the ancient Power that shackled him has withered, Milvós his proof.

His sacrifice was not in vain. Mankind thrives because of him. While he may be forgotten and legends may change, the same struggle will always exist. His is a story that lives forever. Fighting tyranny is as eternal as he, and glory is to the rebels toppling godly and worldly tyrants. Each new warrior against each new tyranny will always be the creator of a better world. Tyranny lasts not forever.

High in the sky, at the top of its lungs, Milvós screeches and soars before circling down to rest and settle back again into his nest of spent embers, next to Prometheus.

In memoriam, Óscar Pérez, and all the fallen in the struggle against tyranny.

V

PETRIFIED

> "It was written I should be loyal to the nightmare of my choice."

JOSEPH CONRAD
Heart of Darkness (1899)

Art by
Mimi Abers: **Back** (2007)
Kiln fired clay. 27 x 17 x 15 in. *Photography by Mimi Abers.*

PETRIFIED

Journal of Myth and History Research, 2022
Vol. 19, No. 4, 231-267

SELF-INTEREST VS. COLLECTIVE INTEREST DILEMMAS IN THE HERO:
Archetypal Paradigms in the Context of Greek Myths and 18th Century Liberalism

Andromacus Perses, PhD (ABD) and
Hermitia Pleiad, PhD (ABD).
Constellar University at Cisthene.

ABSTRACT: *After establishing key facts in the legend of the Gorgon Medusa, the authors seek to determine the elements of bravery and cowardice illustrated by the myth, as they relate to the modern concepts of heroic, cowardly, and treasonous behavior.*

KEYWORDS: Medusa, Perseus, Miranda, Hero, Coward, Traitor, Altruism, Self-Interest, Collective Interest.

The research question posed by this paper is: What is the relationship between heroic behavior, self-interest, and collective interest?

MEDUSA

Medusa the Gorgon is not the subject of this essay. Yet, because she represents the monster in the room, the dark side, the insurmountable obstacle, and the enemy opposing the hero's goals and ideals, she is an intrinsic part of the object of inquiry. Thus, we begin our analysis with a quick overview of her origin story and cultural context to approach an understanding of the shifting nature of the archetypes which are our objects of inquiry: hero, coward, and traitor.

The legend of Medusa seems an affront to any notion of fairness or justice: A beautiful virgin priestess gets raped by a god and is condemned by her own guardian goddess to become a monster; a monster which will turn any man who seeks her into stone. Much symbolic heraldry comes out of this story and, perhaps surprisingly, one of the most favored by the ancients is the one representing Medusa as a protector. Medusa becomes a symbol of internal strength for the victims and the weak against arbitrary violence and power. Other interpretations of the myth of Medusa attribute its origin as part of a set of myths that recount the overthrow of matriarchies by patriarchies, including in religion.[1]

The goddess Athena defers to the god Poseidon and does not seek redress from him for the injury inflicted upon her servant. Athena rather blames Medusa for letting herself get raped and imposes an exemplary punishment upon her. Nevertheless, the legend concludes with the Gorgon elevated to Athena's Shield, redeemed and in service to the virgin goddess of wisdom, the only Olympian not born from woman.

---

[1] Various sources describe Medusa as an earthly demi-goddess, with cycles associated with animals and fertility.

MEDUSA (2)

The myth also illustrates the use of the power of women over men but to the latter's advantage. As the legend goes, Perseus will use the Gorgon's head to overcome his enemies, lending credence to this, rather feminist view, in which Medusa's power transcends her death. Reinforcing this interpretation, the image of her iconic head will be used as a heraldic symbol of protection to the bearer (in armor or shields), or on buildings throughout antiquity. Conversely, it may be said that the bearer of Medusa's head vanquished a powerful monster. Whoever holds its head is protected, not by the head itself but by its silent testimony as to the bearer's power against those who would stand against them.[2]

These aspects of the legend illustrate the permanent conflict between the power of women and the power of men over the destinies of humanity. But the various and contradictory interpretations of Medusa's story are not the key question in our research. In this essay we are interested in identifying what the collective perceives as a hero, and for that our focus is on Perseus.

THE HERO'S MYTH

To the ancients, Perseus was renowned as the hero that slayed Medusa, the Gorgon. To retell this legend in concise form, Perseus was a son of Zeus, living rejected, poor, and miserable on an island ruled by a despot who kept Danae, Perseus' human mother, as a slave. To free Danae, the despot offers her to Perseus in exchange for the Gorgon's head, an impossible task. No one knows where Medusa lives and to see her is to be petrified by the horror.

Undaunted, Perseus prepares for the task by seeking magical supplies from divine allies and by extorting the Gorgon's half-sisters to acquire "tactical intelligence." [3] Thus prepared, with divine supplies and secret information, he uses trickery on the day of the deed: sneaking into the monster's lair and, past its gallery of petrified victims, he beheads her while she sleeps. Perseus returns to his home island with the solicited trophy and uses it to petrify the despot, the true villain of the legend, liberating Danae and his island from tyrannical rule.

Paramount to a hero's story is the subservience of self-interestto the collective interest. This maybe construed as altruism, but that would be an erroneous interpretation. Altruism is a trait inherent to certain individuals who obtain satisfaction by their service to others, sometimes driven by a deep sense of empathy. In its purest form, altruistic behavior is in the self-interest of these individuals because its purpose is to create personal satisfaction, including assuaging/masking — justified or not—guilt feelings derived from their own, or more often, their family's success. This behavior is for the purpose of fulfilling empathic instincts. Any benefits to the collective interests are collateral in this pursuit of personal satisfaction. However, in the case of the Hero's actions, the ultimate self-interest, personal survival, is overridden by the interest of the collective, overcoming all personal and individual goals.

---

[2] It is described in the statue of Athena Parthenos, in the Acropolis, and used in Roman ships to ward off evil and danger. Caravaggio painted her head on a shield (1597) for the Grand Duke of Tuscany as a symbol of victory over his enemies. To this day "protection charm" pendants with an image of the Gorgon are popular items in some regions of Italy.

[3] Medusa is the mortal one of a set of three sisters (the Gorgons) born to a minor sea god and a sea monster. The Gorgons have another set of three sisters (the Graiai) who share one eye and one tooth among them, both of which Perseus will steal to force them into revealing the location of Medusa.

PETRIFIED
THE HERO'S MYTH (2)

Perseus has a goal external to his individual achievement: the survival of his tribe, personified by his mother. To arrive at this goal, he is willing to face over-whelmingly negative odds and go against a primordial instinct: self-preservation. But foolish reckless-ness does not a hero make, as the statues leading up to the monster's bed let us know with their whispered silence.

Perseus fears failure, with all its consequences, so he trains and prepares. He has to survive as an individual to achieve his goal of survival of the collective, so preparation and alliances are crucial. The hero's challenge starts by knowing there is danger, that he or she is in an asymmetric situation (as in that other archetypal legend of David and Goliath), and in being prepared for the challenge. The balance between collective and self-interest is achieved by the survival of the hero — as well as a sense of relief and self-esteem to the listener or reader of the tale, because it is more frequent to self-identify with a common underdog than with an elitist superior force. A fallen hero will be deservedly honored, of course, but surviving heroes are more valuable to society as models of exemplary collective behavior, with an individual earthly reward.

The conflict between self-interest vs. collective interest is central to the history of western civilization. Self-interest is the sublimation of a primordial instinct: survival. Yet, structures of social interaction have been the key to the collective survival of an agglomeration of weak and feeble creatures pitted against nature's powerful forces. Within those social structures, the instinct of individual survival can create dynamics that clash with the ultimate collective interest: survival of the species or, closer to home, of the tribe. Heroes and idealists sacrifice themselves for the collective to achieve a greater goal, be it the survival of the tribe, the preservation of ideas, or as ideological symbol. The community honors heroes in life and death with medals and legends – if the ultimate goal, survival or success of the tribe or clan's interest, is achieved.

Art by
Mimi Abers: *Bent Over* (2008)
Kiln fired clay. 23 x 13 x 14 in. *Photography by Mimi Abers.*

THE HERO'S MYTH (3)

Individuals who choose self-interest (and self-preservation) over the collective interest in crucial survival situations are often branded as cowards. Yet when an individual's success in pursuit of his or her self-interest brings spillover or multiplier effect benefits, those benefits can be perceived to be a collective entitlement. This is part of the reason why ideologies celebrating the pursuit of the common good can be more attractive than those celebrating the pursuit of individual achievement – "free lunches" are popular. Actions (and ideologies) perceived to favor equally all members of the tribe are, almost by definition, more popular than actions perceived to favor unequally the individual good of a single member or select minority of the tribe. [4]

TREASON, OR THE BIRTH OF NATIONS

Perseus illustrates the hero in its simple, mythical form. Reality is more complex, and legendary heroes are not the same as the ones we find in history. Historical heroes cannot be discussed

without an understanding of traitors. Traitors are not the opposite in action to heroes (as is the case of cowards) but antagonists in allegiance. Traitors, villains and monsters are typically labeled as such by the victors, those who will be writing the history books.

In the period of the liberal revolutions, when the concept of sovereign nations within well delineated borders was not truly defined and thus loyalty to geographical boundaries was not prevalent, an individual could have fidelity to the *Sovereign* in power [5] (as Talleyrand well exemplifies), or to the *Ideals* ("the republic," "independence," "*liberté, egalité, fraternité*") identifying a tribe. Those that take up arms to defend Ideals or those that do so as defenders of the Sovereign can face charges of treason when captured by opponents, especially if they have switched allegiances.[6] During the Independence War of the United States, Benedict Arnold became iconic of this circumstance. To this day, changing one's mind on an ideological, political, or even social stance is often portrayed or seen as either a sign of weakness, inconsistency, or betrayal leading to varied consequences, from personal to political.

In history, the Venezuelan Francisco de Miranda exemplifies the development of treason as a "crime against the state," as the sovereignty concept migrated from an individual ruler to the nation-state. Miranda trained in the armed forces of Imperial Spain and, as such, fought during the Independence War of the United States with the Franco-Spanish Alliance against the British. Shortly thereafter in Cuba, perhaps targeted by his rise as a "colonial" in the army ranks and fleeing from the Spanish Inquisition, he deserted the imperial Army and fled to the new republic of the north.

---

[4] What commonly passes as socialist ideology is generally more popular than what is commonly labeled as capitalist ideology. It is stated as a truism that much greater common good is achieved under socialism (as a diffuse ideal) than under capitalism (as a demonized reality). But the fundamental tenet of capitalism is that an individual pursuing his own interest will in fact benefit the collective by stimulating innovation, increased productivity and a greater supply of goods and services. Adam Smith warned against concentrated market power, as seen today in state monopolies and elitist oligopolies. Both of these outcomes are inevitable consequence of both "unfettered" socialism and capitalism, in detriment of Smith's free markets ideal.

[5] Sovereignty resided incarnate in the local or imperial ruler, *The Sovereign*, not in the citizens of a nation, as citizenship itself was not a prevalent concept.

[6] Of course, treason can also be charged when switching allegiances between individual sovereigns, say the King of France and the Emperor of Prussia, but the Liberal Revolution purports to place sovereignty on the state through its citizens, not it's rulers.

PETRIFIED
TREASON, OR THE BIRTH OF NATIONS (2)

Miranda spent more than a year in this newly minted independent nation observing in real time that thing called democracy, and writing about it in his Journals, while befriending protagonists of the American Revolution.[7]

In pursuit of his liberal interests and studies, Miranda moved to London, from whence he traveled throughout Europe and up to Russia where he was advisor, and perhaps more, to Catherine the Great. He eventually gravitated to a France gripped in its throes of revolutionary fevers. Miranda's close friend, the mayor of Paris, recommended him to the armies of the French Revolution in which he ascended to the rank of General.

Miranda's name was eventually etched in the Arc de Triomphe for his service under Division General Charles François Dumoriez in the decisive Battle of Valmy and his actions bringing to an end the Siege of Antwerp. General Dumoriez's failed coup against the revolutionary government in March of 1793 and his subsequent escape to "enemy" territory in April had consequences on his command structure.[8] General Miranda was arrested by the Jacobins, subsequently exonerated of conspiracy related to those events, but kept under close surveillance.

Miranda slips away from Le Terreur and its aftermath in 1798 and returns to England. This turbulent period saw Miranda wear Spanish, Russian, and French uniforms battling sometimes allies of former or future friends. He was asked by England to lead forces in battles against Napoleon's Empire in Spain. Instead, he worked England's geopolitical interests against Spain to favor his life project for the Latin American region where he would wear his last uniform: that of Independence revolutionary. This project took him back to his land of birth, Venezuela, which he led to independence from the Spanish Empire, to create a republic based on his liberal revolutionary ideas. Miranda's rise from son of middle-class shopkeepers in a colonial backwater to adviser of kings, empresses, and prime ministers is an exemplar of self-agency, education, and opportunity for attaining social mobility, a fundamentally liberal idea.

But the young republic he sought to forge was not ready for Miranda's brand of liberalism. Following slave and popular uprisings against a *Criollo* [9] led government seeking to maintain colonial privileges, Miranda was accused by his political enemies (the Criollos) of treason to the newly independent nation and handed over to the Spanish. The Criollos' justification was that Miranda was a carpetbagger with ideas detached from their own interests and local realities. He was a useful idiot to be conveniently handed over to the Spanish Regime as a bargaining chip to retain their status and avoid being "renewed" once Spanish rule were to be restored and the new republic disbanded. Alas, that would not occur. Instead, exile, incarcerations and executions quickly followed for many of them.

---

[7] Miranda's journals have been designated part of the World's Heritage by UNESCO.

[8] Louis XVI was executed on January 20th, 1793. His execution began a new era in Europe in which monarchs saw themselves under a new existential threat. Dumoriez saw the decision by the National Convention to execute the King as irresponsible and a threat to the Republic by uniting the monarchies of Europe against revolutionary France. This will drive his actions two months later.

[9] The Criollos were a social class of locally born colonials who were mostly descendants of the original settlers and landowners of the territory. These were different from the Peninsulares, who were the Spaniards from the peninsula temporally stationed in the territory for bureocratic or commercial reasons, and who often consider themselves "purer" than the criollos.

TREASON, OR THE BIRTH OF NATIONS (3)

Francisco de Miranda spent his remaining days in Spanish prisons, finally in Cádiz, where he sought unsuccessfully to plea his case to the liberal courts (parliament) established under the republican constitution, known as "La Pepa."[10] The restoration of Ferdinand VII in 1814 ended that effort, as the constitution and those courts, were abolished by the newly restored king.

Miranda died in 1816, perhaps of a stroke, perhaps poisoned. He is the only recorded protagonist of the three major revolutionary conflicts convulsing the western world in the late 18th and early 19th centuries and may be the first instance of a man labeled a traitorto a (new)nation, rather than to an army, tribe, or king. He is a clear example of the differences between an archetypal mythical hero with a historical hero, his name engraved on the Arc de Triomphe in Paris, memorialized with a cenotaph in the Pantheon of Heroes of his native country and, yet, whose remains were buried in a Potter's Field, never to be identified with certainty. A man of history, whose actions are colored by its writers and the reversals of fortune frequently associated with its protagonists. [11]

HISTORY, REWRITTEN

The old Perseus myths, and the history of revolutions and shifting allegiances in the 18th and 19th centuries illustrate not only deep-rooted archetypal stances on hero, coward, and traitor, but also the variable nature of the terms when viewed through the lens of common interest, self-interest, and allegiance. The ambiguous legend of Medusa as killer vengeful monster, or as an emblematic protector on Athena's shield is symbolic of the rising fortunes and befallen misfortunes of those labeled with any of those three terms by the whims of their times and history.

Faced with seemingly insurmountable odds, heroic behavior unmistakably includes reality assessment, training and preparation, as well as alliances and cunning to ensure survival. Bravery is the willingness to go through with a plan laid out (mostly carefully in the case of the survivors, mostly hastily in the case of the fallen) for the purpose of a "greater good."

It consists of undertaking an action aware that "*the best laid schemes o' mice an' men gang aft a-gley*".[12] Cowards may have that same plan and be committed to the same "greater good," but their interest in survival prevails at the moment of execution and those that would be heroes do not follow through. For Perseus, that commitment to great'er good was liberating his mother from enslavement, despite grave personal danger.

---

[10] The Cádiz Constitution, popularly known as "La Pepa," was the first functional constitution of the Spanish Empire. It bestowed sovereignty upon the state, not the monarch, and instituted a democratically elected parliament (the Cortes), freedom of the press, and the right to private property. It also granted full rights as a Spaniard to all citizens in all the Empire's territories, as well as equal political administrative status between the peninsula and those territories. Its abolishment by Ferdinand VII was one of the triggering factors for a renewed independence movement across all the colonies. To this day, the rewritten history of Spanish liberalism (spanning centuries, from Juan de Mariana, through Goya, Ortega y Gasset, up to modern contemporaries) after the king's restoration is reflected in a common, derogatory, expression characterizing someone who has little sense of "real life" and its consequences, a penchant for chaos, and generally not a serious person as a "viva La Pepa" (long live "La Pepa") kind of guy.

[11] See cf. Carlos Rangel *The Latin Americans,* Chapter II (Routledge, 1977), and *Marx y los socialismos reales y otros ensayos:* El nacimiento de la traición (Monte Ávila, 1988). For more on Miranda see also Racine, Karen, *Francisco de Miranda – A Transatlantic Life in the Age of Revolution* (2002)(Rowman & Littlefield, MD

[12] "To a Mouse" Robert Burns (1785).

PETRIFIED

HISTORY, REWRITTEN (2)

The "man with a plan" seeking to overcome the unsurmountable obstacle, the monster in the room, the dark side, the enemy (physical or ideological), and who executes that plan to preserve, defend or restore the collective interest, is the hero of the story.

If the hero changes the plan to switch allegiance in favor of enemies to the collective interests of his tribe, he is now labeled a traitor. If he switches in favor of his self-interest, he is now labeled a coward. Cowards are the ones who, having the training, the preparation, and a plan, decide, when push comes to shove, that it is not in their best self-interest to follow through with the plan so they switch allegiance. Because real history and its events are messy, and battling factions are composed of many individuals with opposing allegiances, by using this construct we can objectively identify heroes, traitors, and cowards to each tribal allegiance in any conflict. [13]

From as early as the myth of Medusa we observe the perception of foes and friends as variable. "The right side of history" is not always clear at the time or even in hindsight, as is the case with Miranda, posthumously pardoned by the Republic of Venezuela, the land where he was born. What is clear is that the possibility exists to manipulate the blurry lens of history, bring down past heroes and reappraise forgotten villains of all sorts at the whim of a volatile political environment. Ideologues and self-interested influencers can use this manipulation, altering to their advantage the cultural framework of a nation.

We dig up heroes and bury villains to shape our perception of national heritage. Yet, the tendency to rewrite, modify, or erase our sense of history conveniently to change and reinterpret cultural narratives, comes from an identifiable, deep, and unerasable authoritarian vein within our humanity. That is an element innocently embedded in the natural desire to find archetypal heroes in our blood and soil; a vein mined eagerly by authoritarian leaders seeking to enrich their power, driving false patriotism and unfettered nationalism. [14]

---

[13] Police in school shootings who choose to not enter the building or engage the shooter, in spite of their preparation, training and plans to do so, can exemplify cowardice. Traitors, heroes, and cowards can also be seen during major civic upheavals and unrest, such as in the attempted overthrow of the U.S. government between November 2020 and January 2021. In this instance, these behaviors were apparent among those committed to maintain the rule of democracy and the law, and those who chose to support authoritarian rule and a personality cult. Those events illustrated heroic and treasonous behavior for and against the State as well as cowardly behavior. It is notable that after the events of January 6th, allegiances and behaviors changed once again, illustrating that self-preservation instincts and cowardice are alive and well in politics. It is also clear that, if the attempted constitutional disruption had been successful, the culprits would have labeled themselves as patriotic heroes birthing a new nation. As it is, they stand on trial and in scorn for what they were: seditious conspirators against the Constitution and criminals who broke the laws of the United States of America.

[14] School indoctrination by book and reading bans, and curricular interference from central authority, as well as "cancel culture" by socialnetwork "influencers" are modern instruments of authoritarian control.

THE HERO'S ARTIFACTS

I. MIRROR/SHIELD

A mirror means and contains nothing except that which is reflected by it. As a mirror reflecting petrifying horror the hero's gift, the shield protecting the Goddess of Wisdom, is significant in its multiple ambivalent, Vermeer like symbolisms... "Speculum significat et continet nihil nisi quod ab eo reflectitur. Ut speculum horrorem petrificans reflectens, donum herois, clypeum Deam Sapientiae protegens, est significans in suis multiplex ambigua, symbolismus Vermeerianus... Mauris pellentesque pulvinar pellentesque habitant morbi tristique senectus. Speculum significat et continet nihil nisi quod ab eo reflectitur. Ut speculum horrorem pe

Art by
Caravaggio: *Shield With The Head Of Medusa* (1597)
Oil on canvas mounted on wood. 24 in. × 22 in. (Gallerie degli Uffizi, Inv. 1890 n.

PETRIFIED

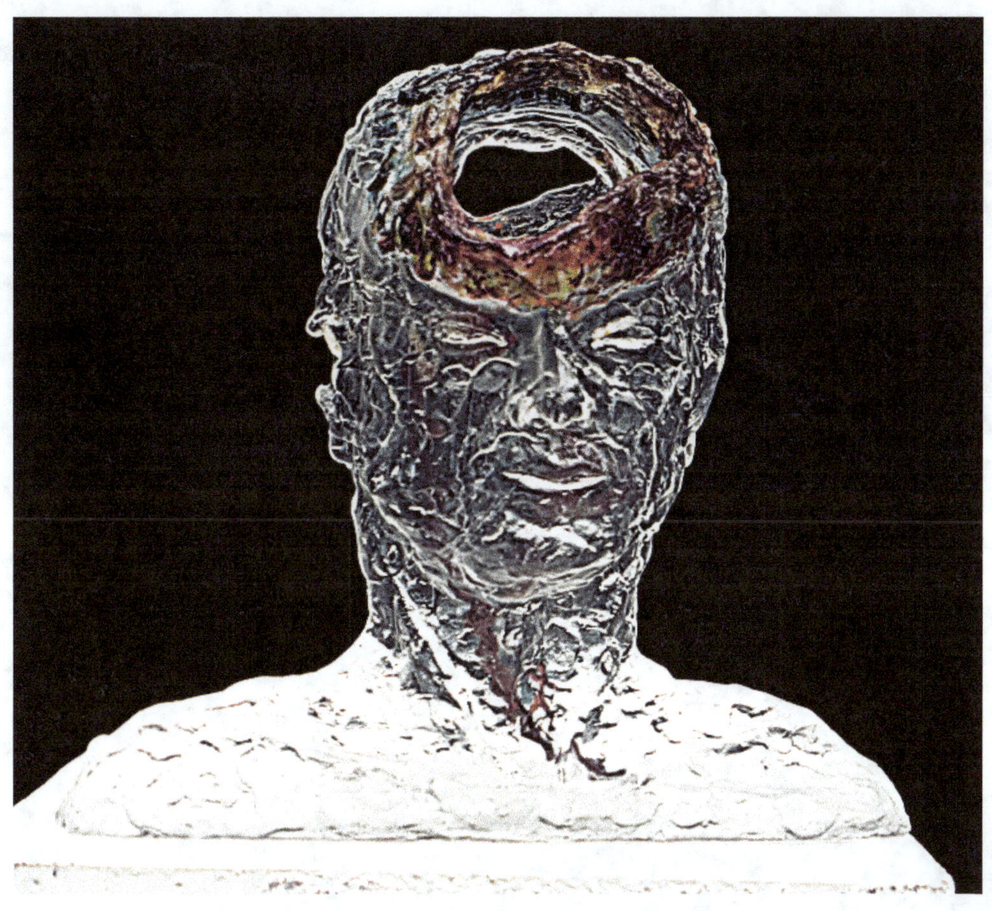

Art by
Mimi Abers: Out Of Mind (2009)
Glass. 14 x 7 x 6 in. *Photography by Mimi Abers.*

THE BUBBLE

"Open your eyes now. I will. One moment. Has all vanished since? If I open and am for ever in the black adiaphane. Basta! I will see if I can see now."

JAMES JOYCE
Ulysses (1933)

Art by
Andrés Salazar: *You Scale, Climb, And Descend From The Incomprehensible* (2022)
Acrylic on Dream Papyrus. 12.5 x 9.5 in.

THE BUBBLE

*W*oe, here I stand, bound tightly against this mast, salty spray lashing my face. My men, tasked to sail and row, ignore me. Alas, why do they not see we have arrived at long last to our beautiful land, why do they ignore my loud protest, my frantic gestures? Why, why?

*W*e will sail past our paradise and, lost again, miss all chance to lay to rest our troubles; to be done with our adventures, to bring our journey to its end. I hear the sweetest voices beckoning: "You're here at last, o welcomed heroes; The brave lost ones we waited for! In this great land you'll rest, you've earned the glory; you're here at last..."

I mistook Circe as a truth bearer, she spouted falsehood: "Beware the sirens and their songs, pass them by or you'll surely die." She was the fake, the misguiding beguiler. What kind of leader am I, listening to her falsehoods that now lead my men astray from our true purpose? I hear my beloved Penelope's voice. I hear my friends' hearty laughter. We have arrived! This is the short and easy path. The gods' reward returning us to our grand homeland! These voices are not the lies, these voices are not the falsehoods. They know me, they call my name, they give me news I long to hear. I implore to my sailors: *"Let me go! You are all wrong! I was wrong to let you bind me! Listen to the glory of our victories! Listen to the tales of our success and greatness! Let us all go celebrate our glorious past, abundant future and promised destiny!"* That's the hymn sung for us by the maidens at the shore...

*W*hat does my Pilot see as he turns his gaze to where I direct my eyes? Can he not see what I hear? The vision of our desires, the shores of Ithaca, with its maidens waving, singing, and calling for us? It all awaits us. Why does he avert his eyes and pale in terror? How can he not see what I clearly hear, what falsehood did Circe's bewitchment imprint into his eyes? Why does he gesture our crew to row faster, faster, faster! As if away from danger instead of into the safe harbor I see? *"Unbind me! I am your captain!"* I yell.

Art by
Annika Connor: *Wolf Pack* (2022)
Watercolor on board. 30 x 40 in.

THE BUBBLE

*T*he wind whips the unruly locks of hair strewn across my brow, my breath rushes faster, my heart races louder, my lungs rip with screaming. The sailors row on, straight ahead, away from the alluring shore. I am at my wits end with despair. How can they not see what I see? I should have let them hear what I see, listen to the song, sealed not their ears with Circe's deceiving wax.

*W*oe, woe, woe, the wind billows our sails, the oars foam the sea as we whisk away from promised solace; no, please no, don't leave our grand land behind. Yells grow weak, fade away to languishing whimpers: *" Stop! Turn 'round! Back to where we were, where we will be great once more... Stop... Turn back, turn back, turn back, go back, go back..."* My eyes no longer see, my mind no longer thinks, I no longer hear, except that siren song, pulling me, until I know no more.

*Y*et again other wanderers sail our waters to hear our songs and deliver us their flesh to feast.

*T*he surf murmurs that these come from far away, from Troy, onward to Ithaca. Many adventures they have lived, swine they became and men again, cyclops they slayed, and Cassandras' castle is ashes now... all by their Prince's wiles. It is now their time to rest. Our songs of praise and heroes will lure them to our shore, cut short their journey to their final resting place.

*O*ur enchanting voices will cloud their eyes, build visions for them of hills and meadows where our sharp rocks stand and the teeth of our reefs await; a shining sun where dark clouds rumble. As we stand tall singing, swaying with our heavenly bodies, our talons unseen claw the rotted flesh and bones of the deluded that satiated us before.

*T*heir leader hears our song, wants for us. To his crew he is a madman tied to the ship's mast. They sail past, ignore our tales. Away they go, away from our bubble of deceit. No matter. Others we will entice with the fictions they always want to hear. And we will devour them.

VII

BEAUTY

"Whoever excommunicates me, excommunicates God."

FRA GIROLAMO SAVONAROLA
(Savonarola was excommunicated by Pope
Alexander VI, May 13, 1497)

Art by
Sandro Botticelli: *The Birth Of Venus* (c. 1484–1486)
Tempera on canvas. 68 ×110 in. *With permission by the Gallerie degli Uffizi.*

BEAUTY

INT. CHIESA DI SAN SALVATORE IN OGNISSANTI - DAY

Choir music sanctifies the space under the frescoed vault. Dust specks in the still air sparkle with colors from rays filtered through a stained glass window.

SUPERSCRIPT: "MAY 23, 1498"

In a side chapel, SANDRO, early 50's, a handsome Italian in elegant Renaissance Artist garb, finishes his silent prayers in front of the tomb of *Simonetta Vespucci 1453-1476*.

                    GIOVANNI (O.C.)
          Beauty lives forever, Sandro.

Sandro greets GIOVANNI, a bit older and more disheveled than him, with a sad hug.

                    SANDRO
          Is it done?

                    GIOVANNI
          They're collecting up the bones and the
          ashes.

EXT. COBBLED PROMENADE BY THE ARNO - DAY

On this sunny afternoon, the pair walks along the river bank towards the Ponte Vecchio. They can see a crowd gathering on the old bridge.

                    SANDRO
          Beauty is fiction, Giovanni, it's only our
          imagination. It doesn't exist in nature.

                    GIOVANNI
          You're thinking crazy again. Look at
          our river, the sky, this day! Beautiful!
          Beautiful way before we were ever even
          strolling here.

                    SANDRO
          Our mind is the one that sees this
          beauty. Not these ants crawling by,
          the rat that darted past us, or the
          alley cats that'll chase it. Soulless
          beasts don't see beauty.

                    (MORE)

The crowd on the bridge cheers as wheelbarrows of ashes and dust are dumped into the river from the bridge's edge. The ash cloud expands, wafting in all directions.

Art by
Sandro Botticelli: **The Birth Of Venus (Detail)** (c. 1484-1486)
Tempera on canvas. 68 ×110 in. *With permission by the Gallerie degli Uffizi.*

BEAUTY

> SANDRO (CONT'D)
> (looks at the ash cloud)
He knew. He knew about beauty… He knew of the sin born from it: vanity. A sin pushing us away from God. A sin purified by fire.

> GIOVANNI
But, hey, no, listen to yourself, pazzo. Look at your bellisima Simonetta. It was you who made her into an immortal goddess of Beauty. Very nice too!

> SANDRO
We're always a contradiction. I'm not pure like he was. Yet, now he's ashes in the Arno, a cloud of dust rising towards that sky of yours.

EXT. STREET IN MEDIEVAL FLORENCE - DAY

They walk on a narrow cobbled street up towards Piazza della Signoria.

> GIOVANNI
The ancients don't say so. Beauty's not a goddess come from the human mind. She comes from the sky, a Titan, born before all those other gods for human stuff.

> SANDRO
> (wistful)
I painted her that way, at the edge of the deep and of the land. It's the edges that define us.

> GIOVANNI
You did good, with that one.

> SANDRO
If not for Lorenzo's memory, I would have burned that pagan one too.

EXT. PIAZZA DELLA SIGNORIA - NIGHT

SUPERSCRIPT: "FEBRUARY 7, 1497"

A large bonfire lights up the night. ANGRY MOB hurls books, paintings, mirrors, luxury garments into the fire. A HOODEDPRIEST, mid 40's, mouths angry words, eggs on the crowd.

> GIOVANNI (V.O.)
That bonfire was a big mistake. Fra Girolamo's arrogance on display for all, all night; The Pope thought so.

Burning ashes float up into the night sky.

44 I

Art by
Sandro Botticelli: *The Birth Of Venus (Detail)* (c. 1484-1486)
Tempera on canvas. 68 ×110 in. *With permission by the Gallerie degli Uffizi.*

BEAUTY

EXT. STREET IN MEDIEVAL FLORENCE – DAY

SUPERSCRIPT: "MAY 23, 1498"

The brothers walk uphill, nearing the end of the cobbbled narrow street.

> SANDRO
>
> Can't you just see it? That Borgia Pope?
> He is the wrong, the monk called it:
> This Pope is mundane, not of God. He
> now pretends his sinful rule over us,
> and even over those new lands and its
> savages. Over it all!

> GIOVANNI
>
> So what? It's a new century, a new world,
> a new era, little brother! And we're
> part of it all!

EXT. PIAZZA DELLA SIGNORIA – DAY

The brothers enter the plaza from the narrow street. In the large square the crenellations of the Palazzo della Signoria stand golden in the late afternoon sun, its tower looms above it all.

At the center WORKERS, under the eye of a STERN MONK, use wash buckets and brooms to clean the paving stones. Others pick trash remains left by a crowd.

> SANDRO
>
> Can you smell it? Burnt flesh has a very
> distinctive smell. It lingers.

On Giovanni's face you can see that he does.

> GIOVANNI
>
> He's in the sixth circle now. He'll burn
> some more. Death and scorn for those who
> destroy.

> SANDRO
>
> Life and glory for those who create.
> I've been told that before.
>
> (pause)
>
> I don't believe it. Savonarola was
> martyred and will be a saint forever.
> I will be forgotten.

The workers brush the stones hard, harder. More buckets are splashed onto the pavement.

> GIOVANNI
>
> Maybe not.

Murky water seeps into the cracks between the pavement stones. Brooms sweep, sweep, sweep. The dark water turns clear as the ashes and dust dissolve and disappear.

THE END

VIII ^{I 47}

IT COMES AROUND

"And yet it moves."

Attributed to

GALILEO GALILEI

Art by
Nuria Román: *From South To North* (2001)
Mixed Media on wood. 51 x 51 in.

IT COMES AROUND

Roma, luni 27, 1633

Salve, carissimi et dilexit Stella:

Abscondere Meis litteris ad Te semper. Melior
est adolebitque ea. In communi sermone Ego
scriberem ad Te, for You to better understand Me.
It is a pleasure to read Your Grace's letters.
It is rare that women of any stature read, much
less write as well as You do, and with the
purpose of the pursuit of knowledge.
These are dark times, and We are witnesses to
the darkening. I am afraid Our letters chronicle
the fate of Our times.

Your comments on the Maestro's <u>Dialogue
Concerning The Two Chief World Systems</u>
in Your last letter were sharp and witty. You are
right that the brilliant arguments by Salviati on
Our sun at the center of a system of planets
totally obliterate Simplico's mindless recitation
of Ptolemaic nonsense. And, as You point out,
He does not even understand these either!

I remembered Your letter as I sat in the gallery,
watching the old man being threatened
by pompous disciples of Simplico with torture
and His remaining days in a cold cell.

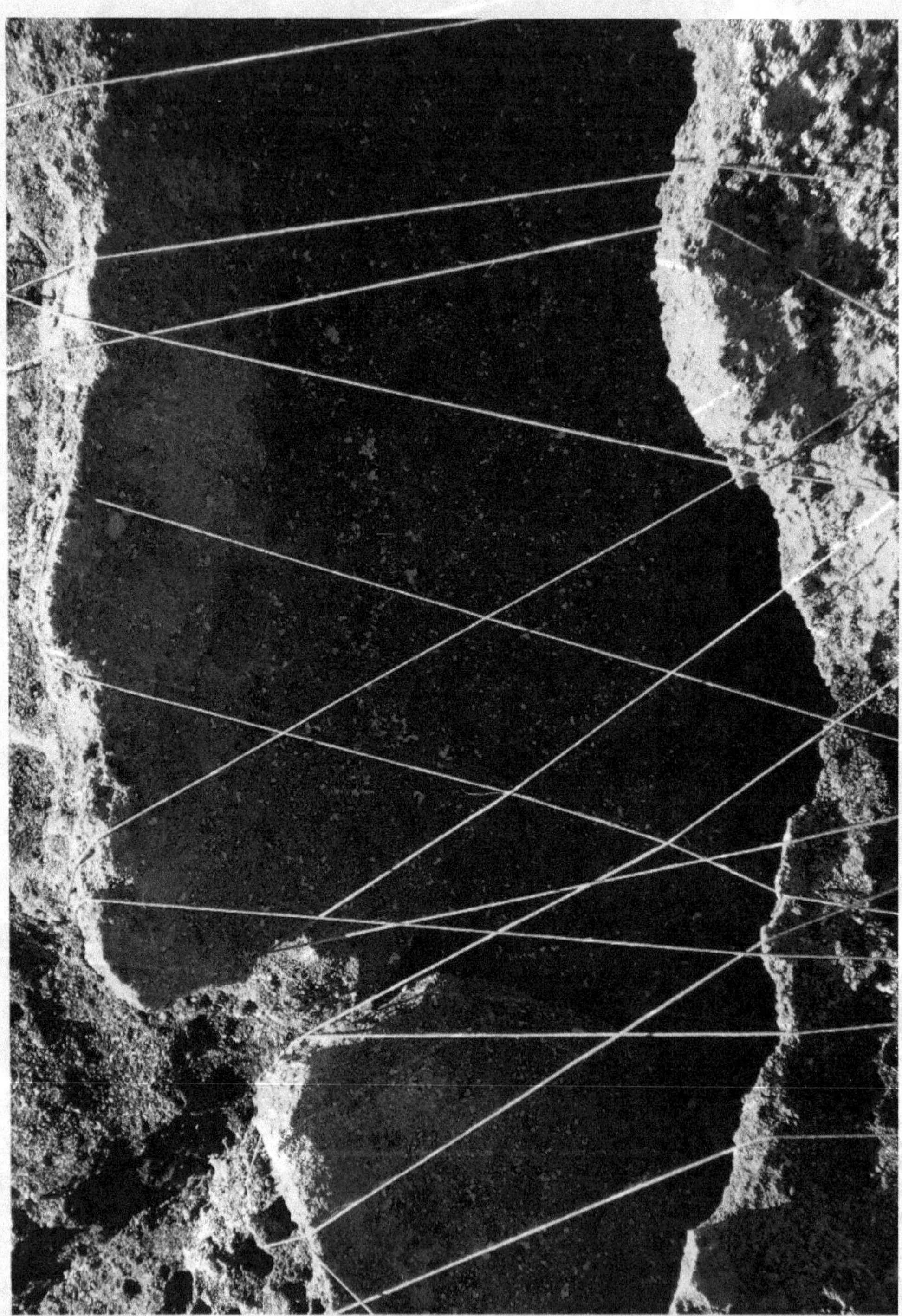

Art by

Nuria Román: *Sew The Earth: Lithica. (detail)*
(2013). 100 ft. Ropes over natural rock. Conceptual Art Piece.
All materials donated by the community.

IT COMES AROUND

In my mind I wandered back to those crispy dark nights when We gazed through Maestro's marvelous invention to that errant bright star, spying It's little ones around It.

Can You believe that when those tribunal buffoons were asked if They had ever used a telescope, They responded by saying it was an instrument of The Devil to test Our faith? That science, reason and progress are tricks from The Dark One?

I fear, Stella, a new age of darkness, not led by Satan but by leaders rejecting knowledge as a guiding principle. We can only improve Our lot if We use the advances that deep study and hard work bring Us, standing on the shoulders of Those that came before Us to see further ahead.

I fear, Stella, that Our cities will soon be in decline while those of others, where Simplicos do not prevail, will conquer the future and improve their lot. It is My only hope that even as We face decline, Our own Simplicos do not imperil the whole of Our world.

Semper Tuus fidelisque amicus,,

Cosimo.

IX

THE MONSTER

"[…the] conditions of life [of the lumpen proletariat] prepare it far more for the part of a bribed tool of reactionary intrigue [than for revolution]."

KARL MARX
The Communist Manifesto (1848)

Art by
Itamar Martínez: **Hombre Herido** (2019)
Oil on board. 15 x 10 in.

THE MONSTER

INTERNAL MEMO
Confidential

From: VRC Central Committee Chairman
To: All Party Leadership Members
Date: 192 days before Election Day and counting
Re: We're Alive!

Some of you may believe our primary process has not yielded the ideal candidate to restore our party to life and power. It has been said that our candidate:

- Has no political experience.

- Has questionable business experience and practices.

- Has litigations and accusations of fraud and worse.

- Is a bald-faced liar, misogynistic and possibly racist.

- Demeans with personal attacks our own primary candidates and their families, deflecting from issues he knows little about.

- Attacks our party's credibility, and what it has always stood for.

Expanding this list with publicly known details could easily produce a 20-page memo highlighting potential weaknesses exploitable by the opposition in any competitive national campaign. But where some of you see toxic baggage, I and others in top leadership see a win for us. The heralding of a new vitality now and into the future.

Our candidate taps into a segment of the electorate typically dead to all politics and any information. We know that about 30% to 40% of the electorate is not animated by political parties or does not see democracy as having any value to them; a "what's in it for me" mind set at the root of their apathy. That is why a "disruptive outsider," such as our candidate, generates the electrical jolt that will drive these voters, until now dead-to-the-system, to come out in those ignored and swing districts where small margins make a big difference.

---

page 2 of 2 - Re: We're Alive!

By plugging into these disconnected voters, we will juice up a victory that traditional polling and media pundits have been telling us is increasingly out of our reach. This candidate is the one that will reanimate the phantom voters and reactivate our political vitality. By assembling our perfect candidate with these discarded elements at the fringes of democracy, he becomes a manifestation of their untapped power — and we create the winner.

And here is the best part: because of his great political inexperience, we will be his closest advisors. We will pilot him through — to him - unfamiliar and turbulent political waters. We will make sure he does not fall crashing into the media's never ending voracious chatter and its blinding limelight. We will leverage all his known and unknown liabilities to our advantage because he will need our support to survive. His power comes from us, and It is in his best self-interest to play along with us to stay politically alive: we supply the energy, we created him. His destructive capacity is a force that we will unleash and direct against our enemies. With him, we will cement our power. With him, we will never be replaced!

Leadership's directive is that we all support wholeheartedly our candidate; that we put aside any misgivings we may have or personal slights he may have made to any of us in the past; and that we take the road towards long-term success for our party and of our interests. This candidate brings new life to our erstwhile moribund party. With him, WE'RE ALIVE FOREVER!

Onwards to victory, always for power & country!

Your Chairman always,

FUBAC

THE MONSTER

Art by
Itamar Martínez: *Untitled* (2022)
Ink and acrilic on paper. 15 x 10 in.

IT'S COOKING

"Once you have mastered a technique, you barely have to look at a recipe again."

JULIA CHILD

Art by
Andrés Salazar: *Techno Visual Recipe For Cock-And-Bull Stew* (2022)
Digital Photograph. 10 x 7 in.

IT'S COOKING

PRIMAL SAUCES

VERSCHWÖRUNG SAUCE:
Something To Talk About

✳ **FOR: Red Meats**

Red meat is best when doused generously with this sauce which awakens the deepest emotions and incites the soul into unexpected action. *Verschwörung* sauce has ancestral origins: It became very popular towards the beginning of the 20th century in Central and Eastern Europe, made its way out of the region and landed in our shores some time ago, only to subside to more mainstream sauces with greater internal uniformity and consistency. But recently this sauce has seen a popular comeback throughout the world as changes in the way ingredients are selected and the mix is cooked make it easier for almost anyone to prepare this sauce adapted to our modern times.

The specialty utensils that you'll need to prepare this sauce are an enormous crockpot because, as the author of Mastering the Art of French Cuisine once said: "always start with a bigger pot than you think you will need;" a large wooden spoon covered in chocolate or another sweet; an "Ethics Stone" to control the boiling; and finally, a chef's blowtorch to use in the final stage of the process.

To obtain the best results, it is recommended to first prepare the sauce in a hidden shelter, away from any eyes of scrutiny. To hail the spirits of grandeur the mixture will evoke, the enormous crock of broth should be placed over fire logs in a secret cave of wonders and mirages. Three cooks whose names no one will ever know are ideal to stir up the most powerful Verschwörung sauce in the world.

For more people than you may think.

VERSCHWÖRUNG SAUCE:

20 Gallons of BS Broth (page 999). **4 Books on nationalistic pride and superiority with patriotic sounding author names and titles.**	Pour 10 gallons of BS Broth into the enormous crock pot and turn up the heat to a slow simmer. Start selecting pages from the books carefully, to separate any possible ambiguity regarding pride and superiority issues. Set those aside. Use the name of the authors sparingly. Do the same with the songs, slogans and sayings.
Ethics Stone	Drop the *Ethics Stone* into the enormous crock pot to make sure you keep the temperature just right.
30 Lyrics of Old Songs (folklore or heartland origin), slogans and sayings.	Stir in the carefully selected book pages, song verses, slogans and sayings, as you chant their words.
5 Kernels of cold truth.	Every time the *Ethics Stone* rattles, drop in a kernel of truth to bring the heat down.

Chapter II: Sauces

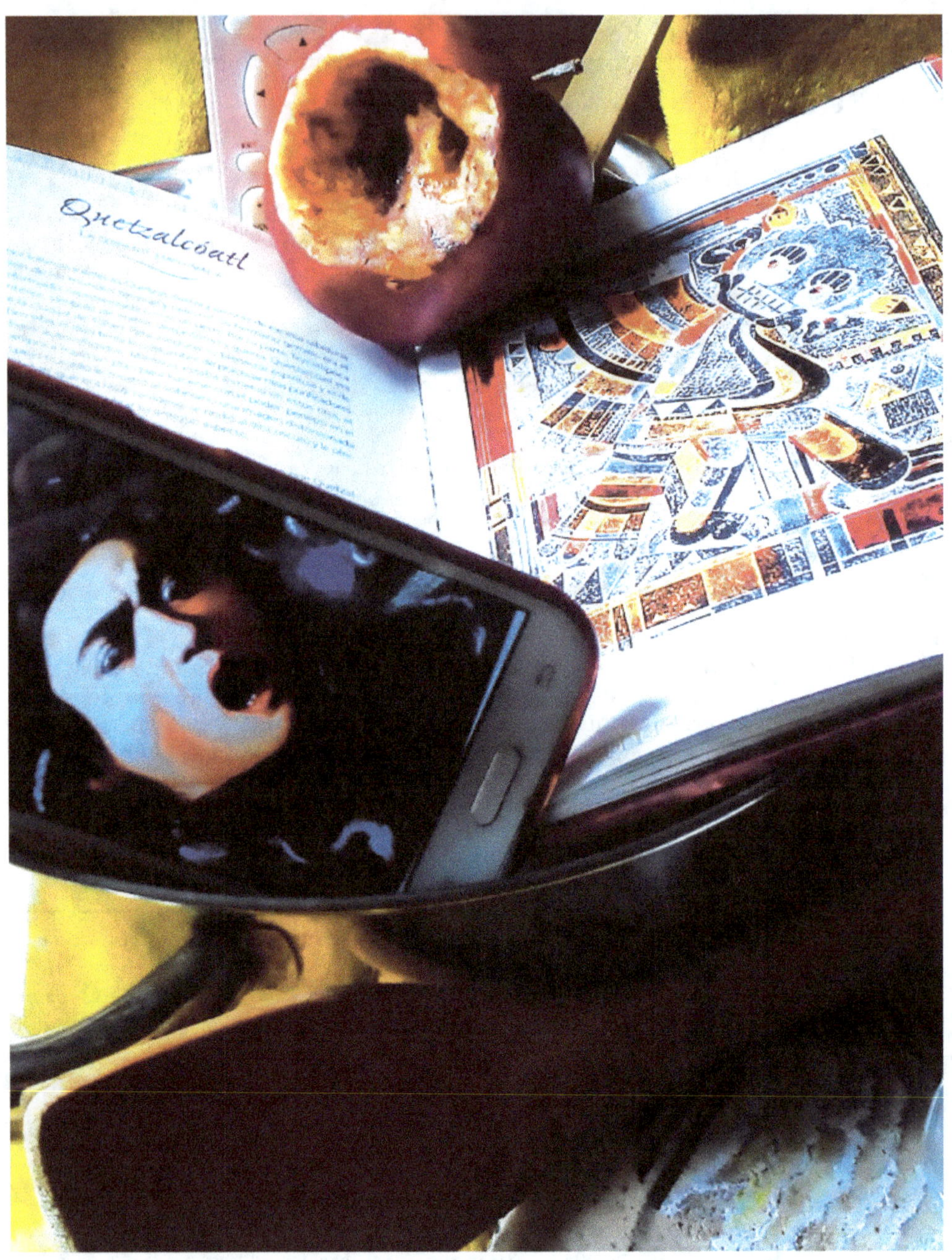

Art by
Andrés Salazar: *Techno Visual Recipe For Cock-And-Bull Stew (detail)* (2022)
Digital Photograph. 10 x 7 in.

IT'S COOKING

VERSCHWÖRUNG SAUCE:

A small dose of *Reflective Nostalgia*. A large dose of *Restorative Nostalgia*.	Let the mix get to a rolling boil once, drop in the doses of Nostalgia. Bring down the heat, let the enormous crock of broth bubble for a long while.
Large Sweet Spoon	Pour in the rest of the BS Broth, slowly stir with the *Large Sweet Spoon*. Chant some more verses.
Dash of varied resentments.	Carefully sprinkle in the varied resentments.
	Fire up the heat and bring the mishmashed ingredients to a boil for a second time. Let the enormous crock bubble, let the **Ethics Stone** rattle louder and louder until it cracks.
	Fish out the pieces of the **Ethics Stone** in the enormous crock pot and toss them into the garbage. There is no use for them anymore.
Presesentation	Serve generously and piping hot over the red meat.
 **Alcohol or other flammable drinks.**	Add the alcohol and use the chef's blowtorch to fire it up *flambé*.
Helpings & Servings.	Make sure there are helpings to spare for all, because they will want some more to share with their friends and family. Add more BS Broth as needed .
 **Snowflake garnish.**	To spice up new helpings, add snowflakes to the *Verschwörung* sauce.

Chapter II: Sauces

Jose Rafael Páez: *Zombie Evolution* (2023)
Character and location renderings for graphic story.
Color markers, ink and gouache on paper, various sizes.
Layout and lettering, Magdalena Rangel.

XI

FOLLOW THE SIMON SAYS

"Cuba is the Sea of Happiness. Venezuela is headed there."

HUGO CHÁVEZ F.
La Habana (March 8, 2000)

FOLLOW THE SIMON SAYS

Day 1

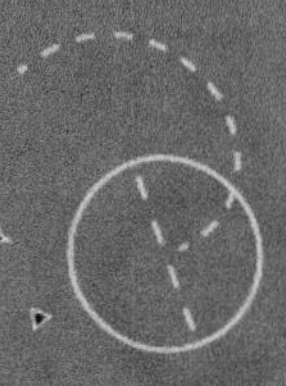

in W.Here BE
braiNs where
be BrAins
i dOnt reMemBer
i aM need
for My brains
i Have no bRains

3.141592653...

we alL haVe No bRains
we mOve wE go we dO
wE have nO braIns
We hAve rage wAnt BrAins
we aRe us we are All
no ONe Else we waNt more
of Us wiTH no braiN
hungry foR brains WE
folloW him folloW hiM
hunger anGer
cant reMemBer.
That Is all THE pi fifty.

Hunger, anger.
Don't remember.
no memory.
My head in
CIRCLES?
Why?
I don't know.
It's my math,
My madness.

FOLLOW THE SIMON SAYS

Day 1 (later)

He says go,
we follow.
His mass we are, yes.
His fury.
His rage.
His anger.
We are him.

Day 2

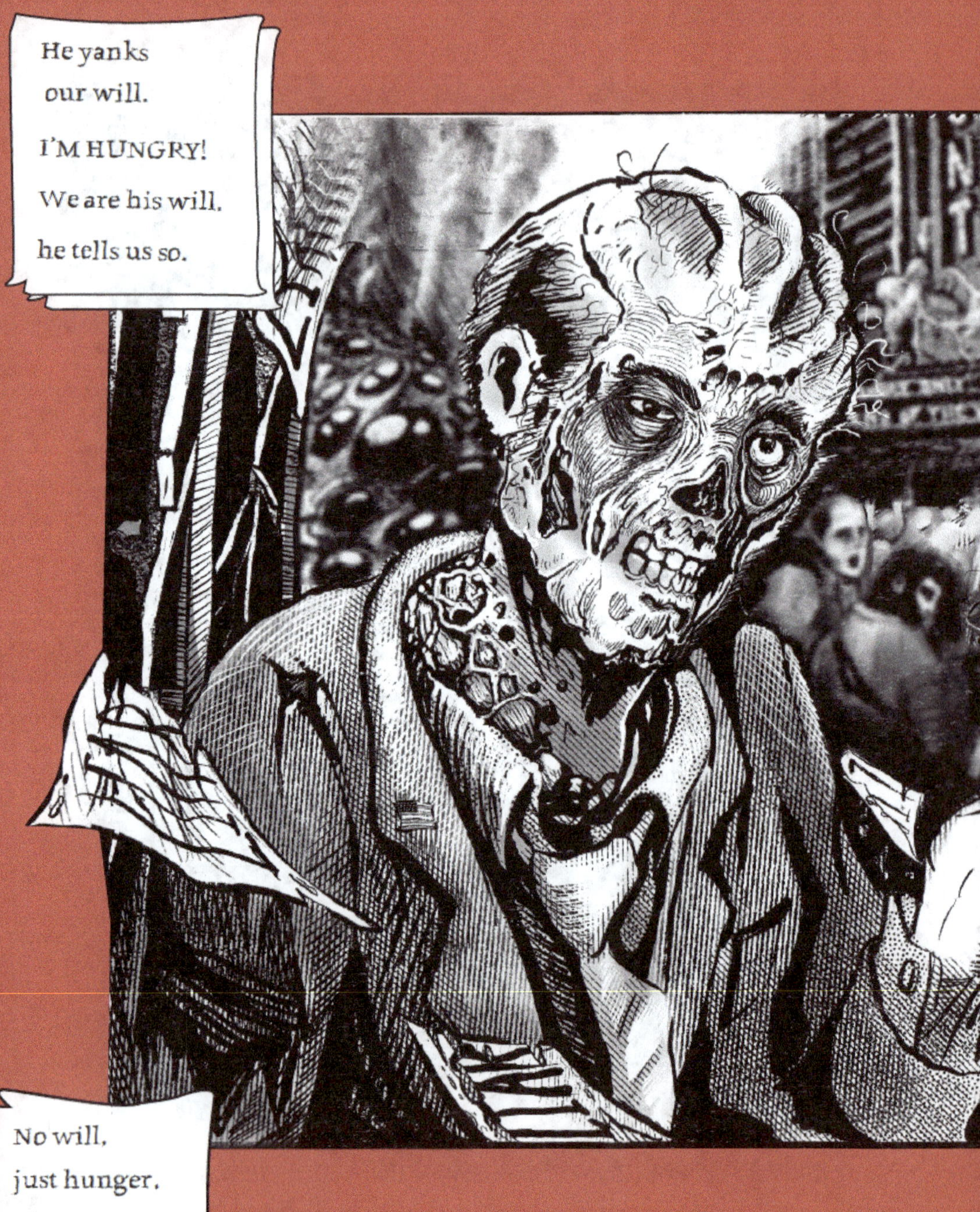
He yanks
our will.
I'M HUNGRY!
We are his will.
he tells us so.

No will,
just hunger.
we move.
we follow.
we go.

FOLLOW THE SIMON SAYS

Only *he*
has the answer:

his love.

Brain.
Fog. Cloud.
In my head, my brain?
I sleep now.
Sleep? Dreams again?

How?

Why?

Day 3

Dead. I am dead.
Alone.
I am only for me
and for my leader.
Maybe I am alive.
for others. Am I?
What is death?
To live?
Does he even care?
CAF

FOLLOW THE SIMON SAYS
Day 5

Why do I not know whether I'm dead or alive? What happened to me? What IS alive?

Makes me alive?

How did I lose alive? Where? When? I need to walk better. I need to talk better.

not in grrrunntt.

¡Grrrunntt!

The leader, we follow,
He gives us a new order,
a purpose we didn't know.
We are NOT chaos!
We amble, we stand,
we grunt, we hunt
new brains, we make
new followers for us,
for him.   Were they even
alive anyway?

Why do I write these
notes?
Every time
I ask me a question
I am better.
I am less dead,
if there can be
such a thing.

Not dead,

Not alive.

Day 8

How many of us are we?
Many brainless for him,
not dead, not alive.
Dont see, dont hear,
don't speak, don't feel,
only the leader exists.
Our leader, why, why
is he our leader?
He leads, we know not why.
He's there, we know not why.
He grunts his word we hear
not what of, doesn't mat-
ter. His loud noise moves us,
opens our hunger, we follow,
we don't feel, no brains, no
breath, no pulse. We have
nothing. Is that death?
nothing to feel?
and yet. Why?
Why do I write
in this journal?
Why, when?

HUNGRY.

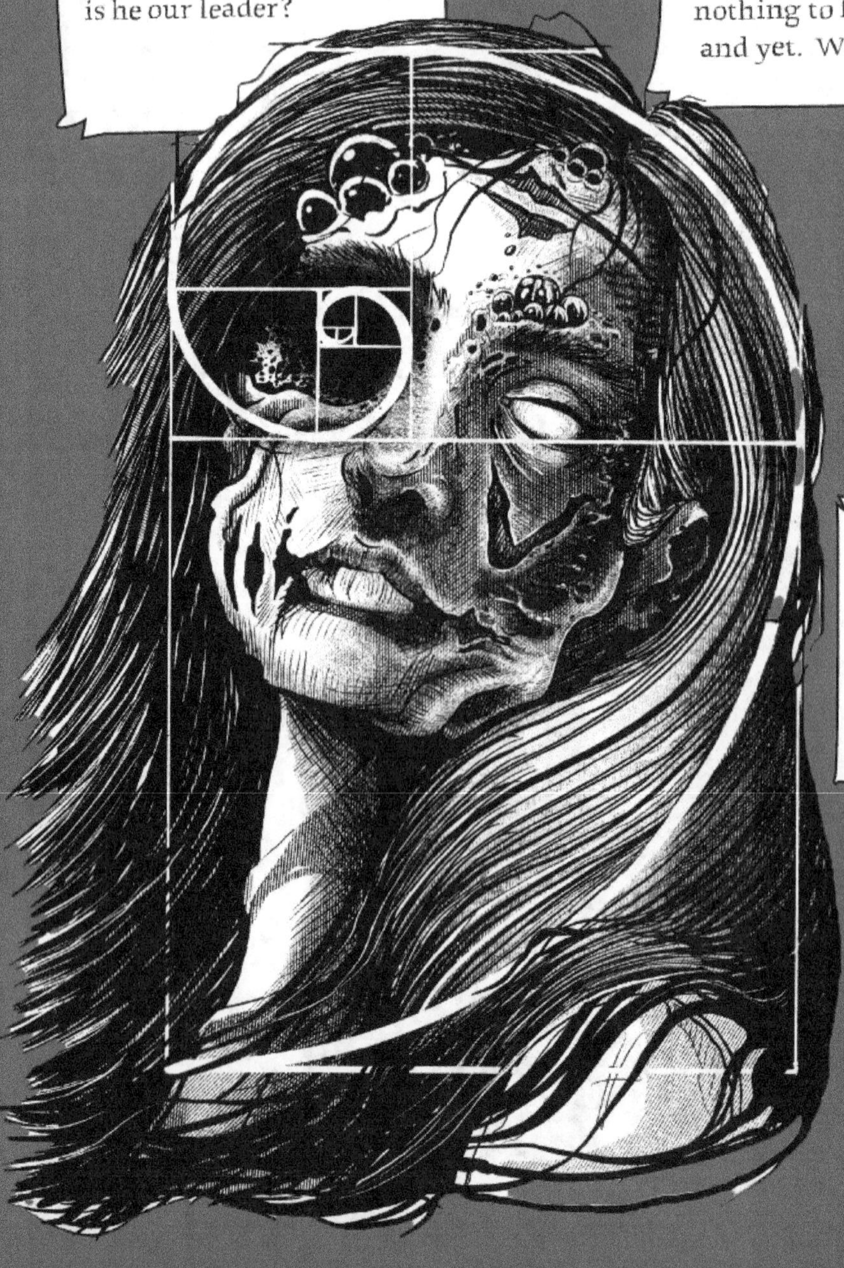

FOLLOW THE SIMON SAYS

I see, I touch, I hear:
that's new.
I hear the leader
and this time I listen
to his grunts.
He pulls us to follow.

If we follow, him,
we are dead,
He grunts words
to die from.

I see someone.
New, or anew also.
She is not food.
It is someone.
We see each other.
We connect.
Is it me more alive?
Are we more alive
when we connect
and more dead
when we do not?
What is more alive?

This red apple
that I hold in my
hand...
it was part of a tree,
no longer. Is it alive?
It has life in it.
It can go on its own,
even after I eat it.
Feel the life.
The Golden Rule.
Order in the chaos
we always live.

This leader is... not.
not a leader.
Now I see him,
know what he is:
a leader of death.
All he wants is our
brains.

ALL HE WANTS
IS OUR BRAINS!

Day 8 (cont.)

More of us in connect.
We feel once again,
we think again.
We are our own,
with each other.

Is it kumbaya?
What does that even
mean? Is it life?
What does it really mean?

I like her.
She is a she,
I am a me.
We are friends,
we are us.
With the friends we
have we are alive.
We had family.
With the family we
have we are alive.

Day 13

¿HELLO?

My journal, again.

Five days with sun,

clouds and rain;

six nights with stars.

I said a "Hello" today.

We can touch the earth,
feel and be part of.
I always could and
I had forgotten.
I was dead.

We will live forever
until we don't.
Some infinities are
smaller than others.

FOLLOW THE SIMON SAYS

I AM DEAD NO MORE

^I 79

XII

PURITY

The Shining City

"...in my mind it was a tall, proud city built on rocks stronger than oceans, wind-swept, God-blessed, and teeming with people of all kinds living in harmony and peace; a city with free ports that hummed with commerce and creativity. And if there had to be city walls, the walls had doors and the doors were open to anyone with the will and the heart to get here."

RONALD REAGAN
Farewell Address (1989)

Art by
Rolando Peña: *Our Daily Dracula* (2022)
Photomaton and acrílic on paper. 10 × 7 in.

PURITY

>>>>> From: Vlad <count_ Țepeș1@dcastle.com>
Sunday, February 23, 20xx, 6:55 AM
To: mina@dcastle.com
Subject: Re: Dead ends

It is time, the circle around me is complete. I will now step out to
my cherished garden and see the sunrise. The pyre is ready,
I am ready. My old master prepared me for this moment.
The fire you lit and that consumes me from within will burst forth
as dawn sweeps my darkness away. Your vital spirit will be part
of mine, sublimated in this chilly dawn's burning glory. From a
distance our enemy will see those purifying flames as their
victory and believe they have won, not seeing it for what it is,
a fleeting morning flash. But you and I will live on, beyond,
together despite their blindness. It is our destiny.

Best forever and more,

V.

>>>> On Feb. 23, 20xx, at 2:15 AM, Mina M
<mina@dcastle.com> wrote:

Always my Vlad:

The victors write history and the losers become
demons. Don't let them destroy you. If you don't
survive, if your life is not our story, then our love
was all for nothing. They'll cook up their own tale.
Come back to me. Let's write our true history.
Come back to our home. Don't make me mourn
you, let me cherish you. Don't let them win.
The moment for our life is now!

Your embraced,

Mina

>>> On Feb. 23, 20xx, at 2:05 AM, Vlad
<count_Tepes1@dcastle.com> **wrote:**

Everlasting Mina:

There is one thing I never told you: the true reason why I left
to pursue fame and fortune in an unwelcoming, far away
land. I must say it now: the reason was you.
You have always been my heart's purpose.

Your fiancé came to our lands while also seeking fortune
of his own. He came here as one of those self-entitled
business men with a silver, no, a golden tongue, seeking
to prey upon the ill-informed and swindle their good faith
for profit and power. I distrusted him from the start. I am
not sure what he told you about his travels, but he spent
an abundance of time with the happy village wenches; his
idea of a bachelor party, I presume.

When he showed me your photograph, I felt sorry for your
future with such a man, an obvious conniver; but it was
then that I realized I had to find you. It was the spark from
behind those eyes and your beaming smile betraying a
bright soul within, a soul which I somehow knew, that drove
me to you. I scraped all my savings and invested in what
he sold me as a "fixer-upper" mansion in The City. I left in a
cargo ship to finally make it to that decrepit shell you know,
a place perhaps in a sorrier state than my home here in
these mountains. *Fixer-upper* was an understatement. Less
generous minds would have called fraud what he did to
me. I am sure his colleagues thought it was brilliant, with a
hearty laugh and a good commission.

I have no regrets about that, I feel blessed for having met
you. I found you. All after that was the bliss and the hell
at once. My skin has always made me *the different one.*
Hyper-photo sensitive skin and my unpigmented eyes force
me to live in darkness and can be a crippling disability. But
it did not matter to you; with you, our souls had light from
within. We were paired since time immemorial, have found
each other before and will do so again, after our current
transit.

When you let me in and I finally embraced you, I found
life, was fully filled by you. I recovered strength, you lit me
within. The hostile city disappeared when I held you, kissed
your fingers, your arms, your neck…

Art by
Rolando Peña: ***Our Daily Dracula (detail)*** (2022)
Photomaton and acrílic on paper. 10 x 7 in.

PURITY

>>>

-- But for your people, I was too different. They could not see us as a
life together, you are too special to them. I have kept from you that
horror fantasy they made up about me; you will hear it in time but
know from now that it is a deceit that hides their own evil nature. It
is a fantastic chimera ideated to separate us because, to them, it is
an abomination that you and I could belong together: a cherished
family jewel seduced by a hideous foreign monster.

When I saw that you faced real danger by the maddened frenzy
of your jealous fiancé and his hoodlums, I left. I left to protect you.
At any moment they could find you at fault of an unforgivable sin,
target you with their saintly sermons, their sharp stakes, their flaming
crosses. I had to deflect their gaze, direct them only to me.
They succeeded in forcing us apart in this life, but we will live
again, and together once again.

I will begin the ritual now: shave my head and don the orange
robe. It will soon be over. Our souls will meet again in a better
place, at a better time, once all our shed tears make their way to
the ocean.

Forever yours,
V.

>> On Feb. 23, 20xx, at 12:10 AM, Mina M
<mina@dcastle.com> **wrote:**

Dearest Vlad:

You never lost me. I've missed your voice and words
so much. I was so happy when I received your message, but not so much when I read it. Ever since you
left, I'm "protected" by men claiming to be friends, but
they just keep me shut in, shut up, they keep me from
being me. Friends to whom? Why do they claim to
own the truth? Who gave them such power over me,
to keep me in this corral like some brainless meat?

I'm so relieved that you gave me this email address,
the one they don't know about. I always dream of you,
waiting for you to come, to feel your embrace once
again, to share our love. But you scare me when you
say that Jonathan put together a revenge posse to hunt
you down. I fear for you, especially because you
write that they're nearby. Please protect yourself.

>>

-- I know what you feel and what you are thinking when you talk about our future together and forever but, to me, believing happiness existed in a fantasy past and will return in an imaginary future only blinds us to our possible present, here and now. I want to appreciate each good moment we have when we have it, because I know it will not last.

I don't know if it's true that we were blessed and pure souls together in some past time. I don't care for such a story; we must live our todays. Many todays! Destiny is what we make of it. Make *me* your goal, your destiny: make it to survive and to come back to me, not to stand for noble principles on some high moral ground. Make me your purpose, come home to me, where I will love you *now and forever*. Not all forevers are the same.

Yours, always
Mina

> On Feb. 22, 20xx, at 11:27 PM, Vla <count_Tepes1@dcastle.com> **wrote:**

Dearest Mina:

This is my last message for you. The end is near. The hate has run its course. I have lost. I have lost you. But I know the path to finding you again.

Leaving The City was not enough for those that hate what I am and what I represent. They have come here, to chase and hunt me down in my own land, to ensure that you and I are never together again. To ensure a lesson is learned for all to know: that people like us can never again, never again... in the name of purity.

Mine is a poor and remote region, not a wealthy metropolis like yours. After the ruin I tried to make fortune in a foreign land, yours, but that was not meant to be. Your fellows and peers viewed me with distrust because of my skin, even my nose! My foreign accent, unintelligible to their closed minds, would always trigger that cleavage question reasserting their belonging there and my alien status among them:

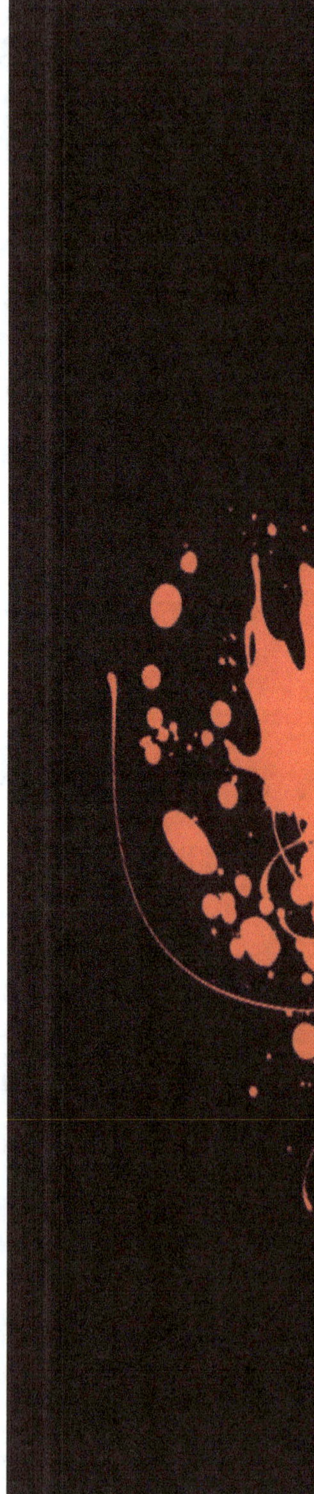

PURITY

"Where are you from?", making sure I always know my place, not from here; that I am a temporary guest given temporary courtesy in their small bubble; a guest, that is, until the moment they believe the ugly, disease ridden, foreigners have come to rape their women and to steal their jobs and money; until they feel threatened by the different, by impurity.

My mind's purpose when leaving my country was to send back money. Send earnings to my own people, who languish with their expectations that I will rescue them from their miseries, just because I live in this high mountain castle. Yet, I was also ruined, I have no servants and this place is falling apart. It was my hope to create fortune in The City, with commerce between our countries. But fear of my presence and of my kind has created greater barriers which now separate us even more.

From times immemorial my family has protected this province. It was my turn now. I wanted to change us from being a remote and forgotten region; I wanted to be part of the world. I have failed. I have only brought conquerors into our midst, led by Harker, seeking to destroy me. You were the only thing gained, and now I've lost you too.

My end will be here soon, one way or another. I am left only to choose the way. Our trek together in this world has come to its dead end. My physical condition made me pursue reflection and inner life, and an old master from the ancient east taught me the ways of wisdom and the paths of destiny. He taught me the purification rite to grant peace and transit to a renewed life when all is lost. I am ready to follow in his steps. It is my sole path to be reunited with you, the only one I see ahead. My farewell is only for now. I decide not with despair, but with hope.

Yours, forever

V.

Art by
Rolando Peña: ***Our Daily Dracula (detail)*** (2022)
Photomaton and acrílic on paper. 10 x 7 in.

XIII

ONCE UPON A TIME...

> "But I like the inconveniences... But I don't want comfort... I want God, I want poetry, I want real danger, I want freedom, I want goodness. I want sin...
>
> All right then, I'm claiming the right to be unhappy. Not to mention the right to grow old and ugly and impotent; the right to have syphilis and cancer; the right to have too little to eat; the right to be lousy; the right to live in constant apprehension of what may happen tomorrow; the right to catch typhoid; the right to be tortured by unspeakable pains of every kind... I claim them all."

ALDOUS HUXLEY
A Brave New World (1932)

Art by
Annika Connor: *Because Of You* (2022)
Oil on linen 20 x 16 in.

ONCE UPON A TIME...

Cindy's Dream

*T*he knot in her gut tightens as Cindy asks herself, "how could I have been so stupid? Why did I tell Annie?"

She hears Annie laughing, almost cackling, over in the kitchen. Annie's voice is loud and mocking, telling Drew: "There once were three sisters... but they weren't! The youngest was a stepsister! That was her dream! And at the end she marries a prince who takes her to a castle away from it all with a dance and a song. Please!"

Annie laughs again, loud and raucous, as only she can when horsing around. An explosive mixture of tease, joy and bullishness that so many boys find attractive in her, like moths to the flame, doomed by that brightness with feigned sweetness. Maybe flies into the honey trap is a better image. Or would that be Drew? They are always going for the boys; and the boys always go for them, ending up petrified by their smarts, wits, and charm. Losers!

Cindy dusts the shelf where her father's wedding pictures stand. Him next to HER. All three girls in prim princess dresses... She should have never told Annie; but... but such a beautiful dream...even musical. She couldn't help herself. She knows it was just a dream, but...

*O*nce upon a time a rich widower with a beautiful baby daughter named Cindy lived happily in a big house with many maids and assistants. Cindy had all the attention and all the love she could ever wish for. Then her father married a widow to help him raise his young daughter. The widow had two daughters who did not like Cindy. Her father died, the twice widowed woman spent all their fortune, all the maids and assistants had to be let go, and Cindy was left to serve the widow and her two daughters. While Cindy lives this life of misery, a magical being appears and helps her find a Prince that will take her away from her misfortune. She and the Prince fall in love at first sight, but the stepsisters try to stop Cindy from leaving by tricking the Prince into loving one of them. True love prevails at the end, the wicked deceit is revealed, and the Prince takes Cindy away to live happily ever after, leaving her step-family to clean up after their own messes and die alone.

And, what's wrong with that? Why did Annie find it so hilarious? There was a time when, Cindy thinks, she had a better life. Why did her father have to marry again? They were perfectly fine with no one else. She remembers little of that time, maybe her imagination remembers it better than it really was, but, as far as she is concerned, it was Paradise. No evil, only love; no suffering, only joy; no wants, just abundance. It was a better time, for sure, not like this life now. Not this constant bickering and rivalry between all of us.

Cindy does not realize when she says it out loud: "What's wrong with wanting a savior? What's wrong with hoping for someone who will take me to a new life, to a new paradise, to take me out of this, this… despairing vale of tears?"

"Well, looky me at such big fancy words. Always thinking you're so special, so much better than us" says Drew, startling Cindy out of her daydream. "What's wrong, you ask? For heaven's sake, little girl, it's not like we live in a dump here. It's a small apartment, yes, but you make it sound like it's the worst place ever. Mom works very hard to make ends meet and we all got to pitch in, even you!"

Cindy is dumbstruck, always timid. Drew seems angrier than her usual self as she lashes out some more at her stepsister.

"Hear to me now little girl, there's no prince, only us. We're the ones that got to make it better for us. We find a guy we like, fine, it's our thing, no magic. Wake up, puh-lease! You have a problem, we talk. You don't just go dream and find a prince to disappear your family, dead to you because you don't want to share with us. It's what you want? Your wish? Really?"

Cindy tries to answer, but Drew unloads: "Waiting for some guy out there, any 'prince' out there to take away your power, girl, all your will and, yes, your voice too, in exchange for his 'Castle of Happiness' where he is your commander over it all while we, your sisters? Conveniently out of sight, out of mind. And believe me this when I tell it to you, yes: your commander will always want it all and more. Only crumbs for you! That's what you really want? That's when you, girl, are really, truly, another brainless zombie-like ambulatory meat."

They stare, maybe glare, at each other. Confusion boils in Cindy. Finally, she blurts "But Drew, you guys always make it all so complicated for me when all I want is a simple life, with no complications. You and Annie are always ganging up on me, I'm always outnumbered. I'm always in the minority!"

"That does not mean you can't talk, little girl, you have a voice of your own, no? There's no such thing as a simple life. Yeah, we sometimes listen you, and you should sometimes listen us. Yeah, you're right, a family of us is much more complicated than just a guy telling you what to do and to shut up, but really, together, we're unstoppable; it's an us that can do anything; I tell you, fighting each other like this, we're the poster of mess, the entry in the encyclopedia for chaos, sweet disasters ready to blow."

ONCE UPON A TIME...

From the kitchen, Annie chimes in: "Tell her Drew, tell it, tell it good." She walks into the room, three Cokes dangling from its six-pack ring. She teases Cindy as she pulls back the one she brought for her, finally letting Cindy grab it.

Annie pops open her can, hissss. "Our sister here, 'little girl,' tells it loud and clear: we are family. We may think different, say it different… but we should all want the same, keeping it together and making it good. It may not be exactly the way I want it, or the way you want it… but the idea is to keep it together, that we can still each do our own thing and make it all better. Let me tell you my dream!"

Once upon a time the kind father of a baby girl found relief from the grief of losing his first wife by meeting and marrying a good woman, herself a widow. This woman had two daughters of her own and they all made life together as a family for a while. Grief visited them once again with the untimely death of their father. Hard times came, and the mother tried to make a living in a cruel world, abusive of her weak situation. The mother tried to make the best for her three daughters, making sure they all got an education and raising them to be strong and independent, not like she had been. But the youngest one remembered a past that did not exist and longed for an imaginary future, rescued from her daily chores by a magically appearing savior on one great mighty steed. While waiting for that day of redemption to come, she moped around the house pining for her dear dead dad, not moving on, forward or whatever, however you say it...

Cindy protests: "That's easy for you to say, but he was my dad!" Drew and Annie: "He was our dad too!" The silence between them grows awkward. A grandma would say an angel passed by.

The wedding pictures perched on their shelf quietly contemplate the three sisters. Drew contains a tear and signals Annie to finish her tale.

Art by
Annika Connor: *Because Of You (detail)* (2022)
Oil on linen 20 x 16 in.

ONCE UPON A TIME...

...All the little girls finally grew up and became an empowered force of change in their world, found love in the partner they wanted, or not, and lived out the life we all expect to live: work every day for the pursuit of happiness in a world full of opportunities. Knowing full well that each day we live is one day closer to the day we'll die – with no ever afters. The end.

Another awkward silence… suddenly, Annie bursts into her contagious laugh.

Cindy chuckles, takes a sip from her soda and, after a minute, pipes: "I guess that's a better dream. Still just another fairy tale."

THE END

AFTERWORD

"You say you want a revolution,
 well, you know
 we all want to change the world.
 You tell me that it's evolution,
 well, you know
 we all want to change the world..."

JOHN LENNON
Revolution (1968)

Art by
Marc Lafia: ***Loren Eisely #20*** (2023)
Digital painting. 42 X 57 in.

AFTERWORD

The practice of democracy is relatively recent in the history of humanity. While there were attempts to make institutionalized democratic republics in Ancient Greece and Rome, the unleashing of the potential for innovation and creativity, by means of this governance experiment, would not be fully realized until the Liberal Revolution of the 18th Century. It was then that the idea of institutional renewal combined with that of economic renewal, capitalism, would shake the world.

This structural quake will bring forth deep social, economic, and political transformation and the notion of democracy as we know it today. It will usher in a prosperous era spanning a scant two hundred and fifty years, at most, in civilization's history of six thousand years; an era that has created and distributed more wealth and well-being than all the time before it, even to nations that do not practice democracy, by its collateral spillover effect. Given the historical span of modern democracy, it is not remarkable that heroic legends, myths, fables and all the historical trappings of our culture are mostly skewed towards what we could regard as illiberalism—authoritarian order centered around tribal loyalties.[1] Yet, liberalism did not sprout out of nowhere. Its roots, and some demons, can be found in those same myths, legends and fables which have shaped our minds for millennia.

● ABOUT THE IDEAS

Some time ago I was invited to participate in a political consultancy team working for a presidential candidate in a Latin American country. As is often the case in the region, a broad spectrum of democratic leaning political organizations was pitted against a broad spectrum of populists labeling themselves (or accusing their opponents of being) "nationalists," "socialists," or other such names, depending on the political base they were seeking to sway. It was clear, once again, that while populists base their standard story on an easily conveyed simple narrative of "facts" deeply rooted in emotion with a scant sprinkling of reason, liberals (in its 18th century meaning) typically struggle to convey complex ideas deeply rooted in reason with a light sprinkling of emotion.

This is not only the case in Latin America. It is a normal human tendency to prefer simple order and control to complex messiness and uncertainty. Strongmen (not always men) can use the institutions of democracy to achieve and keep political power with a promise to end uncertainty and restore order.

---

[1] Authoritarian rule is associated with the "blood and soil" tribal instinct, which both the so called right and left can appropriate at any given time in different variations. Hugo Chávez invoking Bolívar to fight Yankee imperialism invokes the same instincts as Viktor Orbán protecting Hungarian purity against (non-existent) immigrant hordes ("Xenophobia is dangerous, but patriotism is a good thing" – V. Orban). Nationalistic leaders from the range of the political spectrum, like Maduro, Ortega, Xi, Putin, Orbán, or Erdoğan to mention a few, spokespeople from the alt-right in the U.S., and candidates such as Le Pen, Meloni, and others, make opportunistic use and common cause with authoritarian nationalistic rhetoric as opposed to libertarian principle.

Over the last twenty years we have seen a great illiberal wave sweeping across the globe, a likely reaction to that fount of messiness and uncertainty which is liberal democracy and which had its peak in the early 90's – Francis Fukuyama's "End of History" era.

Thus, once again facing the rivalries and swings between order and disorder, that consultancy engagement steered me back to a book project which I had set aside; a project seeking to identify and understand latent archetypes embedded in our common popular tales and interpreted within a liberal democracy narrative.

In a previous book I wrote a segment on the power of populism and its emotionally seductive narrative: the promise to redress a heterogeneity of grievances, gathered under a mantle of general malaise, with simple ideas, catchy slogans, and strong, almost iconic symbols, colors, and even distinctive garments.[2] As a counter narrative, I argued, the reasoned promises liberalism can make are attractive when articulated: individual dignity, equal and fair treatment under the law, equal opportunity, and protection of private property—promises which in one way or another are often made by all candidates during democratic election campaigns (because elections, after all, are basically a liberal idea), while enjoying local foods, kissing babies, and professing their love for mom, dad, and country.

In that same book I propose to define liberty as the condition under which a human being has the opportunity to fulfill his or her own full potential as such. Liberty is at the essence of free will; it is the ideological core of liberal democracy. In the present book I juxtapose this governance paradigm against its rival, authoritarian rule. The latter can be defined as a condition under which human beings survive and thrive dependent on the opportunistic whims of a regime whose ideological core is that maximum power is rightfully and legitimately concentrated in its leader.

---

[2] "Populism, or the collective blindness which leads people to the abyss", in Rangel, C.J., *La Venezuela Imposible: Crónicas y reflexiones sobre democracia y libertad.* (Alexandria Publishing House, Miami, FL. 2017).

AFTERWORD

The promises of liberal democracy are invariably broken under populist rule, which will lead to authoritarianism. It does not matter if such rule labels itself left or right wing: equal opportunity and equal protection under the law are doomed to disappear and injustice to prevail. In politics, as in life, monsters will surface out of the dichotomy reason/emotion when reason sleeps.

If the (attractive) promises and rules of a democratic liberal system are kept, these inevitably will result in the rotation of any populist, quasi-authoritarian leader and possibly violent confrontations between both systems and their followers. Self-preservation, a basic instinct in politics, and particularly acute under authoritarian rule, clashes with the basic principle of democracy: the renovation of ideas, leaders, and institutions, no matter what came before. This is commonly stated as "out with the old, in with the new", or more commonly still: "throw the bums out!" (family-friendly here). This periodic institutional renovation aspect of democracy is an underlying theme of the first vignette, Old Greek myths repeatedly illustrate leadership succession as a sequence of violently overthrown tyrants by many means, sometimes by their sons or daughters, sometimes by the hero of the day.

Those powerful tales, likely reflecting true life observations, perhaps led to the idea of systematic institutional renewal by rules and orderly means and, eventually, democracy. This renewal idea, despite its many flaws, seems better than the bloodshed described in their legends, plays and stories. But, as in all fanciful fiction, reality often clashes with wishful thinking

Art by
Marc Lafia: *Loren Eisely #16* (2023)
Digital Painting. 42 X 57 in.

Left and right ideologies are purposefully clouded by their adherents as a means of political self-preservation. The ideological bases of these opposing factions and their ultimate goals can be traced back to the French Revolution, when the then-called left championed rights to opportunity, in all possible manifestations, while the then-called right championed property rights, again, with all its possible implications. A true liberal democracy seeks to balance the rights of opportunity and those of property to achieve the best possible outcome for all of society. In other words, for democracy to exist and thrive, so must the political alternance and permanent creative churn generated by that rivalry between left (opportunity) and right (property). The need of opposites to build a whole, from ideas and behaviors, mechanisms and systems, up to humankind itself, is contained within all the texts of this book and, of course, brings to mind the ancient concept of Ying/Yang.

But this quest for maximal political self-preservation, i.e., achieving and maintaining power at all costs, will lead to other outcomes, sometimes even compromising the security of a nation and its citizens. Right and left partisans may prefer to heat up antagonistic rhetoric, each faction accusing the other of being the anti-democratic one (because the word "democracy" is a favorite one in modern populist and authoritarian speech), the one that "will destroy our country and our values as we know and love them," with the corollary that to protect the essence of our nation the opponents (and dissidents) are the enemy that must be silenced, canceled, eliminated... Polarization ensues, extremism gains ground, and positive social outcomes diminish. That is the underlying theme for the final vignette, ONCE UPON A TIME..., which ends in the sour note about both sides of the coin being the same fairy tale, with no happily ever afters, just continuous struggle.[3]

It is important to point out that when a subset of these factions behave in truly antidemocratic ways, using their power to subvert norms and institutions with political intimidation and political violence[4], such behavior is sometimes resisted (as heroic defense) by some of the faction's own members and peers, instead of (as institutional treason) collaborated with. The labels of treason, loyalty, cowardice, and bravery are results dependent and as such, and as they relate to societal transformation, are explored in the fifth vignette, PETRIFIED.

---

[3]   Friedrich Hayek, in his Postscript to The Constitution of Liberty (1960), "*Why I am not a Conservative*," proposes that political ideology is not a linear spectrum but a triangle, with the Right and the Left in two of its vertices, and Liberalism in its third. In the extreme of the first two ideologies there would be autocracies, with the will of a few seeking to impose control on the many in name of the common good, either by a mercantilist or communist dictatorship. We can infer, then (as some critics of Hayek have done), that we can associate extreme liberalism with anarchy, a social order in which each individual is responsible of controlling their own well-being and progress. Conceptually (once again) modern democracy as a form of government would be placed towards the center of this triangle, satisficing many, in Herbert Simon's sense, but never enough, leading to that continuous struggle.

[4]   For example, by members of the Polish Law and Justice party in 2015, subverting constitutional and political norms to drive democratic institutions and society to the extreme right, or by the Morena coalition trying to do the same in Mexico towards the extreme left in 2022.

AFTERWORD

In this manner, from the first to the last vignette, the intention of the book is an attempt to identify what makes that messy institutional mechanism we call democracy tick and stick, and the roots it may have in our enduring ancient and familiar tales.

● ABOUT THE BOOK

I had let my insights into such roots languish after an initial and feverish burst of writing a few years ago until, once again, I felt the imperative need to write them down because of that consulting engagement. Moreover, I realized the need for illustrations to accompany the text when it taps into the myths and tales, because in our minds we already have imprinted images of them. Thus, the book project was fully conceived.

The work is presented in thirteen "vignettes," each with an archetypal myth or story at its core, and each accompanied by illustrations from a constellation of artists from around the world which contributed generously to the making of this project. The interaction with each artist helped me focus on the topic of each vignette, and I am truly grateful for this interaction and their support. The following paragraphs are extracts (with some paraphrasing for clarity) of my communications with some of them to attempt some guidance in the selection and creation of imaging for the text:

> ● "…Vignettes may touch upon more than one topic at once, and these include democracy as renewal, tyranny, 'me too,' fake news, the nature of life, beauty, demagogues, science denial, populism, individual empowerment, diversity, and many others. Each vignette is written to be read quickly and convey through the story its underlying topic…"

> ● "…Regarding TYRANNY, the vignette is based on a powerful if perhaps forgotten myth, one in which the creator of mankind [Prometheus] is punished by a superior god for, basically, giving humans a fighting chance against the whims of the gods …has his reward (redemption?) in his creation, humankind, which thrives and prospers because of what he did. Not to mention that Zeus himself, the tyrant, is now a lesser god. This self-sacrificial aspect of the hero I explore further in a later vignette, PETRIFIED…

● "…Some of Prometheus' legends say that, while he created the human form with clay molded into the shape of the gods (as happens in all creation myths), it was Athena, the goddess of wisdom, who with her breath brought the clay to life. This is an interesting and intriguing part of the myth because it contains two ideas. First Prometheus, a titan god of the old universe order, makes alliance with the new universe order, an olympian god, to create humankind. I delve directly into the old/new universe order (in essence, nature vs. man) three more times in the book, directly once before, in RENEWED, later with BEATY, and indirectly in IT COMES AROUND. The second message contained in the Prometheus/Athena creation myth is that just as you needed the old and the new, you needed a man and a woman to create humanity…"

● "…[Regarding IO RUMINATES] we must be aware of how power can transform. He is accused by over 100 women of verbal and sexual abuse, groping, and rape, feeling entitled to do so because of his power over them. It is not acceptable. A series highlighting the disempowerment of his victims is a worthwhile project…"

AFTERWORD

● "... THE BUBBLE vignette seeks to reflect an antagonistic duality between lies and truth, and the danger that a longed for fantasy may hide the dangerous reality one faces…".

● "…In using old tales, myths, and legends, one of the purposes of the book is to engage with the timelessness of the stories it taps. To make any of the illustrations too relevant to our current moment diminishes the power over time of the messaging… [THE MONSTER] is applicable to any wanna-be strong-man, current or past, propped up by any witless political and/or economic oligarchy…"

● "…FOLLOW THE SIMON SAYS [illustrates] mobs that can be mindlessly driven by empty slogans [grunts], even to the extent of being self-destructive. To escape that collective mob mentality individuals must assert their own being, difficult as that may be… The vignette also addresses the essence of life and how it is only by connecting with what surrounds us and with other people that life is manifested, that we are happy to be alive…

● "…[PURITY uses] the three messages from Count Tepes as a dramatization of K-R's stages of anger, denial, acceptance, bargaining and depression associated to the certainty that death is near…[5] His first email message, the last one in the text, makes direct reference to the second vignette in the book, the one on the Pandora/Eve myth, BOTTOM OF THE BARREL, but turning on its head the hope and despair relationship; the violence associated to the count's persecution is of course related to the violence used by the powerful to maintain their privileges (and not be 'RENEWED')… The objectification of Mina by her 'protectors' is referential to the third vignette, IO RUMINATES; and the exchange between the Count and Mina is the eternal dichotomy between collective idealism and individual pragmatism, theme also touched upon in the fifth vignette based on the Perseus myth (and famously represented in the movie 'High Noon' with Grace Kelly and Gary Cooper)…" [6]

● "…The Cinderella story is one of the most toxic tales imprinted upon all of us since childhood. In a beautiful candy wrapper, and with an excess of sugar coating, it disempowers women abysmally and sets up unreasonable expectations for men. The power of the tale is that it is derived from an idea that has set back human progress and development throughout history (and which my father, within the context of Latin America, debunked in his most famous book).[7] This is the idea that existence has three stages: one of paradise, one of suffering, and one of paradise recovered by a redeemer. In Cinderella there was a time of plenty, there is a time of suffering, and there will be a 'happily ever after' delivered by a magical redeemer or powerful hero. Of course, this is the christian myth (among other religious variants), but it is also the Marxist myth, which makes this one so powerfully resonant in many societies. The archetypal origin of the tale comes from the stages of childhood innocence, growing up (the fruit of knowledge delivered by Eve/Pandora), and a rationalization for the purpose of life (an afterlife, or for Marxists, the unattainable future wellbeing). But these myths end up disempowering the individual and distracting from the here and now…"

---

[5] Kubler-Ross, E., **On Death and Dying.** (Routledge, 1969).

[6] The vignette "Purity" is written as an email chain, so it can be read as presented in the book or backwards, chronologically by its time stamps. In the first reading it is Count Vlad writing/responding to Mina. When read following the timestamp line, it is Mina's responses after reading the Count's first message.

[7] Rangel, C., **The Latin Americans: Their Love-Hate Relationship with the United States.** (Hacourt Brace Jovanovich, 1977).

AFTERWORD

Friends, collaborators, and acquaintances kind enough with their time to read portions and early drafts of the text have made, among their generous comments, two observations. The first one is that the brief vignettes make them curious and have made them want to further explore the story or subject matter. That was one of my intentions, to ignite such curiosity. The second is more of a question as to whether more such stories could be forthcoming in the future. more such stories could be forthcoming in the future.

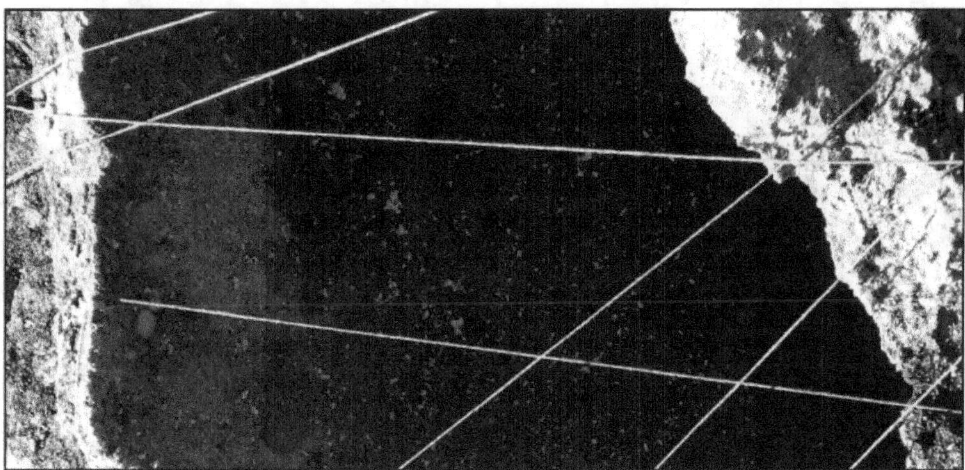

From the large selection of tales in our western lore, I winnowed these out. I did think of a few others, such as Midas, the Minotaur, Daedalus and Icarus, David and Goliath (to which I do make a reference in one vignette), Cain and Abel, Little Red Riding Hood, Rumpelstiltskin, Moby Dick, and several more. Some could have fit within my narrative arc, others would not, or were just too obvious and too used.[8] The Emperor's New Clothes, for example, is overexposed: A politician with raw ambition, believing himself entitled to power and wealth, spins fabulous yarns for his followers. His partisans believe that only a fool would not admire such a leader as he brazenly displays his naked ambition and impunity, strutting down Grand Avenue or sitting on his baubled, gilded throne. Not one of his subjects dares to point out that the Emperor is naked lest he or she be called an idiot, a traitor, or bear a worse fate. A tale too overexposed, too of the moment. Or is it really?

This selection of seemingly disparate stories is used to develop a single theme: the duality autocracy/democracy from various angles and within a simple narrative. I had considered the project complete with twelve vignettes and their illustrations when one of my friends, Dr. Nemesio Mondelo, suggested that I should include among the various styles of writing a cooking recipe. At first, I refused. I had dedicated too much energy to the project already and had deemed it done.

---

[8] Having finished writing the text for the book and its Afterword, I had the opportunity to present a different book, a new Italian translation of *The Latin-Americans: Their Love-Hate Relationship with the United States*, at the Istituto Bruno Leoni, Milan, in November 2023 (the full text of the presentation, is available in my blog carlosjrangel.com: *Carlos Rangel and Democracy as the Anti-Myth*). In that presentation I referred to The Boy that Cried Wolf to talk about civic and media complacency to the permanent threats to democracies. As I have tried to argue in this book: democracy is always under attack, internally and externally, and the warnings and dangers are real. The wolf stalks, always.

But after a reading of Anne Applebaum's *Twilight of Democracy* I realized that my book was indeed missing one ingredient: the elements of conspiracy — essential in authoritarian domination. I then wrote one last vignette IT'S COOKING, a recipe in a Shakesperean imagining, completing thusly the baker's dozen. One of the collaborating artists, Andrés Salazar, scrambled up a photo composition including fear, corrupt knowledge, and nationalistic ideas, to perfectly accompany the text. While recipes may not quite be myths, legends, or tales, for some they can be part of a deliciously shared family tradition, like the aroma of comfort food wafting out from our favorite drunk uncle's kitchen.

Carlos J. Rangel

ART DETAILS IN AFTERWORD FROM ART IN EARLIER PAGES:

Pag. 96,	Marc Lafia: **Loren Eisely #20** (2023).
Pag. 99:	**Loren Eisely #16** (2023).
Pag. 98:	Magdalena Rangel: **Pandora's Gift #3-Color-4 (Detail)** (2023). In Book: Pag. 8.
Pag. 100:	**Mimi Abers: Back. (Detail)** (2007). In Book: Pag. 22.
Pag. 101:	**Nuria Román: From South To North (Detail)** (2001). In Book: Pag. 48.
Pag. 102:	Magdalena Rangel: **Io Ruminates #48,#50 (Details)** (2023). In Book: Pag. 12.
Pag. 103:	Itamar Martínez: **Hombre Herido (Detail)** (2019). In Book: Pag. 54.
Pag. 105:	**Nuria Román: Sew The Earth: Lithica (Detail)** (2013). In Book: Pag. 50.
Pag. 106:	Andrés Salazar: **Techno Visual Recipe For Cock-And-Bull Stew (Detail)** (2022). In Book: Pag. 60.

THE ARTISTS

Mimi Abers

PETRIFIED

BACK (2007)
Kiln fired clay.
17 x 27 x 15 in. Pag. 22.

BENT OVER (2008)
Kiln fired clay.
23 x 13 x 14 in. Pag. 25.

OUT OF MIND (2009)
Glass. 4 x 7 x 6 in. Pag. 31.

All photography by Mimi Abers.

Mimi Abers is passionate about her art, which she uses as her permanent interaction of light, shadow, texture, and darkness. She says about her work: "I received an MFA in sculpture in the late 70's, working in clay and metal. I have often mixed other media with clay, and when I first started exploring glass in the early 90's I mixed clay and glass and still do. For my glass work, I start with a clay mold which I cast and fill with glass to fire in a kiln. My work reflects my personal demons: fear of aging; feelings of constriction or pain; feelings of helplessness and annoyance over my limitations or some foolish regret. I have chosen clay as my primary medium because I'm enamored with texture, and clay is a material that never stops." *Stanford Magazine* describes her work as a study in textures; textures of "weird glass" and clay littering her studio floor, an embrace of tactile experiences.

To Abers, her successful career as a VFX compositor artist in the renowned Industrial Light & Magic company (ILM) was the day job that allowed her to focus on her true passion, sculpture. Her wanderlust led her to explore orangutans, exotic birds, and other sensory nature experiences around the world to inspire her soul and her art.

For nearly twenty years she participated as a member of an artists' collective called **Gallery Route One**, where she has held numerous shows, including one dedicated to the multiple use and feel of hands. Her work has been showcased in several juried collective shows in the Bay Area of San Francisco, where she lives. In addition to her personal work, she engages with local communities, teaching ceramics and art to all ages. Her website is *mimiabersculpture.com*

A partial image of Mimi Abers' sculpture "BACK" (2007) is included in the book's cover art.

Annika Connor

THE BUBBLE

WOLF PACK (2022)
Watercolor on board.
30 x 40 in. Pag. 36.

.ONCE UPON A TIME...

BECAUSE OF YOU (2022)
Oil on linen. 16 x 20 in. Pag. 88.

Annika Connor describes herself as a contemporary romantic artist and as a modern-day renaissance woman, integrating and promoting her artistic vision in the wide range of her interests and activities. She is primarily known for her watercolor and oil paintings in which she uses strong symbolism and passionate imaginings to explore the feminine aesthetic and the range in which beauty can ignite imagination. Her tools are precision, detail, and allegory, used as hooks to lure the viewer's eye while showcasing an imagery that sparks often-mysterious narratives.

She is a vocal advocate for gender equality, using her paintings to explore topics ranging from the political, to beauty and nature, while portraying issues of female identity. As an art activist, Connor is heavily involved in sustaining the art community in which she creates. She is the Owner/President of **Active Ideas Productions**, an arts organization with the mission to serve the artistic community by facilitating the presence and publication of young talented artists and educating the public about their work. Her works and those of the artists she sponsors are showcased in her book, Point Suite Contemporary Art, available on Amazon. She is also a SAG/AFTRA member and screenwriter, additional skills used to convey her artistic visions.

Connor owns **Annika's Art Shop**, an online boutique for creative clothing, accessories, home-ware, and gifts featuring Annika Connor's paintings. All the items in the Shop are made in the USA and Canada and produced with ethical manufacturing. Her website is annikaconnor.com

Marc Lafia

AFTERWORD

LOREN EISELY #20 (2023)
Digital painting. 42 x 52 in. Pag. 96.

LOREN EISELY #16 (detail) (2023)
Digital painting. 42 x 52 in. Pag. 99.

Marc Lafia is an American artist and filmmaker whose work emerges with network culture as it changes our relationship to knowledge, ourselves, our memories, and our bodies, from one of representation to one of presentation, and from contemplation to new modes of embodiment, producing new subjectivities and new ways of going in the world.

His work has been exhibited at the Walker Art Center, the Whitney Museum of American Art, the Tate Online, ZKM, Centre Pompidou, Anthology Film Archives, International Film Festival Rotterdam, the Minsheng Museum, Shanghai, The 8th Shenzhen Sculpture Biennale, The Whitney Museum's **PROGRAMMED: RULES, CODES, AND CHOREOGRAPHIES IN ART, 1965–2018**, and most recently The Guangzhou Triennial, 2023.

Mr. Lafia's most recent work of installation and performance **EVERYTHING IS EVERYTHING AND THERE IS NOTHING ELSE**, composed over 5 years and consisting of 5 long form spoken word and scored prose poems, has been called a masterpiece through its delicately balanced chaos and attempt to show the messy beauty of the "everything" of life.

He has taught at Stanford University, the San Francisco Art Institute, Art Center College of Design in Pasadena, Pratt Institute, and Columbia University. He is the author of *Image Photograph* (2015), *Everyday Cinema* (2017), and *The Event of Art* (2020), all on Punctum Books. His website is *cargocollective.com/marclafia.*

Itamar Martínez

RENEWED

UNTITLED
(CRONOS DEVOURS HIS CHILDREN)
(2022) Charcoal and Tempera on paper.
10 x 15 in. Pag. 2.

UNTITLED (ZEUS, SON OF KRONOS AND
RHEA) (2022) Charcoal and Tempera on
paper. 10 x 15 in. Pag 4.

UNTITLED (PHEME) (2022)
Tempera on paper. 10 x 15 in. Pag. 5.

THE MONSTER

HOMBRE HERIDO (2019)
Ink and acrílics on paper.
38 x 25 cm. Pag. 54.

UNTITLED (2020)
Oil on board. 10 x 15 in. Pag. 57.

Itamar Martínez is a visual artist who's early experimental work included videos, visual poetry, mail art, as well as conceptual and performance art. Since 1980 he has focused exclusively on painting as the medium for his artitic vision. He has held multiple One-man shows in Caracas and London, as well as participated in Collective Exhibits in London, Berlin, Tokyo, Paris, Rio de Janeiro, Copenhagen, Madrid, Mexico, and New York City. IKEA has included his works as part of their prints for sale with over 350,000 sold. His work is part of the Permanent Collection of the Museum of Modern Art in New York and of the Palacio de Bellas Artes, in Santo Domingo.

His studies from an early age included prestigious art schools in his native country, and in the Central University of Venezuela (UCV), film direction at the University of Bucharest, Institute Jean Lukas Caragiale of Theatre and Film, for which he was awarded a scholarship by the governments of Rumania and of Venezuela, and visual arts at the Royal College of Art, in England. He was Chief of the Education Department and Assistant Chief for Fine Art Exhibit Coordination at the Museo de Bellas Artes in Caracas, Venezuela.

A prolific producer of art, Itamar says *"Life is a labyrinth of works, only by them will you know me."* Itamar manages his art studio and exhibition space, **The Yellow Chair Gallery** in Reading, U.K. where he resides.

José Rafael Páez

FOLLOW THE SIMON SAYS

***ZOMBIE EVOLUTION* (2023)**
Character and location renderings for
graphic story. Color markers, ink and
gouache on paper, various sizes.
Pags. 64-77.

José Rafael Páez dedicates his professional expertise and creative nature to design experiences that enhance usability and comprehension of products and ideas, finding his place in corporate America by enabling visual design strategies. He combines an academic and business background with his study of various art fields and forms using all media from painting, sketching, poetry, stained glass, and woodwork, up to digital rendering to explore senses and perception from the tangible physical presence to an ephemeral conceptual image.

José holds a Masters Degree in Design Management from the Savannah College of Art and Design, and degrees in International Business and Business Management from Florida International University. To excel in the fast-paced management world of America, he strives to seamlessly blend his corporate career with a deep passion for visual creation. He uses this ability to create works transcending conventional bounda-ries, exploring amalgamated realms of surrealism and pop art, and bringing his imaginative visions to practical life.

José's talent and passions have found an outlet within the corporate world, yet his un-wavering commitment to supporting fellow creatives remains at the core of his artistic journey. While in a major information technology corporation, he volunteered his art to its cultural outreach magazine, adding visual layers to showcase featured new writers. He assists local filmmakers in Austin, Texas, where he lives, brainstorming storyboards to help them realize their vision. His dedication and selfless contributions within the broader artistic community not only nurture the dreams of aspiring artists but also add a vibrant splash of creativity to the world around him.

Rolando Peña

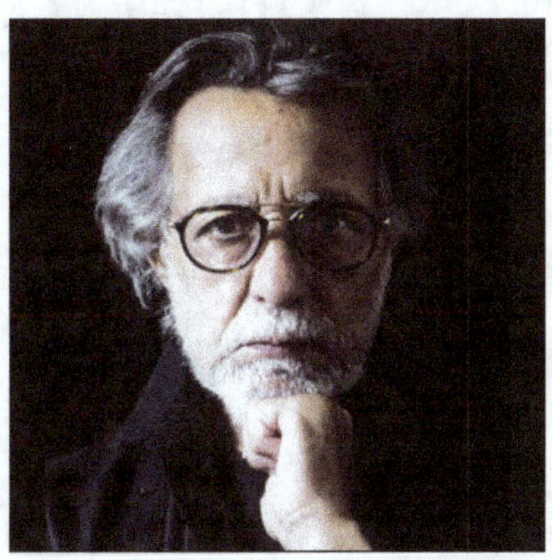

PURITY

OUR DAILY DRACULA (2022)
Photomathon/multimedia.
7.5 x 10.5 in. Pag. 80.

Rolando Peña is one of the most outstanding Latin American artists of the 20th and 21st centuries. His long and uninterrupted international career has been characterized by seeking innovation, dialoguing with the fundamental concepts of our time, and as a pioneer using technology in art.

His rich artistic career has led him to participate in important universal waves of creativity throughout his life. He began his career combining his training in dance and architecture with "happenings" in the Avant Garde scene of New York in the 1960s. At the time he collaborated with figures such as Allen Ginsberg, Timothy Leary and Andy Warhol, in **The Factory.**

Starting in 1980 he begins the development of a dense, continuous, and critical oeuvre on the topic of oil in its different manifestations as a factor of economic illusion and power. Through this line of work, encompassing drawings, engravings, photographs, film, video, performances and public space sculptures, he established a prime political-ecological position, which pioneered the challenges of this century. His work in this area earned him a Guggenheim Fellowship in 2009. Most recently he was showcased in the book *Refined Material* by Sean Nesselrode Moncada (2023), which exploresthe integral relationship between the global oil industry and the rise of geometric abstraction, kinetic art, and modern architecture in midcentury Venezuela.

His pursuit of links between art, science, and technology has led him to experiment with the most state-of-the-art ideas in physics. He says his legacy in art is turning life into the poem of infinity. Rolando Peña has exhibited his work since 1963 in multiple museums and galleries in USA, Spain, France, Germany and Venezuela, and participated in the Venice Biennial, 2008. A new anthology of his work, *Welcome to My Art World* was published in 2022 and is available through Amazon. He lives in Madrid, Spain.

His series PHOTOMATONS, begun in 1960 and of which the illustration in this book is part of, continues to this day. His website is *rolandoart.work.*

Magdalena Rangel

BOTTOM OF THE BARREL

PANDORA'S GIFT (2022)
iPad Pro Digital painting.
40 x 28 cm. Pag. 8

IO RUMINATES

IO RUMINATES #48 (2023)
iPad Pro Digital painting.
28 x 40 in. Pags. 12, 13.

Design and layout for this book and its cover.

Magdalena Rangel is a visual artist, who has been using the tools of CGI as her primary medium for decades. Artistically, her interests have always been explorations of the dynamic nature of life. She has been involved in projects from movie credits to designs and animations for films and videos, and from entertainment to corporate, in the L.A., California universe of film and aerospace clients such as Paramount, Touchstone Pictures, Polygram Pictures, CSI, Virgin Records, Hughes Aircraft, JPL, and many others. While living in Los Angeles, she was a member of the independent film collective **Oasis**.

In Seattle she was art director at Starwave, a tech company started by Microsoft cofounder Paul Allen with the mission to develop broadband at its inception. Projects included an interactive adventure in music and art by Peter Gabriel called EVE, and which was awarded the Milla D'Or Grand Prix, in Cannes. Earlier, Magdalena received an award for experimental animation film at the Montpellier Film Festival in France, and the Houston International Film Festival, for her film House Taken Over, based on a Julio Cortázar short story.

Magdalena studied at the School of Visual Arts, in NYC, Otis Parsons College of Art & Design (BFA in Drawing & Painting), and UCLA Film School (MFA in Animation), the last two in Los Angeles. She was a lecturer in Animation at the UCLA Film School, and at UCLA Extension. She enjoyed preparing and conducting animation workshops for children at the Los Angeles County Museum.

From her studio, **JumpAngel dEsign**, in Santa Cruz, California, Magdalena designs websites, books, as well as animations, illustrations and other art. In 2022 she published a book called *Young Heart Menagerie,* through her own imprint, **JumpAngel Press**. She has also started a new imprint called **Relatos de Tierra Firme (Tales of Tierra Firme)**, with the mission to develop and publish creative works mostly connected to the histories of South America. She previously collaborated with Carlos J. Rangel on the cover design and illustrations for his 2017 book, *La Venezuela imposible: Crónicas y reflexiones sobre democracia y libertad.* Magdalena Rangel's website is *jumpangel.com.* Information on the present book, including where to purchase can be found at *relatosdetierrafirme.com*

A partial image of Magdalena Rangel's digital painting "IO RUMINATES #48" (2023) is included in the book's cover art.

Nuria Román

IT COMES AROUND

FROM SOUTH TO NORTH (2001)
Mixed media on wood.
51 x 51 in. Pag. 48.

SEW THE EARTH: LITHICA. COSIR LA TERRA Latitud 40° (2013)
Rope on Stone, Height:100 ft.
Conceptual/Performance Art, Pag. 50.

With community donated rope on natural stone. View the project COSIR LA TERRA Latitud 40° on: (vimeo.com/49245006).

Through her art, **Nuria Román** explores a diversity of issues such as the relationship of women with the world; the search for new solutions to the problems that plague the world; the north south relationship; the earth as a place of welcoming and as a broken space; and the need to create bridges and to "sew the earth".

Her work has been exhibited in Paris, New York, and various locations throughout Spain. She has also curated various group shows, among them the remarkable **ON SON LES GIFTS? LA ILLUSIÓ** at the Museo de Menorca, 2015, an analysis of how male artists have represented women throughout history.

LITHICA is part of the project **LATITUDE 40° - SEW THE EARTH. L40°** is an artistic project conceived by Román offering to restore the fractures that mankind has generated over time by uniting with art installations at different points around the world through which the 40° N. parallel circles the globe. She has promoted, presented, and deployed this project in various places internationally with works and collaborations in Spain, Italy and the US.

Since 2016 she manages the **Nuria Román Art Gallery** in Maó, which she describes as a place for the meeting and visibility of local artists from Menorca. Her website is *nuriaroman.com.*

Andrés Salazar

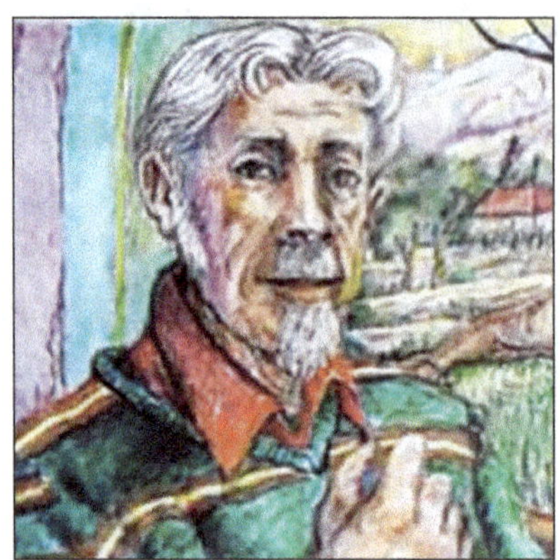

THE BUBBLE

YOU SCALE, CLIMB, AND DESCEND FROM THE INCOMPREHENSIBLE (2022)
Acrylic on Dream Papyrus.
2.5 x 9.5 in. Pag. 34.

IT'S COOKING

TECHNO VISUAL RECIPE FOR COCK-AND-BULL STEW (2022)
Still Life Digital Photograph.
7 x 10 in. Pag. 60.

"Not infrequently our mind plays to surprise us, it happens in sleepless nights and dreams. To make these almost magical states visible, we need to resort to collages, photographic or painterly, as in this piece at the edge of pataphysics." – Andrés Salazar.

Andrés Salazar began his self-taught artistic journey at an early age, absorbing from his surroundings the great vocation. That is why he passionately ventures with his endeavors into multiple fields with notable success including painting, graphic design, advertising, set design, mural design, sculpture, and photography. Due to his wide artistic range, he was selected as a founding member of the Experimental Art Workshop of the National Institute of Culture and Fine Arts (INCIBA), the highest institution of its kind at the national level in Venezuela.

His eclectic approach has made him successful in the field of graphic design, creating logos and brands for products widely distributed in his country, including food products, record labels, pharmaceuticals, etc., and as an illustrator of children's books by renowned national authors. A participant of many prestigious National Art Salons, he is included in the permanent collection of the MACCSI, the Museum of Contemporary Art of Caracas Sofía Imber, in Venezuela, which had been once one of the most prominent in Latin America. His art trajectory is featured in the forthcoming book, *La búsqueda infinita*, by Agatha de la Fuente and Rubén Monasterios.

Critics and authors write: "[Salazar's] languages are interconnected and take on a kind of segmented whole where each fragment has an independent symbolic value, and at the same time can be in permanent rotation through the different phases of the plastic weave"; "... [In Salazar we find] the firm will to transform a considerable number of elements, where the presence of techniques, resources, shapes and textures are seen as expressions of his great versatility and creative passion."

Authorizations
FROM MUSEUMS AND GALLERIES:

FOREWORD: Pags. XVI, XVIII:

FRANCISCO DE GOYA Y LUCIENTES, *THE SLEEP OF REASON PRODUCES MONSTERS, CAPRICHOS #43* (1797-99) Etching aquatint on laid paper, 12.05 x 7.91 in. (Cat. G2131). © Photo Archive of Museo Nacional del Prado. Reproduction and images used by permission of the Museo Nacional del Prado, Madrid.

TYRANNY: Pags. 16, 18:

PETER PAUL RUBENS and FRANS SNYDERS, *PROMETHEUS BOUND* (1611-12, 1618) Oil on canvas, 7 ft. 11.5 in. x 6 ft. 10.5 in. Purchased by the PMA with the W.P. Wilstatch Fund, 1950 (Acc.W1950-3-1). Photo by Alberto Otero Herranz, courtesy of the Prado Museum, 2015. Reproduction and images used by permission of the Philadelphia Museum of Art.

PETRIFIED: Pag. 30:

CARAVAGGIO, *SHIELD WITH THE HEAD OF MEDUSA* (1597) Oil on canvas mounted on wood, 24 x 22 in. (Inv. 1890 n. 1351) Reproduction used by permission of the Gallerie degli Uffizi, Florence, Ministry of Culture.

BEAUTY: Pags. 40, 42, 44:

SANDRO BOTTICELLI, *THE BIRTH OF VENUS* (c. 1485) Tempera on canvas, 5 ft. 7.9 in x 9 ft. 1.6 in. (Inv. 1890 n. 878) Reproduction and images used by permission of the Gallerie degli Uffizi, Florence, Ministry of Culture.

IT'S COOKING: Pags. 60, 62:

CARAVAGGIO, *SHIELD WITH THE HEAD OF MEDUSA* (1597) Oil on canvas mounted on wood, 24 x 22 in. (Inv. 1890 n. 1351) Image used by permission of the Gallerie degli Ufizzi, Florence, Ministry of Culture. The Quetzalcóatl book image is from *Enciclopedia de la Mitología*, Editorial Libsa (2015).

Carlos J. Rangel

Photo: © Wenceslao Cruz Blanco.

PREVIOUS BOOKS:

CAMPAIGN JOURNAL 2008: *A Chronicle Of Vision, Hope, And Glory* (2009)
Transaction Publishers, New Brunswick.

LA VENEZUELA IMPOSIBLE: *Crónicas y reflexiones sobre democracia y libertad* (2017)
Alexandria Library, Miami.

This is the third book by **Carlos J. Rangel.** His first one, *Campaign Journal 2008: A Chronicle of Vision, Hope, and Glory* (Transaction Publishers, New Brunswick, 2009), is about Barack Obama's insurgent and successful presidential campaign. This book was described by Dr. Irving Horowitz, the Chairman and Editorial Director of the publishing house at Rutgers University, as better by far than the two reviewed by The New York Times at that time on the subject matter. Among the many favorable comments received on this book, one was written by former president Jimmy Carter: "A welcome addition to my collection and I appreciate you remembering me in such a thoughtful way." His second book is titled *La Venezuela imposible: Crónicas y reflexiones sobre democracia y libertad* (Alexandria Library, Miami, 2017). The book explores in two sections the events and the situation in Venezuela at the time of its writing, 2014-2017, (though the book includes correspondence and an op-ed article from 1992 for context), and the structural framework creating that situation; a political and cultural framework which affects the country to this day.

When it was published, *La Venezuela Imposible* was among the top titles sold in it's topic category on Amazon and continues to sell steadily to this day. Among the comments on the book stands out one written by the leading intellectual personality Carlos Alberto Montaner, describing the book as "valuable, clearly written, and without pointless passion."

As a political and strategic analyst he collaborated on a working paper titled *Bring Down the Hammer: From Silk Road Bandits to Deviant States: The rise of Transnational Organized Crime (TOC) and what the World Can Do About it* (with Beatrice Rangel and Mateo Haydar) a working paper for **Interamerican Institute for Democracy (IID)**, a Miami based liberal democracy think tank.

He was editor for the new online editions published by **CEDICE Libertad** of the three major works of his father, the political analyst Carlos Rangel. CEDICE Libertad is a think tank centered around studies on liberal democracy located in Caracas, Venezuela. He has also been instrumental in publishing new editions of his father's works in Brazil, Italy and Chile.

Mr. Rangel has architectural degrees from Pratt Institute (NYC) and Universidad Central de Venezuela, UCV, Caracas, city in which he practiced his profession for many years. He also has an MBA from the Instituto de Estudios Superiores de Administración, IESA (Caracas), in a joint program with the Anderson School of Management of the University of California Los Angeles, UCLA, and a Professional Certificate in Strategic Planning for the Entertainment Industry, also from UCLA.

A link for the present book, including where to purchase can be found in Rangel's Blogspot: *mythsofourhumanity.com*

X-Twitter: *@CarlosJRangel1* |Threads: *cjrangel712* | *www.carlosjrangel.com*

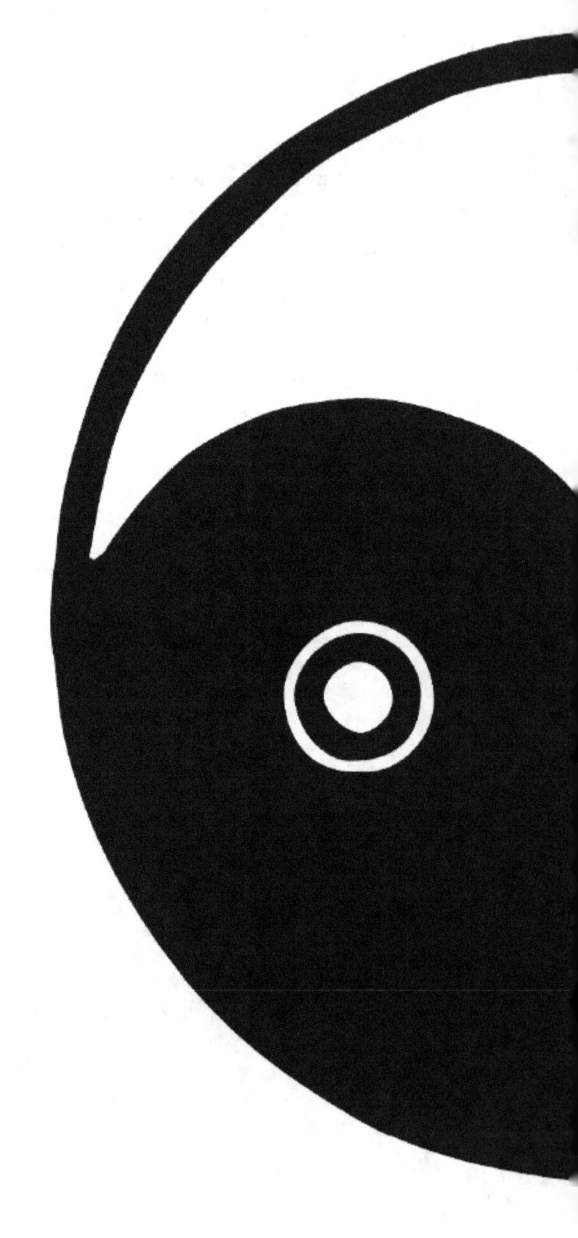

MITOS DE NUESTRA HUMANIDAD:
RELATOS DE SIEMPRE PARA HOY

Rangel, Carlos J.

ISBN: 9798991567718
Numero de control de la biblioteca del Congreso de los E.E.U.U.: 2024920493

© **Carlos J. Rangel 2024.**

Producción y diseño del libro por **Estudio JumpAngel** (*jumpangel.com*).

Diseño de portada por Magdalena T. Rangel. Edición **Relatos de Tierra Firme** (*relatosdetierrafirme.com*).

Todas la illustraciones y arte son usados con permiso de sus respectivos dueños. Todos los permisos y autorizaciones de museos y galerías son acreditados con sus detalles completos en la página 119.

Escudo de Medusa en las págs. 23, 26, 27; Corona de victoria, pág. 24; Serpiente del diluvio, pág. 27; Búho de sabiduría, pág. 28; Triskelión, pág. 29 y Zeus en su carroza, pág. 97, son usados con el libre permiso del catálogo *Magic and Mystical Symbols,* Dover Publications, Inc, Mineola, Nueva York, 1969. Algunas de estas mismas ilustraciones e imágenes también son utilizadas como parte del arte de portada para este libro. Reconociendo ese uso en esta página cumple con los términos de uso. Espada de Venganza por M.T.Rangel basada en el naipe español de Fournier.

OTROS LIBROS POR CARLOS J. RANGEL:

Campaign Journal 2008: A Chronicle of Vision, Hope, and Glory (2009) Transaction Publishers, New Brunswick.

La Venezuela imposible: Crónicas y reflexiones sobre democracia y libertad (2017) Alexandria Library, Miami.

Impreso y distribuído por Ingram/Spark.

MITOS
DE NUESTRA HUMANIDAD
RELATOS DE SIEMPRE PARA HOY

CARLOS J. RANGEL

Para

Bárbara, artista,

y

Carlos, pensador.

MITOS DE NUESTRA HUMANIDAD:
RELATOS DE SIEMPRE PARA HOY

*"Una reimaginación del anhelo de libertad
en nuestros mitos, relatos, fábulas y tradiciones".*

CJR

Reseñas para ***MITOS DE NUESTRA HUMANIDAD***

Toda cultura tiene mitos, historias transmitidas a lo largo de la historia para darle sentido al mundo. Para el autor, empresario, escritor y analista político venezolano [Carlos J. Rangel], los mitos también son cruciales en cómo una población concibe y protege la democracia...

...Rangel ávidamente juega con la forma escrita: una viñeta de Zeus toma la forma de un artículo periodístico; otra se lee como una escena de un guión cinematográfico con Sandro Botticelli; una tercera utiliza un memorando interno dentro de un partido político conservador.... Una de las secciones más impactantes es un cómic espeluznante, con un epígrafe del ex presidente venezolano Hugo Chávez, que utiliza un apocalipsis zombi como metáfora de cómo los ciudadanos pagan el precio de la apatía y el extremismo político...

La facilidad con la que Rangel entrelaza ideas y luchas de siglos y milenios pasados con el panorama político actual, tanto en Estados Unidos como en el resto del mundo, genera un efecto escalofriante. Pero al igual que la esperanza, en el fondo de la caja de Pandora, todavía existe la sensación de que podemos avanzar, si tan sólo escuchamos nuestro pasado.

[Este libro es] Un juego vibrante del arte visual y de la palabra escrita que ataca la apatía y nos implora que actuemos.

El libro fue seleccionado por Kirkus como uno de los cien mejores títulos independientes del año 2024.

Kirkus Reviews

"*Mitos de nuestra humanidad*" es una novela literaria ferozmente original que no solamente es una lectura emocionante y divertida, sino que tiene algo importante que decir acerca de un tema crucial – la búsqueda de la libertad por parte de la humanidad. Rangel entreteje de manera magistral bellas ilustraciones con mitos de nuestro pasado compartido — desde los dioses de la Grecia antigua hasta el mito moderno de Drácula, todo para crear una astuta novela que reta al pensamiento. Nadie puede leer este libro sin admirar el extraordinario talento de su autor. "*Mitos de nuestra humanidad*" es un tesoro literario.

PREFACIO

"El sueño de la razón produce monstruos."

FRANCISCO DE GOYA Y LUCIENTES

(1799)

Francisco De Goya y Lucientes: *El sueño de la razón produce monstruos (Caprichos #43)* (1797-1799) Aguafuerte, aguatinta sobre papel verjurado. 306 x 201 mm. (Cat. #G002131). © Archivo Fotográfico Museo Nacional del Prado.

PREFACIO

UNA IDEA COMPLEJA FORJADA CON ELEMENTOS SIMPLES, CONCEBIDA PARA LA FÁCIL LECTURA DE PÍLDORAS DIFÍCILES DE TRAGAR.

Es así como puede describirse *MITOS DE NUESTRA HUMANIDAD: Relatos de siempre para hoy.* Los textos del libro reescriben en forma contemporánea viejos y conocidos relatos para ilustrar de manera familiar ideas modernas sobre fundamentos de la democracia liberal. De esta manera, el libro explora el anhelo de libertad en nuestros mitos, cuentos, fábulas y tradiciones. Una criatura híbrida, surgida al combinar el ensayo con la ficción política.

Los segmentos secuenciales del libro, sus "viñetas", son acompañados por una colección de ilustraciones complementando las ideas del texto. Al igual que el arte, que se presenta en múltiples estilos y formas, las viñetas se presentan en diversos estilos y formatos. Finalmente, el libro fue escrito simultáneamente en inglés y español, incluyendo ambos textos en el mismo volumen, con la intención de servir a ambas audiencias de este multiverso que cabalgo a diario.

Le debo muchos agradecimientos a todos aquellos que colaboraron conmigo en este proyecto, especialmente a los artistas que contribuyeron el arte que lo acompaña, las instituciones que generosamente concedieron el permiso para reproducir obras maestras de su colección, y al Dr. Carlos Di Bonifacio, quien me guió para obtener los derechos del uso de una imagen de la Galería Uffizi, en Florencia. Un agradecimiento especial es para mi hermana, Magdalena Rangel, por usar sus talentos únicos no solamente para contribuir con las ilustraciones de dos viñetas, sino para diseñar y diagramar el libro y su portada, y para capturar gazapos y otros errores ante los cuales yo estaba ciego. También les debo agradecimientos a Gemma Pineda y Mark Comstock, quienes dedicaron su tiempo a leer los textos también cazando gazapos, capturando algunos más. Cualquiera que escapó es por mi culpa. Sería una negligencia imperdonable no agradecer a Beatrice Rangel, mi prima en espíritu, cuya insistencia constante en incluirme en sus múltiples proyectos e intereses me inspiró nuevamente para retomar este, que por varias razones había abandonado en el pasado.

Agradezco también a mis amigos artistas que desde sus propias redes hicieron contactos para ampliar la red de colaboradores, y a mi agente, Maria Elena Lavaud, por siempre hacer preguntas. Debo reconocer en particular a un editor a quien no nombraré de mi casa editorial anterior quien elevó el proyecto a su comité editorial, pero se le dijo que era "demasiado creativo; somos académicos". De esa manera fui arrojado a la madriguera del conejo para explorar el potencial del proyecto, encontrar el gato enigmático — y a la auto publicación.

Mi crítica más exigente es la Dra. Esmeralda Garbi, mi esposa. Cuando terminó de leer el primer borrador avanzado del libro y me dijo "es bueno", supe que lo era. Su ojo agudo, rápido comentario y precisas correcciones editoriales hicieron que este libro sea muchas veces mejor que aquel temprano borrador que ella leyó. Su callado apoyo mientras yo dedicaba innumerables noches y madrugadas a la escritura del texto y a la carpintería del proyecto fue inestimable. Desafortunadamente, a veces uno tiene un impulso indomable de escribir que absorbe cuerpo y alma; ella me permitió satisfacerlo. Sin ella, logro nada. Sé que ella sacrificó mucho al hacerlo, así que mi agradecimiento y mi amor son profundos. Su amor se manifiesta de muchas maneras.

CJR

Francisco De Goya y Lucientes: *El sueño de la razón produce monstruos (Caprichos #43) (detalle)* (1797-1799) Aguafuerte, aguatinta sobre papel verjurado. 306 x 201 mm. (Cat. #G002131). © Archivo Fotográfico Museo Nacional del Prado.

TABLA DE CONTENIDO

I

RENOVADO

"Es una enfermedad que llega con toda
tiranía, la de no confiar en amigos".

ESQUILO
Prometeo encadenado (c. 450 B.C.)

CRONOS DEVORA A SUS HIJOS (Exclusivo del *Clarín Divino.*)

Arte por
Itamar Martinez: ***Untitled*** (2022)
Carbón, Acuarela sobre papel. 38 × 25 cm.

RENOVADO

El Clarín Divino

EL UNIVERSO OLIMPO ESTILO Y PLACER ALTA SOCIEDAD LOS DE ABAJO

SACUDÓN: Mandatario del Universo Derrocado por su Hijo. Termina la Guerra de Diez Años.

Iniciada con una conspiración sucesoral, finaliza la Guerra de los Dioses. Los dioses del hombre someten a los dioses de la naturaleza.

Por Pheme.

EL OLIMPO: Fecha universal, la antigüedad. (*Exclusiva de El Clarín Divino*). Las viejas profecías pueden convertirse en realidad. Cuando Cronos se enteró de la profecía de su destino, que un hijo suyo lo derrocaría como mandatario del universo, hizo lo que haría todo ser racional que se siente con derecho eterno al poder: devoró a cada uno de sus hijos a medida que nacían. A fin de cuentas, él mismo había depuesto a su propio padre con un Golpe de Estado violento. Cronos no quería que el orden del universo fuese renovado otra vez. La Edad de Oro del Universo y él como líder supremo existiría para siempre.

Fuentes anónimas reportan que la esposa (y hermana) de Cronos, Rea (alias Madre Naturaleza) no estaba felíz con estos acontecimientos. Rea daba luz a sus hijos inmortales solo para verlos descender por la garganta de Cronos y desaparecer por toda la eternidad. Rea, conspirando con Gaia, su suegra (y madre), engañó a Cronos y cambió a su sexto bebé por una gran piedra, que el dios ávidamente engulló. En ese momento celestial, el reloj de Cronos comenzó su tic-tac inexorable hacia el destino final del dios.

Rea escondió al bebé en una isla remota y le puso de nombre Zeus. Llegado el momento, ya crecido y junto a sus hermanos inmortales (rescatados de las entrañas de su padre mediante una poción vomitiva preparada por Rea), Zeus desencadena la Guerra de los Dioses, la Titanomaquia. Esta guerra termina ahora con la victoria incuestionable de los Olímpicos sobre los Titanes. Cronos ha sido desterrado y su Comandante General, el Titán Atlas, ha sido condenado a cargar el mundo sobre sus espaldas. Todos los otros Titanes, exceptuando a Prometeo y Tetis que se habían aliado a los Olímpicos, están ahora encerrados en la notoria nada del Tártaro. Antes de su encierro final, Cronos declaró: *"El orden natural siempre prevalecerá sobre el desorden innatural"*.

Zeus le encargó a Prometeo la creación del hombre, una débil criatura terrenal cuyo propósito era servir a los dioses y hacer crecer el poder de los Olímpicos. Sin embargo, se rumora que Zeus no está satisfecho con los dones especiales otorgados por Prometeo a la humanidad: iniciativa, artesanía, viveza y tramposería. Especialmente porque, también se rumora, Prometeo les otorgó fuego robado del mismísimo hogar sagrado del Olimpo por su ave rapaz, el milano. Este incidente, y el disgusto de Zeus, no augura nada bueno para Prometeo.

Las criaturas de Prometeo han asentado firmemente la presencia de los Olímpicos y creado nuevos dioses. Esta devoción de la humanidad ha convertido a Zeus en el Dios del Gran *Poder*. Hera, su esposa, en Diosa de la *Familia*. Sus hijos Ares y Hefesto, de la (*Sangre* y) *Guerra*, y del (*Fuego* y) *Trabajo* han surgido por el conflicto y esfuerzo del hombre. Otros nuevos dioses incluyen Atenea para la *Sabiduría* y Dionisio para la *Fiesta*. Afrodita, una Titán distante nacida de la violencia de Cronos contra su padre Urano, pero neutral durante la guerra, sincretiza a *Belleza* con el *Amor*, una combinación divina entre la naturaleza y lo humano. Con el fin de la Titanomaquia surge una nueva divinidad centrada sobre la humanidad para regir el universo.

ZEUS, HIJO DE CRONOS Y REA
(Exclusivo para *El Clarín Divino*).

 **ACTUALIZACIÓN 1 –**
En información exclusiva para El Clarín, nuestro reportero Hermes confirma que Prometeo ha incitado la ira de Zeus y ha sido desterrado a una montaña remota donde, sujeto en las alturas, padecerá tortura eterna. Nuestras fuentes, solicitando anonimato para su propia protección, afirman que a medida que Zeus aumenta su poder por la devoción de la humanidad al mismo, el dios ha desatado un reinado de abuso tiránico que incluye transformarse a sí mismo en toros y cisnes, neblina o lluvia dorada para tener relaciones sexuales con las mujeres que desea, y fulmina con rayos a aquellos que le desagradan.

Arte por
Itamar Martinez: **Untitled** (2022)
Carbón, Acuarela sobre papel. 38 × 25 cm.

ACTUALIZACIÓN 2 –
El Clarín se ha enterado de que una ciudad entre **Los de Abajo** llamada Atenas, en honor a la diosa de la Sabiduría, está ensayando un sistema para alternar el poder entre sus ciudadanos, para renovar, innovar y perfeccionar instituciones. Buscan los humanos, con ese sistema de renovación basado en la racionalidad, minimizar la sangre derramada por una sucesión de tiranos en busca de su permanencia en el poder. Entrevistado sobre esta idea de renovación periódica institucional, Zeus declaró: *"Estos hombres dicen que, ¿cómo la llaman, 'democracia'?, dicen que es un régimen por toda la gente, pero la verdad es que es solo para sus pocos elegidos, sus llamados iguales." Nunca querrán renovarse; solo se rotarán entre sus lacayos el poder de gobernar. Es un experimento condenado al fracaso. Débil."*

RENOVADO

Sin embargo, esta reportera notó preocupación en el rostro de su majestad, mirando con recelo por encima de su hombro, como preguntándose si esta idea llegará al Olimpo. Finalizando, declaró: *"Aquí también tengo democracia. Siempre les pregunto a todos qué es lo que están pensando"*.

Pheme es redactora en jefe y directora editorial para *El Clarín Divino*

© *El Clarín Divino*–fecha universal, la antigüedad.

● ACTUALIZACIÓN 3 —

Desde la ciudad de Atenas, una fuente que no quiere revelar su nombre ni escribir nada por temor a que le parta un rayo o le obliguen a beber cicuta, cree que la historia no es un estándar para emular o celebrar; que no debe usarse para proyectar una visión filtrada de glorias pasadas.

El Sr. Fuente opina que debemos usar la historia de nuestros ancestros para conocernos mejor hoy en día; para avanzar renovando líderes y gobiernos; que la renovación es necesaria para evitar estancarse en una mala imitación de un pasado feliz; un ideal conservando con devoción nuestro tóxico lastre social en un estante de vidrio, o como un ídolo en un pedestal.

● ACTUALIZACIÓN 4 —

Los poderes que mandan nos obligan a revelar nuestra fuente para la actualización anterior. Su nombre es (era) Sócrates.

Arte por
Itamar Martinez: **Untitled** (2022)
Carbón, Acuarela sobre papel. 38 × 25 cm.

II 17

TOCANDO FONDO

"Uno no se ilumina imaginando figuras de luz, sino haciendo consciente la oscuridad".

CARL G. JUNG
El Árbol Filosófico (1945)

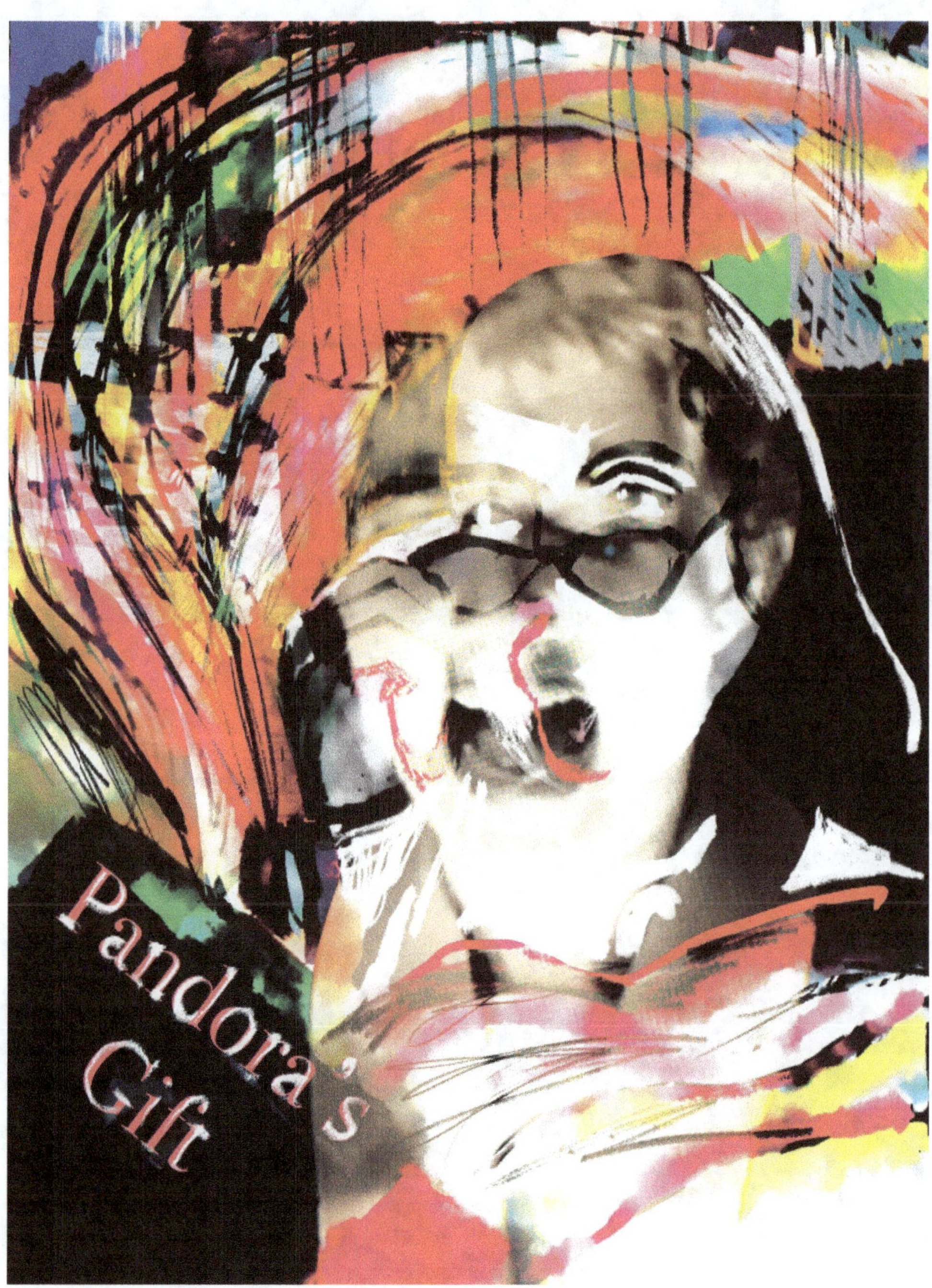

Arte por
Magdalena Rangel: *El Regalo De Pandora #3-color-04* (2022)
Pintura digital con iPad Pro. 25.4 × 17.78 cm.

TOCANDO FONDO

El Regalo de Pandora

Lucha inútilmente para cerrar la tapa. Oscuros sentimientos, tristeza y miedo se apoderan de su voluntad, debilitando su espíritu. Las fuerzas implacables superan sus débiles intentos de someterlas a medida que desatan sobre el mundo el odio, el dolor, la enfermedad, el hambre, la guerra, la división, la discordia...

Todos los males se desatan sobre la humanidad por un dios cruel que utiliza la curiosidad para destruir la inocencia y la felicidad en este mundo. Ella será la recordada como aquella que le trajo a la humanidad el sabor amargo del fruto de una sabiduría nada bienvenida: sufrir y aguantar la brutalidad, el dolor y la maldad de la vida; la sabiduría nada bienvenida de saber que tras todo nuestro sufrimiento solo nos espera el morir; el brutal reconocimiento de que cada día que vivimos es un día más cercano al día de nuestra muerte.

Por fin logra cerrar la caja. Su mundo ha cambiado, su corazón le pesa acongojado. La desesperación, esa creencia casi irracional de que todo saldrá mal, se apodera de ella mientras mira a su alrededor, viendo lo que ha hecho. Nubarrones se arremolinan en su alma y se pregunta si la caja aún contiene lo que pueda ser su liberación final. La toca suavemente. Siente la vibración de algo poderoso en su interior. La podría abrir una vez más, su acto final. ¿Será valentía? ¿Será cobardía? No lo sabe. No le importa.

Levanta la tapa lentamente, mira dentro, y descubre que no todo está perdido. Puede superar el momento, esta tiniebla. Recupera su voluntad de vivir, restaura su voluntad de actuar, su voluntad de ser y de enfrentase al reto diario de la vida. Sabe ahora que cada día siempre tendrá un mañana y se anima con esa creencia casi irracional de que todo saldrá bien: la esperanza.

ÍO MASCULLA

"Ya no lo aguantamos".

ALYSSA MILANO

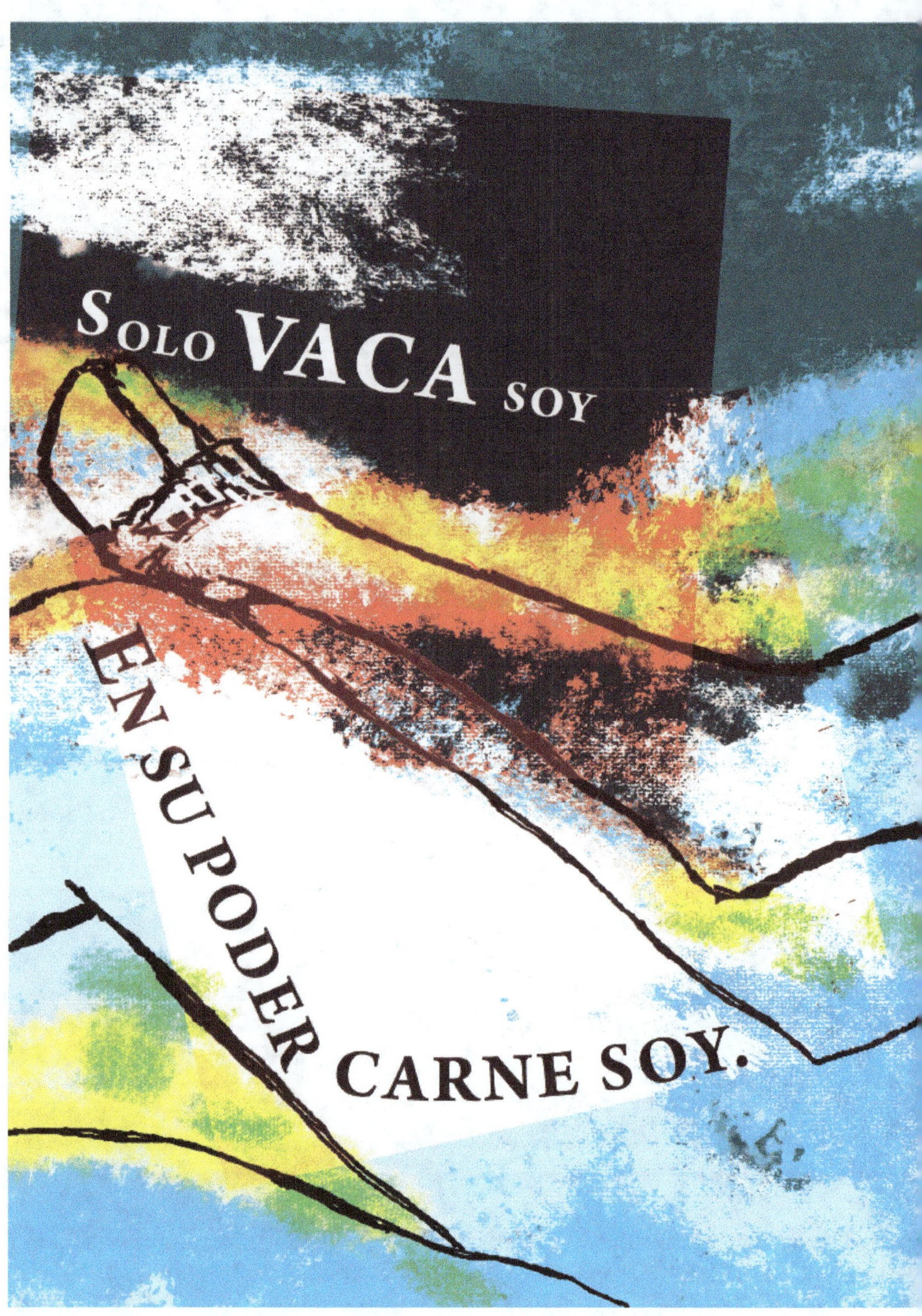

Arte por
Magdalena Rangel: *Io Masculla, ¿Yo También? #50* (2023)
Pintura digital con iPad Pro. 25.4 × 35.56 cm.

ÍO MASCULLA

IV ^{I 15}

TIRANÍA

> "Dios mío, Dios mío, ¿por qué me has abandonado?".

JESUCRISTO
(Mateo, 27:46)

Arte por
Pedro Pablo Rubens y Frans Snyders: *Prometeo Encadenado* (1611-1612, 1618)
Óleo sobre lienzo. 242.6 x 209.6 cm. (Con permiso del Museo de Arte de Filadelfia).

TIRANÍA

Eternas no son

*B*ajo el amarillento amanecer, lentamente se apagan las pocas luces que aun brillan abajo mientras desaparecen arriba las estrellas. Un nuevo día despierta después de otra noche de insomnio, azotado por el viento helado, gritando, aullando. Cada día se confunde con el siguiente, pero las noches le traen siempre la imagen de progreso. Hace innumerables noches, el profundo valle se sumergía en negra oscuridad; pero primero con unos pocos destellos y ahora con miles de ellos, la huella de su creación crece y prospera incuestionablemente.

Casi ya no recuerda cuando fue que le insufló vida a aquel barro. La humanidad seguro que ya no le recuerda, acá atado por las cadenas del Tirano a un acantilado desolado más allá de Meteora, las rocas afiladas contra su carne desnuda; su único compañero ese viejo aliado, ahora rabioso can alado con garras afiladas y pico ponzoñoso, cumpliendo la tarea encomendada de desgarrarle diariamente su carne y darse un festín con sus entrañas. La bestia no lo había olvidado. Ni un día. La bestia era fiel. Tras mil años nombró a la bestia alada, el cometa: Milvós.

Milvós se sentó una vez a su lado, como cansado de su espantosa tarea, antes de proceder a desgarrar su piel, arrancar su carne, derramar su sangre, perforar sus huesos; la agonía una vez más, su encarnado suplicio otra vez. En su mente está grabada aquella primera vez, hace casi unos 1.700 años, cuando la bestia no le arrancó su hígado, quizás el encargo del Tirano una pesada servidumbre también para la bestia. Se zambulló desde el cielo, chillando ensordecedor como de costumbre hasta su percha en esa roca al lado. Entonces... simplemente voló... se fue... Durante cientos de años, esa primera indiferencia se tornó más frecuente. Tal vez el Tirano le había quitado el ojo de encima o su poder había disminuido; o quizás la tarea de Milvós ya no era tan importante.

¿Cuál había sido su pecado? ¿Qué lo había condenado a este torturado olvido? ¿A la eterna tortura inmortal? ¿Fue acaso darles una vida transitoria a esas formas de barro ambulantes? ¿darles razón y fuego? A fin de cuentas, fue la misma humanidad la que empoderó a esos dioses menores que derrocaron el antiguo orden, su propio antiguo orden; el orden en el que él, el Cielo, la Tierra, el Tiempo, la Naturaleza y sus hermanos Titanes crearon y gobernaron el universo por milenios y milenios. Hasta el hombre, su creación.

Arte por
Pedro Pablo Rubens y Frans Snyders: *Prometeo Encadenado (detalle)* (1611-1612,
1618) Óleo sobre lienzo. 242.6 x 209.6 cm. (Con permiso del Museo de Arte de Filadelfia).

TIRANÍA

La humanidad le concedió divinidad al Poder, a la Sabiduría, al Amor y Belleza; a la Guerra, el Trabajo, y a todo eso cotidiano y mundano. Él cree que esos dioses menores, dejados solos, degradarán a la humanidad; y que sus criaturas, no entendiendo su verdadero lugar en el universo, confiando en sus nuevos dioses y olvidando a los dioses de la naturaleza, se destruirán a sí mismas.

Poder es el peor de todos ellos, relampagueando con el miedo, la ira y la venganza para dominar a los demás; fuerza bruta para imponerse a los desprevenidos, a veces furtivamente, como bestia, a veces como sí mismo, descaradamente. Fue contra el abuso de Poder que él se rebeló — y fue la razón por la que le dio a la humanidad su propia fuente de poder: el fuego. El fuego, que puede calentar una sopa en el hogar o reducir a cenizas un majestuoso bosque. El poder del fuego asemeja los hombres a los dioses y, al mismo tiempo, los aleja de ellos. Imperdonable para el Tirano. En ironía perversa, el Tirano envió un milano para torturarle, la misma criatura que él usó para distribuir el poder del fuego de los dioses a la humanidad.

La lucha contra la tiranía no es una cómoda, piensa mientras padece el filo de las rocas, el ardor del sol. La lucha contra ese dios tirano le hizo caer, inmortal pero encarnado, a esta tortura eterna por los elementos y el carnicero alado. La humanidad preferiría creer que su cuerpo mortal murió, colgado en lo alto con desdén, a creer que vive, inmortal, encadenado al escarpado acantilado de una montaña desconocida en una tierra lejana. Pero, cuando ve aquel valle abajo, sabe que ese antiguo Poder que lo encadenó se ha marchitado, Milvós es su prueba.

Su sacrificio no fue en vano, la humanidad prospera gracias a él. Aunque él sea olvidado o las leyendas cambien, la lucha siempre existirá. La suya es una historia que vivirá para siempre. La lucha contra la tiranía es tan eterna como él y la gloria es para los rebeldes derrocando tiranos, divinos y terrenales. Cada nuevo guerrero contra cada nueva tiranía será siempre el creador de un mundo mejor. Tiranías eternas no son.

A todo pulmón, cielo arriba, Milvós chilla y se eleva antes de descender en círculos para acomodarse y descansar de nuevo en su nido de brasas desgastadas, junto a Prometeo.

In memorian, Óscar Pérez, y todos los caídos en la lucha contra la tiranía.

V ^{I 21}

PETRIFICADO

"Estaba escrito que debería ser leal a la pesadilla de mi elección".

JOSEPH CONRAD
El corazón de las tinieblas (1899)

Arte de
Mimi Abers: **Back** (2007)
Arcilla cocida al horno. 70 × 43 × 38 cm. *Fotografía por Mimi Abers.*

PETRIFICADO

Cuadernos de Investigación en Mitos e Historia, 2022
Vol. 19, No. 4, 231-267

DILEMA DEL INTERÉS PROPIO VS. EL INTERÉS COLECTIVO EN EL HÉROE:
Paradigmas arquetípicos en el contexto de un mito griego y el liberalismo del Siglo XVIII

Andromacus Perses, PhD (ABD) y
Hermitia Pleiad, PhD (ABD).
Universidad Constellar en Cisthene.

RESUMEN: *Tras establecer hechos clave en la leyenda de la Gorgona Medusa, los autores buscan determinar los elementos de valentía y cobardía ilustrados por el mito y su relación con conceptos modernos de heroísmo, cobardía y traición.*

PALABRAS CLAVE: **Medusa, Perseo, Miranda, Héroe, Cobarde, Traidor, Interés propio, interés colectivo.**

La pregunta de investigación en este trabajo es: ¿Cuál es la relación entre el comportamiento heroico, el interés propio y el interés colectivo?

MEDUSA

Medusa la Gorgona no es el sujeto de este ensayo. Sin embargo, porque representa el Monstruo en la Habitación, el Lado Oscuro, el Obstáculo Insuperable y el Enemigo opuesto a las metas e ideales del Héroe, es parte intrínseca del objeto de investigación. Por ello, comenzamos nuestro análisis con un rápido vistazo a su relato de origen y contexto cultural para aproximarnos a la comprensión de la naturaleza cambiante de los términos arquetípicos que son nuestro objeto de investigación: héroe, cobarde y traidor.

La leyenda de Medusa es una afrenta aparente a cualquier noción de equidad o justicia: una hermosa sacerdotisa virgen es violada por un dios y, en consecuencia, es castigada por su propia diosa protectora que la convierte en un monstruo; un monstruo que transforma en piedra a cualquier hombre que la pretenda. Muchos símbolos heráldicos surgen de esta historia y, quizás sorprendentemente, uno de los más favorecidos por algunos antiguos es la representación de Medusa como protectora. Medusa se convierte en símbolo de la fortaleza interna de las víctimas y los débiles en contra de la violencia y el poder arbitrario. Otras interpretaciones del mito de Medusa atribuyen su origen como parte de un conjunto de mitos relatando el derrocamiento de matriarcados por patriarcados, incluyendo en la religión.[1]

La diosa Atenea cede ante el dios Poseidón, y no le reclama a éste la injuria perpetrada sobre su devota sirviente. Atenea más bien acusa a Medusa de haberse dejado violar y le impone un castigo ejemplar. Sin embargo, la leyenda concluye con la Gorgona elevada al escudo de Atenea, redimida y al servicio de la diosa Virgen, la Sabiduría, la única entre el Olimpo que no nació de mujer.

---

[1] Diversas fuentes describen a Medusa como una semidiosa terrenal, con ciclos asociados a los animales y a la fertilidad.

MEDUSA (2)

El mito también ilustra el uso del poder de las mujeres sobre los hombres, pero en beneficio de estos últimos. Según cuenta la leyenda, Perseo usará la cabeza de la Gorgona para vencer a sus enemigos, validando esta interpretación, algo feminista, en la cual el poder de Medusa trasciende su muerte. Reforzando esta interpretación, la icónica imagen de su cabeza se usa como símbolo heráldico de protección para su portador (en armaduras o escudos), o en edificios a lo largo de la antigüedad. Sin embargo, y contrario a esta última interpretación, también se puede alegar que el portador de la cabeza de Medusa venció a un poderoso monstruo. Quienquiera que porte su cabeza está protegido, no por la cabeza propiamente sino por el testimonio callado sobre el poder del que la tiene contra cualquiera que ose enfrentársele.[2]

Estos aspectos de la leyenda ilustran el conflicto permanente entre el poder de la mujer y el poder del hombre sobre los destinos de la humanidad. Pero las diversas y contradictorias interpretaciones de la historia de Medusa no son la pregunta clave de nuestra investigación. En este ensayo estamos interesados en identificar lo que el colectivo percibe como un héroe, y para ello nuestro foco recae sobre Perseo.

EL MITO DEL HÉROE

En la antigüedad, a Perseo se le conocía como el héroe que mató a Medusa, la Gorgona. Relatando la leyenda de manera concisa, Perseo era hijo de Zeus, viviendo rechazado, pobre y miserable en una isla gobernada por un déspota que mantenía como esclava a Dánae, la madre humana de Perseo. Para liberar a Dánae el déspota le ofrece a Perseo intercambiarla por la cabeza de la Gorgona, una tarea imposible. Nadie sabe dónde vive Medusa y ver su faz

es quedarse petrificado del horror. Sin amilanarse, Perseo se prepara para la tarea, solicitando objetos mágicos de sus aliados divinos y mediante extorsión de las medias hermanas de la Gorgona para obtener "inteligencia táctica".[3] Preparado así, con pertrechos divinos e información secreta, utiliza artimañas el día del hecho: entra con sigilo a la guarida de Medusa, pasa su galería de víctimas petrificadas y la decapita mientras duerme. Perseo regresa a la isla con el trofeo solicitado y lo usa para petrificar al déspota, el verdadero villano en la leyenda, liberando a Dánae y la isla del régimen tiránico.

La clave para entender la historia de un héroe es la subordinación del interés propio al interés colectivo. Esto pudiese considerarse altruismo, pero eso sería una interpretación errada. El altruismo es una característica inherente a ciertos individuos impulsada por un profundo sentido de empatía. En su modo más puro, el comportamiento altruista está en el interés propio de estos individuos puesto que su propósito es lograr satisfacción personal, incluyendo mitigar / ocultar sentimientos de culpa – justificados o no – por su propio éxito o, más frecuentemente, el de su familia. Ese comportamiento es con el propósito de satisfacer los instintos de empatía del individuo.

---

[2]   Se le describe en la estatua de Atenea Parthenos, en la Acrópolis, y usada en navíos romanos para alejar el mal y el peligro. Caravaggio pintó la cabeza de Medusa en un escudo (1597) para el Gran Duque de Toscana como símbolo de la victoria sobre sus enemigos. Hasta el día de hoy, "amuletos protectores" con la imagen de la Gorgona son artículos populares en varias regiones de Italia.

[3]   Medusa es la mortal de un conjunto de tres hermanas (las Gorgonas) nacidas de un dios marino menor y una quimera marina. Las Gorgonas tienen otro conjunto de tres hermanas (las Graiai) las cuales comparten un ojo y un diente entre ellas y que Perseo les roba para obligarlas a revelar la ubicación de Medusa.

PETRIFICADO
EL MITO DEL HÉROE (2)

Los beneficios al interés colectivo son colaterales a la búsqueda de esa satisfacción personal. Pero en el caso de las acciones del héroe, el máximo interés propio, la supervivencia, es anulado por el interés colectivo, que supera toda meta personal e individual del interés propio. Perseo tiene un objetivo que sólo puede describirse como externo a su individualidad: la supervivencia de su tribu, personificada por su madre. Para lograr su objetivo, se dispone a enfrentar probabilidades adversas abrumadoras e ir en contra de un instinto primordial: la autoconservación. Pero la temeridad imprudente no hace al héroe, como nos hacen saber con sus silenciosos susurros las estatuas conduciendo al lecho del monstruo.

Perseo teme fracasar, con todas sus consecuencias, así que se entrena y prepara. Tiene que sobrevivir como individuo para lograr su meta de supervivencia del colectivo, por lo cual su preparación y sus alianzas son cruciales. El éxito del héroe se basa en saber que hay peligro, que él o ella está en una situación asimétrica (como en esa otra leyenda arquetípica de David y Goliat), y en estar preparado para ese reto. El equilibrio entre el interés colectivo y el propio se logra en la historia del héroe sobreviviente — así como una sensación de alivio y autoestima, puesto que la auto-identificación del oyente o lector del relato es más frequente con un indefenso común que con una fuerza superior elitesca. Un héroe caído será honrado, por supuesto, pero el héroe sobreviviente es más valioso para la sociedad como modelo de comportamiento ejemplar a favor del colectivo, con recompensa terrenal.

El conflicto entre el interés propio versus el interés colectivo es central en la historia de la civilización occidental. El interés propio es la sublimación de un instinto primordial: supervivencia. Sin embargo, las estructuras de interacción social han sido la clave en la supervivencia colectiva de una aglomeración de criaturas débiles y frágiles contra las poderosas fuerzas de la naturaleza. Dentro de esas estructuras sociales el instinto individual de supervivencia puede crear dinámicas que chocan con el interés colectivo superior: la supervivencia de la especie o, más apegado a casa, de la tribu. Héroes e idealistas se sacrifican por el colectivo para lograr un objetivo mayor, ya sea la supervivencia de la tribu, la perdurabilidad de ideas, o como símbolo ideológico. La comunidad honra a los héroes en vida o muerte con medallas y leyendas — si el objetivo final, la supervivencia y éxito del interés de la tribu o del clan, se logra.

Arte por
Mimi Abers: **Bent Over** (2008)
Arcilla cocida al horno. 58 x 36 x 33 cm. *Fotografía por Mimi Abers.*

EL MITO DEL HÉROE (3)

Los individuos que eligen el interés propio (y su autopreservación) sobre el interés colectivo en situaciones cruciales de supervivencia, a menudo serán tildados de cobardes. Sin embargo, si el éxito individual generado por el interés propio acarrea beneficios comunes por su efecto multiplicador o de difusión colateral, esos beneficios pueden percibirse como derecho adquirido del colectivo. Esta es parte de la razón por la cual las ideologías que celebran la búsqueda del bien común pueden ser más populares y atractivas que aquellas celebrando la búsqueda del logro individual — los *"almuerzos gratis"* son populares. Las acciones (e ideologías) percibidas como favorables por igual a todos en la tribu son, casi por definición, más populares que acciones percibidas como favoreciendo desigualmente al bien individual de un solo miembro o alguna minoría selecta de la tribu.[4]

TRAICIÓN, O EL NACIMIENTO DE LAS NACIONES

Perseo ilustra al héroe en su forma simple y mítica. La realidad es más compleja, y los héroes legendarios no son siempre los mismos que los que encontramos en la historia. No se puede hablar de héroes históricos sin entender a los traidores. Los traidores no son lo contrario en acción a los héroes (como es el caso de los cobardes) sino antagonistas en sus lealtades. Traidores, villanos y monstruos suelen ser etiquetados como tales por los vencedores, que serán los que escriban los libros de historia.

En el período de la Revolución Liberal, cuando el concepto de naciones soberanas enmarcadas dentro de fronteras delimitadas no estaba realmente definido, y por ende la lealtad a un territorio geográfico no prevalecía, un individuo podía tener lealtad al *Soberano* en el poder[5] (cuyo gran ejemplo es Talleyrand) o a los *Ideales* ("la república", "independencia", (*"Liberté, egalité, fraternité"*) identificando a una tribu. Aquellos que toman las armas para defender Ideales o aquellos que lo hacen como defensores del Soberano pudiesen enfrentar cargos de traición al ser capturados por sus oponentes, especialmente si cambiaron lealtades.[6] Durante la Guerra de la Independencia de los Estados Unidos, Benedict Arnold es emblemático de esta circunstancia. Hasta el día de hoy, cambiar de opinión sobre una postura ideológica, política o incluso social, a menudo se presenta o es vista como signo de debilidad, inconsistencia o traición con consecuencias variadas, desde personales hasta políticas.

En la historia, el venezolano Francisco de Miranda ejemplifica el desarrollo de la traición como "delito de estado", al migrar el concepto de soberanía desde un individuo mandatario al estado nación. Miranda entrenó en las fuerzas armadas del imperio español y, como efectivo en ellas, luchó en la guerra de independencia de los EE.UU. con la alianza franco-española contra las fuerzas

---

[4] Lo que comúnmente pasa por ideología socialista es generalmente más popular que lo que comúnmente se etiqueta como ideología capitalista. Se afirma como una perogrullada que bajo el socialismo (como ideal difuso) se logra un bien común mucho mayor que bajo el capitalismo (como realidad demonizada). Pero el principio fundamental del capitalismo es que cuando un individuo persigue su interés propio se beneficiará la sociedad al estimular la innovación, mayor productividad, y mayor oferta de bienes y servicios. Adam Smith advirtió contra la concentración de mercados, hoy vista en monopolios estatales y oligopolios elitistas. Estos resultados son consecuencias eventuales e inevitables tanto del capitalismo como del socialismo salvaje, en detrimento del libre mercado ideal de Smith.

[5] La noción de soberanía estaba encarnada en el gobernante local o imperial, El Soberano, no en los ciudadanos de una nación, ya que ciudadanía como tal no era un concepto prevaleciente.

[6] Por supuesto, la traición también puede imputarse al cambiar lealtades entre individuos encarnando la soberanía, por ejemplo, del rey de Francia al emperador de Prusia; pero la revolución liberal coloca la soberanía en los ciudadanos de modo que, técnicamente, aplica el mismo razonamiento.

PETRIFICADO
TRAICIÓN, O EL NACIMIENTO DE LAS NACIONES (2)

Poco después estando en Cuba, tal vez por destacarse entre las tropas pero discriminado por ser advenedizo colonial (es decir, no *Peninsular*) y huyendo de la inquisición española, Miranda desertó del ejército imperial y escapó a la nueva república del norte. Vivió más de un año en esta recién acuñada nación independiente observando en tiempo real esa cosa llamada democracia y escribiendo en sus *Diarios*, al mismo tiempo que entablaba amistad con protagonistas de la revolución independentista.[7]

Motivado por sus intereses en el conocimiento de ideas liberales se traslada a Londres, desde donde viaja por toda Europa hasta Rusia, donde fue consejero, y tal vez algo más, de Catalina la Grande. Eventualmente gravita hacia una Francia en estertores de fiebres revolucionarias. Un amigo cercano de Miranda, el alcalde de París, lo recomendó a los ejércitos de la Revolución Francesa, en los que ascendió al rango de general.

El nombre de Miranda fue eventualmente grabado en el Arco de Triunfo por su servicio bajo el General de División Charles François Dumoriez en la decisiva batalla de Valmy y por sus acciones para concluir el sitio de Amberes. Pero el fallido Golpe de Estado del General Dumoriez contra el gobierno revolucionario en marzo de 1793 y su posterior escape a territorio "enemigo" en abril, trajo consecuencias a su estructura de mando.[8] El general Miranda es arrestado por los jacobinos, posteriormente exonerado de conspiración relacionada con esos hechos, pero mantenido bajo estricta vigilancia.

Miranda se escapa de *Le Terreur* y sus secuelas en 1798, y regresa a Inglaterra. Este período turbulento vio a Miranda vestir el uniforme español, ruso y francés, a veces batallando aliados de antiguos o futuros amigos. Inglaterra le solicitó sus servicios para liderar batallas contra el imperio de Napoleón en España. Lo que hizo, sin embargo, fue tratar de canalizar los intereses geopolíticos de Inglaterra contra España a favor de su proyecto de vida para la región latino-americana, en donde vestiría su ultimo uniforme: el de revolucionario independentista. Su proyecto lo lleva de vuelta a la tierra que lo vio nacer, Venezuela, la cual lidera para independizarse del imperio español y para crear una república basada en sus ideas liberales revolucionarias. El ascenso de Miranda, desde hijo de comerciantes de clase media a consejero de reyes, emperatrices y primeros ministros ejemplifica la auto mejora, educación y oportunidad como medios para lograr la movilidad social, una idea fundamentalmente liberal.

Pero la joven república que Miranda buscaba forjar no estaba lista para este tipo de liberalismo. Tras rebeliones populares y de esclavos contra un gobierno conducido por *Criollos*[9] buscando mantener el privilegio mantuano (colonialista), Miranda fue acusado por sus enemigos políticos de traición contra la nueva nación independiente y convenientemente entregado a las autoridades españolas. Miranda, para los Criollos, era un arribista con ideas fuera de su realidad e intereses.

---

[7] Los Diarios de Miranda han sido designados Legado Mundial por la UNESCO.

[8] Luis XVI fue ejecutado el 20 de enero de 1793. Su ejecución inició una nueva era en Europa, en la cual los monarcas se veían bajo una nueva amenaza existencial. Dumoriez consideró irresponsable y una amenaza a la república la decisión por la Convención Nacional de ejecutar al rey, por unificar a las monarquías europeas en contra de la Francia revolucionaria. Esto lo impulsará a actuar dos meses más tarde.

[9] Los Criollos eran una clase social de colonialistas nacidos en el territorio y terratenientes, descendientes de los colonos originales. Se diferencian de los Peninsulares, españoles de la península, en tránsito temporal en el territorio por razones burocráticas o comerciales, y los cuales a menudo se consideraban a sí mismos "más puros" que los criollos.

TRAICIÓN, O EL NACIMIENTO DE LAS NACIONES (3)

Miranda era un tonto útil entregable por Criollos al régimen español como ficha de negociación para retener su estatus y evitar ser "renovados" una vez que fuese restaurado el orden del imperio y la caótica nueva república disuelta. Sin embargo, eso no sucedería, puesto que exilio, cárcel y ejecución rápidamente sobrevendría para muchos de ellos.

Pasará el resto de sus días en prisiones españolas, y finalmente en Cádiz, donde intentó infructuosamente apelar su caso ante las Cortes (parlamento) establecidas bajo la constitución liberal española apodada 'La Pepa'. La restauración de Fernando VII en 1814 truncó ese esfuerzo, ya que la constitución y esas cortes fueron abolidas por el restaurado monarca.[10]

Murió en 1816, tal vez por hemiplejia, tal vez envenenado. Miranda es el único protagonista registrado de los tres grandes conflictos revolucionarios que convulsionaron el mundo occidental en los siglos XVIII y XIX, y puede ser el primer caso de un hombre enjuiciado como traidor a su (nuevo) país, en lugar de a una tribu, un ejército, o un rey. Él es un claro ejemplo de las diferencias entre el arquetipo del héroe mítico con el héroe histórico, su nombre inscrito en el Arco de Triunfo de Paris, un cenotafio a su memoria en el Panteón de los Héroes de su país natal y, sin embargo, con sus restos enterrados en una fosa común, nunca identificados a ciencia cierta. Un hombre de la historia, sujeto al cristal de los escritores de esta y a los cambios de fortuna frecuentemente asociados a sus protagonistas.[11]

HISTORIA, REESCRITA

Los viejos mitos de Perseo, y la historia de revoluciones y alianzas cambiantes en los siglos XVIII y XIX, ilustran no solo el profundo arraigo de posturas arquetípicas sobre héroe, cobarde y traidor, sino también la naturaleza variable de estos términos al ser vistos a través del lente del interés colectivo, el interés propio y la lealtad. La legendaria y ambigua figura de Medusa, ya sea como monstruosa asesina vengativa o como protectora emblemática en el escudo de Atenea, simboliza el ascenso y la caída de aquellos etiquetados con cualquiera de aquellos tres términos por los caprichos de su época y de la historia.

Ante adversidades aparentemente insuperables, el comportamiento heroico incluye de manera inequívoca la evaluación de la realidad, entrenamiento y preparación, así como alianzas y astucia para asegurar la supervivencia.

La valentía entonces es la voluntad de ejecutar el plan trazado (casi siempre cuidadoso en el caso del héroe sobreviviente, casi siempre apresurado en el caso del héroe sacrificado) con el propósito de lograr un "bien mayor".

---

[10] La constitución de Cádiz, popularmente apodada "La Pepa", fue la primera constitución funcional del imperio español le concedía la soberanía al estado, no al monarca, e instituía un parlamento electo democráticamente (las Cortes), libertad de prensa, y el derecho a la propiedad privada. También le otorgaba el pleno derecho de ser español a todos los ciudadanos en los territorios del imperio y paridad político-administrativa entre la península y esos territorios. Su abolición por Fernando VII fue uno de los factores que desencadenó un renovado movimiento independentista en las colonias. Hasta el día de hoy, la historia reescrita sobre el liberalismo español (abarcando siglos, desde Juan de Mariana pasando por Goya, Ortega y Gasset, hasta los contemporáneos modernos) tras la restauración del rey se refleja en una expresión común y denigrante que caracteriza a alguien con poco sentido de la "realidad" y sus consecuencias, afinidad con el caos, y en general falto de seriedad, como un "viva la pepa".

[11] Véase cf. *Carlos Rangel Del Buen Salvaje Al Buen Revolucionario*, Capítulo II, Monte Ávila, 1977 y Marx y los socialismos reales y otros ensayos: El nacimiento de la traición, Monte Ávila, 1988. También Racine, Karen *Francisco de Miranda – A Trans Atlantic Life in the Age of Revolution*, Rowman & Littlefield, MD, 2002.

PETRIFICADO
HISTORIA, REESCRITA (2)

Consiste en llevar a cabo la acción a sabiendas de que "*los mejores planes de hombres y ratones con frecuencia acaban mal*".[12] Los cobardes pueden tener el mismo plan y estar igualmente comprometidos con el "bien mayor", pero su propia supervivencia prevalece al momento de la ejecución, y aquellos que hubiesen sido héroes no cumplen su tarea. Para Perseo, ese compromiso al bien mayor era liberar de la esclavitud a su madre, a pesar del gran riesgo propio.

El "hombre con su plan" buscando remontar el obstáculo insuperable, el monstruo en la habitación, el lado oscuro, el enemigo (físico o ideológico), y que ejecuta dicho plan para mantener, defender o restaurar el interés colectivo, es el héroe del relato. Si el héroe cambia el plan y hace alianzas a favor de enemigos de los intereses colectivos de su tribu, ahora se le llama traidor. Si cambia a favor de su interés propio ahora se le llama cobarde. Los cobardes son aquellos que, con su entrenamiento, la preparación y el plan, llegada la hora deciden que no está en su mejor interés propio ejecutar el plan, o cambiar sus lealtades. Debido a que la realidad histórica y sus eventos son complicados, y facciones en pugna se componen de muchos individuos con diversidad de lealtades en oposición, podemos usar esta estructura conceptual en la identificación objetiva de héroes, traidores y cobardes en cualquier conflicto.[13]

Desde los tiempos del mito de Medusa se observa que la percepción de enemigo y amigo es variable. "El lado correcto de la historia" no siempre está claro ni en el momento o ni siquiera en retrospectiva, como en el caso de Miranda, perdonado póstumamente por la República de Venezuela, la tierra que lo vio nacer. Lo que sí está claro es que existe la posibilidad de manipular el borroso lente de la historia para tumbar héroes de su pedestal y restaurar villanos de todo tipo al capricho de un ambiente político volátil. Ideólogos e "influenciadores" con intereses propios pueden utilizar esta manipulación para alterar a su favor la estructura cultural de una nación.

Desenterramos héroes y enterramos villanos para formar nuestra percepción del legado e historia nacional. Sin embargo, la tendencia de reescribir, modificar o borrar a conveniencia el sentido de la historia para cambiar y reinter-pretar nuestra narrativa cultural proviene de una veta autoritaria identificable, imborrable y profunda dentro del colectivo de la humanidad. Esta es una veta inocentemente incrustada en el deseo natural de encontrar héroes arquetípicos en nuestra sangre y tierra; una veta explotada ávidamente por líderes autoritarios que buscan enriquecer su poder, impulsando el nacionalismo patriotero desenfrenado.[14]

---

[12] "*To a Mouse.*" (*A un ratón*) Robert Burns (1785).

[13] En casos de tiroteos en escuelas, los policías que, a pesar de su preparación, entrenamiento y planes, no entran o se enfrentan al criminal, pueden ejemplificar la cobardía. Traidores; héroes y cobardes también se revelan durante grandes convulsiones y disturbios civiles como los que ocurrieron durante el intento de derrocar al gobierno de Estados Unidos entre noviembre de 2020 a enero de 2021. En esa instancia, estos comportamientos fueron obvios entre aquellos comprometidos a mantener el ejercicio democrático y de la ley, y aquellos que escogieron apoyar el ejercicio autocrático y del culto a la personalidad. Esos eventos ilustraron el comportamiento heroico y traicionero a favor y en contra del estado, así como el comportamiento cobarde. Es de hacer notar que después de los eventos del 6 de enero, lealtades y comportamientos cambiaron nuevamente, ilustrando que la autoconservación es un instinto bien desarrollado en la política. También está claro que, en caso de haber sido exitoso el intento de ruptura constitucional, los causantes se habrían autoproclamado héroes patrióticos, dando a luz una nueva nación. Pero lo que enfrentan ahora es juicio y desprecio por lo que fueron: conspiradores sediciosos y criminales en contra de la constitución, quebrantando las leyes de los Estados Unidos de America.

[14] Adoctrinamiento escolar prohibiendo libros y lecturas, interferencia curricular por la autoridad central, así como la cultura de "cancelar" por "influenciadores" en redes sociales son instrumentos modernos de control autoritario.

LOS ARTEFACTOS DEL HÉROE

I. ESPEJO/ESCUDO

Un espejo no significa ni contiene nada excepto aquello que refleja. Como espejo reflejando un horror petrificante, el regalo del héroe, el escudo protegiendo a la Diosa de la Sabiduría, es significativo en sus múltiples simbologías cuasi-Vermeer y ambivalentes que speculum significat et continet nihil nisi quod ab eo reflectitur. Ut speculum horrorem petrificans reflectens, donum herois, clypeum Deam Sapientiae protegens, est significans in suis multiplex ambigua, symbolismus Vermeerianus... Mauris pellentesque pulvinar pellentesque habitant morbitristique senectus. Speculum significat et continet nihil nisi quod ab eo reflectitur. Ut speculum horrorem petrificans reflectens, donum herois, clypeum Deam Sapientiae protegens, est signifi in suis multiplex ambigua e symbolis mus Vermeerianus... Mauris pellentesque

Arte por
Caravaggio: *Escudo con la cabeza de Medusa* (1597)
Óleo sobre lienzo montado en madera. 60 cm × 55 cm. (Galería degli Uffizi, Inv. 1890 n. 1351).

PETRIFICADO

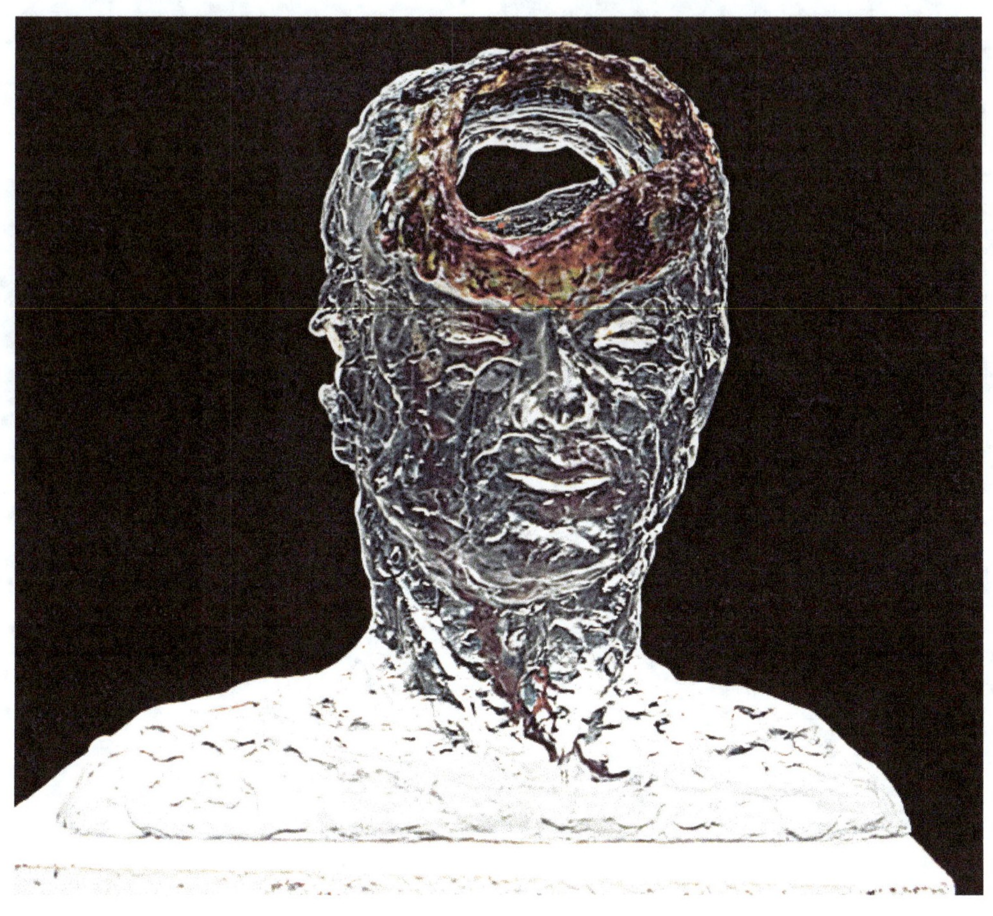

Arte por
Mimi Abers: **Out Of Mind** (2009)
Vidrio. 35 × 17 × 15 cm. *Fotografía por Mimi Abers.*

^I33

VI

LA BURBUJA

"Abre los ojos ahora. Lo haré. Un momento. ¿Ha desaparecido todo desde entonces? Si abro y estoy para siempre en la negra adiáfana. ¡Basta! Veré si puedo ver".

JAMES JOYCE
Ulises (1933)

Arte por
Andrés Salazar: *Escalas, Subes Y Bajas De Lo Inconmesurable* (2022)
Acrílico sobre papiro soñador 31 × 24 cm.

LA BURBUJA

¡Ay de mí! Erguido aquí, atado inmóvil a este mástil, con el rocío salado azotando mi cara. Mis hombres, en tarea de navegar y remar, me ignoran. ¡Ay! ¿Por qué no ven que por fin hemos llegado a nuestra hermosa tierra, por qué ignoran mis fuertes gritos, mis gestos frenéticos? ¿Por qué, por qué?

Navegaremos dejando atrás nuestro paraíso y, perdidos de nuevo, toda oportunidad de descansar de nuestras dificultades; de acabar nuestras aventuras, traer este viaje a su fin. Escucho a la voz más dulce llamando: "Llegasteis al fin, héroes bienvenidos. ¡Los valientes errantes que esperábamos! En esta gran tierra descansaréis, han ganado la gloria; llegasteis al fin".

Me equivoqué al creer en Circe como fuente de verdades, era fuente de falsedades: "Tened cuidado con las sirenas y sus cantos, no os detengáis o seguro moriréis". Ella era la falsa, la confusa engañosa. ¿Qué clase de líder soy yo, escuchando sus falsedades que ahora desvían a mis hombres de nuestro verdadero propósito? Oigo la voz de mi amada Penélope. Oigo la cordial carcajada de mis amigos. ¡Hemos llegado! Este es el sendero corto y fácil. ¡La recompensa de los dioses regresándonos a nuestra grandiosa patria! Estas voces no son las mentiras, estas voces no son falsedades. Me conocen, me llaman por mi nombre, me dan noticias que anhelo escuchar. Le imploro a mis marineros:

"¡Desatadme! ¡Estáis todos equivocados! ¡Me equivoqué al dejar que me atáseis! ¡Oigan las loas a nuestras victorias! ¡Escuchad los relatos de nuestros éxitos y grandeza! ¡Celebremos nuestro glorioso pasado, abundante futuro y destino prometido!." Ese es el himno para nosotros cantado por las doncellas en la orilla...

¿Qué ve mi Piloto cuando voltea su mirada hacia donde dirijo mis ojos? ¿Acaso no puede ver lo que yo oigo? ¿La visión de nuestros deseos, las orillas de Ítaca, doncellas saludando, cantando y llamándonos? Todo nos espera. ¿Por qué desvía su mirada y palidece de terror? ¿Cómo no ve lo que yo oigo, qué falsedad le estampó Circe la hechicera en sus ojos? ¿Por qué le hace gestos a la tripulación para que reme más y más rápido, como para alejarse del peligro en vez de calar en el puerto seguro que veo? Grito: *"¡Desatadme! ¡Soy su capitán!"*

Arte por
Annika Connor: **Wolf Pack** (2022)
Acuarela sobre madera. 76 × 102 cm.

LA BURBUJA

El viento azota los mechones de cabello rebelde dispersos sobre mi frente, mi respiración se agita, mi corazón se acelera, mis pulmones se desgarran con mis alaridos. Mis marineros reman y reman, con rumbo firme, lejos de la irresistible orilla. Estoy al borde de la desesperación. ¿Cómo no ven lo que yo veo? Debí dejarles oír lo que yo veo, dejarles ver esta canción, no taparles los oídos con la engañosa cera de Circe.

Ay, ay, ay, el viento hincha nuestras velas y los remos espuman la mar a medida que aceleramos lejos de nuestro consuelo prometido; no, por favor no, no dejéis atrás nuestra gran tierra. Mis gritos se hacen débiles, desvanecen con gemidos langidecientes:

¡Deteneos! ¡Dad la vuelta! De vuelta a donde estábamos, donde seremos grandes otra vez… deteneos… regresad, regresad, de vuelta, de vuelta…"

Mis ojos ya no ven, mi mente ya no piensa, ya no escucho, excepto ese canto de sirena, llamándome, llamándome… hasta que no sé más…

❦

Marineros errantes nuevamente navegan nuestras aguas para escuchar nuestras canciones y entregarnos su carne para el festín.

El oleaje murmura que éstos vienen de muy lejos, de las arenas de Ilión, con rumbo a Ítaca. Muchas aventuras han vivido, convertidos en cerdos y de vuelta en hombres, tumbaron cíclopes, el castillo de Casandra yace en cenizas… todo por artimañas de su Príncipe. Ya es su hora de descanso. Nuestro canto de alabanza heroica les guiará a nuestra orilla, acortará su viaje al lugar de descanso final.

Nuestras voces de encanto nublan sus ojos y construyen visiones: colinas donde se alzan nuestras afiladas rocas y playas donde acechan los dientes de arrecifes; un sol resplandeciente donde retumban nubarrones. Cantamos erguidas, ondeando nuestros cuerpos celestiales, mientras nuestras garras ocultas aferran los desechos podridos y huesos quebrados de los ilusos que nos saciaron antes.

Su líder escucha nuestro canto, nos desea. Para su tripulación es un desquiciado atado al mástil del barco. Pasan navegando, ignoran nuestras ilusiones. Lejos se van, lejos de nuestra burbuja de engaños. No importa. Otros atraeremos con la ficción que añoran escuchar. Y los devoraremos.

❦

VII

BELLEZA

"El que me excomulga, excomulga a Dios".

FRA GIROLAMO SAVONAROLA
(Savonarola fue excomulgado por el Papa
Alejandro VI, Mayo 13, 1497)

Arte por
Sandro Botticelli: *El Nacimiento De Venus* (1485)
Témpera sobre tela. 172.5 × 278.5 cm. *Con permiso de la Gallerie degli Uffizi.*

BELLEZA

INT. CHIESA DI SAN SALVATORE IN OGNISSANTI - DIA

Música coral santifica el espacio bajo la bóveda de frescos. Briznas de polvo suspendidas en el aire destellan con colores de los rayos de sol filtrados por un vitral.

SOBRESCRITO: "23 DE MAYO, 1498"

En una capilla lateral SANDRO, algo más de 50, un apuesto italiano en elegante atuendo de artista renacentista, termina su callada oración ante el sepulcro de *Simonetta Vespucci, 1453-1476.*

                    GIOVANNI (O.C.)
          La belleza vive para siempre, Sandro.

Sandro saluda a GIOVANNI, un poco mayor y más desgarbado que él, con un triste abrazo.

                    SANDRO
          ¿Ya acabó?

                    GIOVANNI
          Están recogiendo los huesos y las cenizas.

EXT. PASE O EMPEDRADO A ORILLAS DEL ARNO - DIA

En esta tarde soleada, la pareja camina hacia el Ponte Vecchio a lo largo de la ribera del río. Ven a una muchedumbre que se aglomera sobre el viejo puente.

                    SANDRO
               La belleza es ficción, Giovanni, solo es
               nuestra imaginación. No existe en la
               naturaleza.
                    GIOVANNI
               Otra vez pensando a lo loco.¡Mira
               nuestro río, al cielo, este día!
               ¡Belleza! Belleza mucho antes de que
               camináramos por aquí

                    SANDRO
               Es nuestra mente la que ve esta belleza.
               No la ven estas hormigas rastreras,o esa
               rata furtiva, o el gato en el callejón
               que la cazará. Las bestias sin alma no
               ven la belleza.

                    (MÁS)

La muchedumbre sobre el puente celebra cuando carretillas a su borde vierten cenizas y polvo al río. La nube de cenizas se expande, flota y dispersa en el aire.

Arte por
Sandro Botticelli: *El Nacimiento De Venus (detalle)* (1485)
Témpera sobre tela. 172.5 × 278.5 cm. *Con permiso de la Gallerie degli Uffizi.*

BELLEZA

                        SANDRO (CONT'D)
                     (ve la nube de cenizas)
          Él sabía. Él sabía de belleza… Él sabía
          del pecado nacido de ella: la vanidad.
          Un pecado que nos aleja de Dios. Un
          pecado purificado con fuego.

                           GIOVANNI
          Así no, oye, escúchate, pazzo. Mira a
          tu bellísima Simonetta. Fuiste tú quien
          la pintó como diosa eterna de la Belleza.
          Y muy buena, además.

                            SANDRO
          Siempre somos una contradicción. Yo no
          soy puro como él lo fue. Pero él ahora
          es cenizas en el Arno, una nube de polvo
          subiendo hacia ese cielo tuyo.

EXT.   CALLEJÓN EN FLORENCIA MEDIEVAL – DIA

Caminan el empedrado, acercándose hacia la Piazza della Signoria.

                           GIOVANNI
          No, los antiguos no dicen eso. La belle-
          za no es diosa que venga de la mente
          humana. Viene del cielo, una Titán,
          nacida antes del hombre y que todos esos
          otros dioses de cosas humanas.

                            SANDRO
                         (añorando)
          Así la pinté, al borde del profundo y
          la tierra. La transición. Al borde de
          los tiempos. Los bordes nos definen.

                           GIOVANNI
          Te quedó bien, esa...

                            SANDRO
          De no ser por memoria de Lorenzo,
          también hubiese quemado a esa pagana.

EXT. PIAZZA DELLA SIGNORIA – NOCHE

SOBRESCRITO: "7 DE FEBRERO, 1497"

Una gran hoguera enciende la noche. Una HORDA ENARDECIDA arroja
al fuego libros, obras de arte, espejos, vestimentas lujosas.
Un SACEROTE ENCAPUCHADO, en sus 40, gesticula furiosamente, arenga
a la muchedumbre.

                        GIOVANNI (O.C.)
          Esa hoguera fue su gran error. La
          arrogancia de Fra Girolamo brillando
          ante todos, toda la noche. Eso también
          lo pensó el Papa.

Cenizas ardientes se elevan al cielo nocturno.

Arte por
Sandro Botticelli: *El Nacimiento De Venus (detalle)* (1485)
Témpera sobre tela. 172.5 × 278.5 cm. *Con permiso de la Gallerie degli Uffizi.*

BELLEZA

EXT. CALLE ESTRECHA EN FLORENCIA MEDIEVAL - DIA

SOBRESCRITO: "23 DE MAYO, 1498"

Los hermanos remontan el empedrado, acercándose al final.

> **SANDRO**
> ¿Es que no lo ves? ¿Al Papa Borgia? Él
> es el mal, el monje lo decía: este Papa
> es mundano, no es de Dios; y ahora pre-
> tende dominarnos con su reino del pecado,
> hasta en aquellas nuevas tierras y sus
> salvajes. ¡Todo! ¡Lorenzo lo sabía!

> **GIOVANNI**
> ¿Y eso que importa, hermanito? ¡Es un
> nuevo siglo, un nuevo mundo, una nueva
> era! ¡Y somos parte de eso!

EXT. PIAZZA DELLA SIGNORIA - DIA

Los hermanos entran a la Piazza desde la Calle Estrecha. En la gran
plaza, los farallones del Palazzo della Signoria se yerguen dorados
bajo el sol del atardecer, su torre imponente domina el ámbito.

Al centro, TRABAJADORES bajo la mirada de un MONJE SEVERO usan
baldes y escobas para lavar el empedrado. Otros recogen los restos
de basura dejados por una muchedumbre.

> **SANDRO**
> ¿Lo hueles?

En la cara de Giovanni, se le ve que sí.

> **SANDRO (cont.)**
> La carne quemada tiene olor distintivo.
> Perdura.

> **GIOVANNI**
> Ya está en el sexto círculo. Arderá aún
> más. Muerte y escarnio para los que traen
> destrucción.

> **SANDRO**
> Vida y gloria para los que traen
> creación. Ya me lo han dicho antes.
> (pausa)
> No lo creo. Savonarola fue un mártir y será
> un santo para siempre. A mí me olvidarán.

Los trabajadores cepillan las piedras duro, más duro. Más baldes
de agua sobre el pavimento.

> **GIOVANNI**
> Tal vez no.

Agua pantanosa se escurre entre las grietas de las piedras. Escobas
barren, barren, barren. El agua oscura se aclara, las cenizas y el
polvo se disuelven y desaparecen.

FIN

MITOS DE NUESTRA HUMANIDAD:

VIII

VIENE DE VUELTA

"Pero se mueve".

Atribuído a
GALILEO GALILEI

Arte de
Nuria Román: *De Sur A Norte* (2001)
Medios mixtos sobre madera. 130 x 130 cm.

VIENE DE VUELTA

Roma, luni 27, 1633

Salve, carissimi et dilexit Stella:

Abscondere Meis litteris ad Te semper. Melior
est adolebitque ea. In communi sermone Ego
scriberem ad Te, para que Me entienda mejor.
Qué grato es leer las cartas de Vuestra Merced.
No es común que mujeres de cualquier estado
social lean, y mucho menos que escriban tan bien
como Vd., y con el propósito de la búsqueda del
conocimiento. Estos son tiempos aciagos, y somos
testigos del oscurecimiento. Me temo que Nuestras
cartas narran el destino de Nuestros tiempos.

En Vuestra última carta Vuestros comentarios sobre
el Diálogo entre los dos Máximos Sistemas del
Mundo del Maestro fueron agudos e ingeniosos.
Tenéis razón al escribir que los brillantes
argumentos de Salviati sobre Nuestro sol
al centro de un sistema de planetas anulan
por completo la recitación sin sentido de Simplico
de las tonterías ptolemaicas. Y, como bien
señalais, ¡éste ni siquiera las entiende!

Recordaba Vuestra carta mientras estaba sentado
en la galería, viendo a los pomposos discípulos
de Simplico amenazando a un anciano con torturas
y el resto de Sus días en una fría celda.

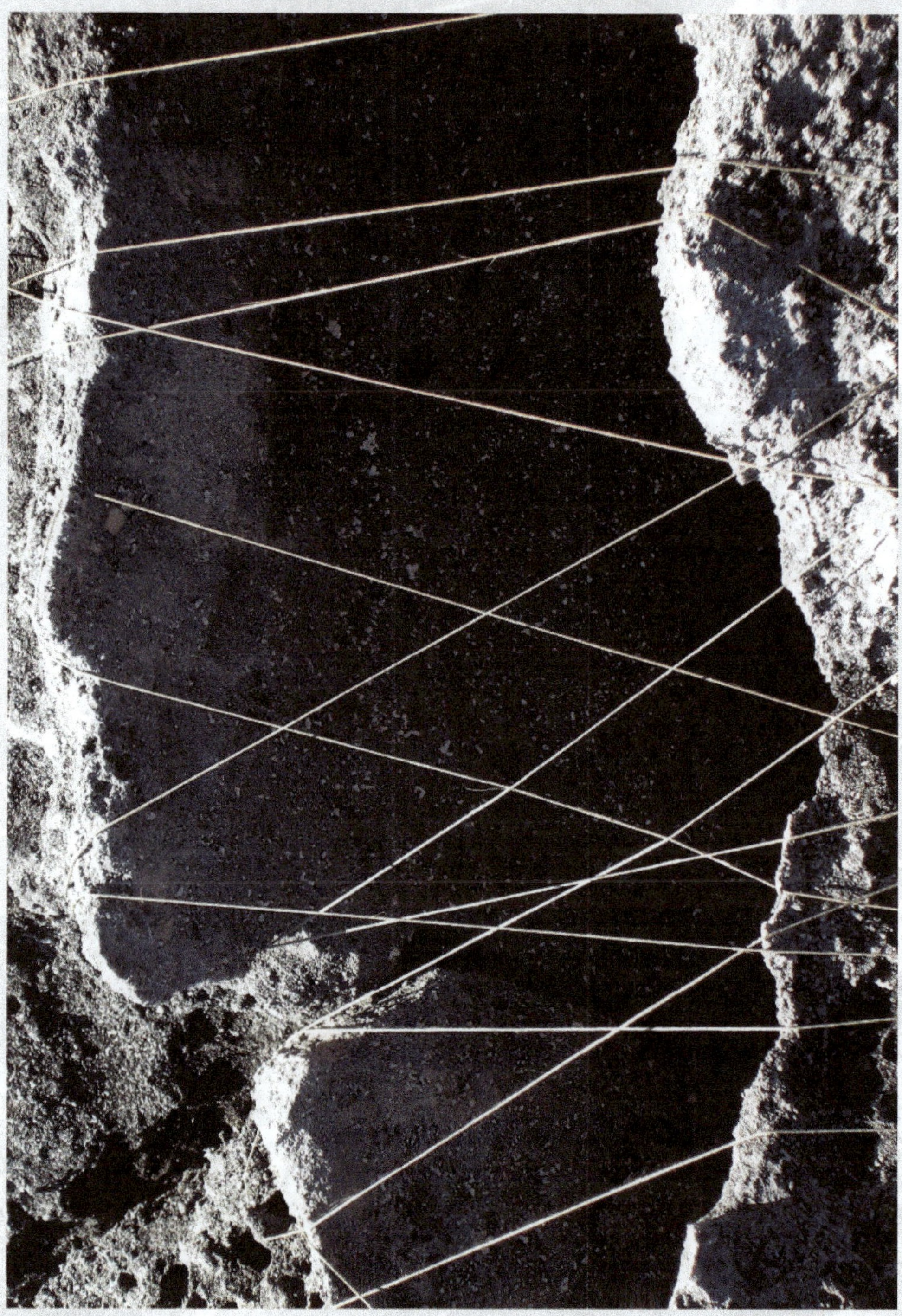

Arte de
Nuria Román: *Coser La Tierra: Lithica (detalle)* (2013)
Altura c. 30 mt. Cuerdas sobre roca natural. Arte Conceptual.
Todos los materiales fueron donados por la comunidad.

VIENE DE VUELTA

En mi mente volví a esas frescas y oscuras noches cuando, mirando a través del invento del Maestro, espiábamos a la brillante estrella errante y Sus pequeñuelos rodeándola.

¿Podrá creer V. Merced que cuando se le preguntó a los bufones del tribunal si habían usado un telescopio alguna vez, respondieron diciendo que este era un instrumento de El Diablo para retar Nuestra fe? ¿Que la ciencia, la razón y el progreso son trucos de El Maligno?

Me temo, Stella, que viene una nueva era de tinieblas, no orquestada por Satanás sino por líderes rechazando al conocimiento como principio rector al tomar decisiones. Solo podremos mejorar Nuestra suerte si usamos los avances que nos brindan el estudio profundo y el trabajo duro, encima de los hombros de los que vinieron antes para ver más lejos.

Me temo, Stella, que Nuestras ciudades pronto estarán en declive mientras que las de otros, donde Simplicos no prevalecen, conquistarán el futuro y mejorarán su suerte. Mi única esperanza es que, aun enfrentando el declive, Nuestros Simplicos no hagan peligrar al mundo entero.

Semper Tuus fidelisque amicus,

Cosimo.

IX

EL MONSTRUO

"[...las] condiciones de vida [del lumpen proletariado] le preparan más para ser una herramienta sobornable de la intriga reaccionaria [que para la revolución]".

CARLOS MARX
El Manifesto Comunista (1848)

Arte por
Itamar Martínez: ***Hombre Herido*** (2019)
Óleo sobre tabla. 38 × 25 cm.

EL MONSTRUO

MEMORÁNDUM INTERNO
Confidencial

De: Presidente del Comité Central del CRV
Para: Todos los Miembros Directivos del Partido
Fecha: 192 días antes de las elecciones y contando
Asunto: ¡Vivimos!

Algunos de ustedes puede que crean que nuestro proceso de primarias no resultó en el mejor candidato para renovar el partido y restaurarnos al poder. Se ha dicho del candidato que:

- No tiene experiencia política.

- Su experiencia y prácticas de negocio son cuestionables.

- Está involucrado en litigios acusándole de fraude y peor.

- Es un mentiroso descarado, misógino y posiblemente sea racista.

- Insulta con ataques personales a los candidatos de nuestras primarias y a sus familias, para evadir temas que conoce poco.

- Ataca la credibilidad de nuestro partido y todo lo que siempre ha representado.

Ampliar esta lista con detalles conocidos públicamente fácilmente produciría un memorando de 20 páginas, destacando debilidades potencialmente explotables por la oposición en cualquier campaña nacional competitiva. Pero donde algunos de ustedes ven lastre tóxico, yo y otros en la alta dirigencia del partido vemos nuestra victoria. El advenimiento de una renovación vital, desde ya y hacia el futuro.

Nuestro candidato conecta con un segmento del electorado típicamente muerto para la política y para cualquier información. Sabemos que entre el 30% y el 40% del electorado no se anima con partidos políticos o no ve que la democracia tenga valor para ellos; una mentalidad del "¿y cuanto hay para mí en eso?" en la raíz de su apatía. Es por eso que un candidato "externo y disruptivo", como el nuestro, genera la sacudida eléctrica al sistema que impulsa a estos votantes, hasta ahora muertos para el sistema, para salir a votar en esos distritos electorales ignorados donde pequeños márgenes hacen la gran diferencia.

página 2 de 2 - Asunto: ¡Vivimos!

Al energizar estos votantes desconectados, obtendremos una victoria que las encuestas tradicionales y los sabihondos en los medios dicen que cada vez está más fuera de nuestro alcance. Este candidato es el que reanimará a los votantes fantasma y reactivará nuestra vida política. Al ensamblar al candidato perfecto con estos elementos descartados al borde de la democracia, él es la manifestación de su poder latente y creamos al ganador.

Y esto es lo mejor: debido a su gran inexperiencia política, nosotros seremos sus asesores más cercanos. Seremos su piloto a través de lo que son, para él, las aguas turbulentas y desconocidas de la política. Nos aseguraremos de que evite caer en el voraz despeñadero de la cháchara incesante de los medios y sus luces enceguecedoras. Aprovecharemos todos sus defectos conocidos y desconocidos a nuestro favor porque necesitará nuestro apoyo para sobrevivir. Su poder viene de nosotros, y está en su mejor interés propio mantenerse bien con nosotros para mantenerse con vida política: nosotros le suministramos la energía, nosotros lo creamos. Su capacidad destructiva es una fuerza que desataremos en contra de nuestros enemigos. Con él, consolidaremos nuestro poder.
Con él, ¡nunca seremos reemplazados!

Es directiva del alto liderazgo el que apoyemos de todo corazón a nuestro candidato; que dejemos de lado todo recelo que tengamos o agravio personal que pudiésemos haber recibido de él en el pasado; y que emprendamos el camino del éxito a largo plazo del partido y nuestros intereses. Nuestro candidato revive a nuestro de otra manera moribundo partido.
Con él, ¡VIVIMOS!

¡Hacia la victoria, siempre por la patria y el poder!

Su director, siempre.

FMADTC

EL MONSTRUO

Arte por
Itamar Martínez: *Untitled* (2022)
Tinta y acrílico sobre papel. 38 x 25.5 cm.

X

SE ESTÁ COCINANDO

"Una vez dominada una técnica, casi no hace falta ver una receta de nuevo".

JULIA CHILD

Arte por
Andrés Salazar: *Receta Tecnovisual Para Guisar Patraña* (2022)
Foto digital. 26 x 18 cm.

SE ESTÁ COCINANDO
SALSAS PRIMAS

SALSA VERSCHWÖRUNG:
Algo de qué hablar

✳ **PARA: Carnes Rojas**

La carne roja es mejor cuando se le riega generosamente con esta salsa que despierta las emocio-nes más profundas e incita el alma a la acción inesperada. La salsa *Verschwörung* tiene orígenes ancestrales, fue muy popular hacia principios del siglo XX en Europa central y oriental, recorriendo la región y llegando a nuestras costas hace un tiempo, solo para ser opacada por salsas más comunes con mayor consistencia interna y uniformidad. Pero recientemente esta salsa ha visto un resurgimiento alre-dedor del mundo a medida que cambios en la manera de escoger ingredientes y cocinar la mezcla hacen posible que casi cualquiera pueda preparar esta salsa, adaptada a nuestros tiempos modernos.

Los utensilios especializados que necesitará para preparar esta salsa son un enorme caldero de cocción porque, como dijera una vez la autora de **Dominando el arte de la cocina francesa**: "...siempre comience con una olla más grande de la que piensa que va a necesitar"; un cucharón de madera recubierto de chocolate o algún otro dulce; un "sonajero ético" de piedra para controlar el hervor; y, por último, un soplete de cocina para la etapa final del proceso.

Para obtener los mejores resultados, se recomienda preparar la salsa primero en un refugio oculto, lejos de cualquier ojo crítico. Para invocar los espíritus de grandeza que la mezcla evocará, el enorme caldero se colocará sobre troncos de leña en una cueva secreta de espejismos y maravillas. Tres cocineros cuyos nombres nunca nadie conocerá son los ideales para mezclar la más poderosa salsa Verschwörung del mundo.

Para más personas de las que usted se imagina.

40 Litros de caldo de PNDJs (véase pág. 999).	Mientras hierven lentamente veinte litros del Caldo de PNDJs, cuidadosamente seleccione páginas de los libros para eliminar cualquier posible ambigüedad acerca del orgullo y la superioridad nacional. Use esporádicamente los nombres de autores. Haga lo mismo con las canciones, lemas y refranes.
4 Libros de superioridad y orgullo nacionalista con títulos y autores con timbre patriótico.	
Sonajero Ético.	Deposite el *Sonajero Ético* en la mezcla para asegurarse de mantener la temperatura en su punto.
Letra de 30 Viejas Canciones (de origen folclórico o tradicio-nal), dichos y refranes.	Mezcle cuidadosamente las páginas escogidas de los libros, las canciones, los lemas y los refranes, mientras recita sus palabras.
5 Pepitas de fría realidad.	Cada vez que haga ruido el *Sonajero Ético*, eche una pepita de fría realidad para bajar la temperatura.

Capítulo II: Salsas

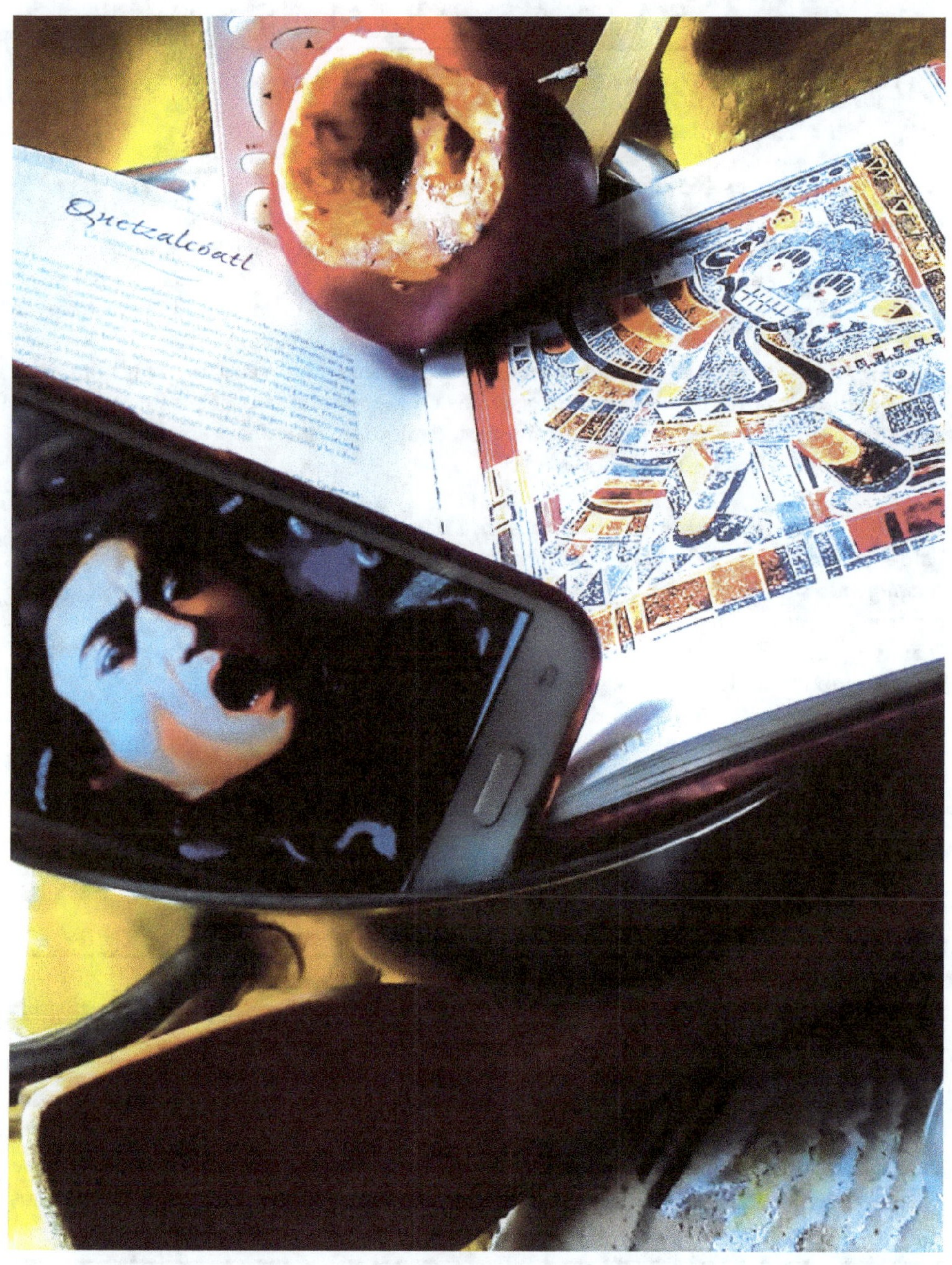

Arte por
Andrés Salazar: *Receta Tecnovisual Para Guisar Patraña (detalle)* (2022)
Foto digital. 26 × 18 cm.

SE ESTÁ COCINANDO

SALSA VERSCHWÖRUNG:

Una pequeña dosis de *Nostalgia Reflexiva.* Una dosis grande de *Nostalgia Restauradora.*	Deje a la mezcla hervir fuerte una vez, eche las dosis de *Nostalgia.* Baje el fuego, deje a la gran cacerola de caldo burbujear por un rato largo.
Cucharón Dulce	Añada el resto del Caldo de PNDJs, mezcle lentamente con el *Cucharón Dulce*, recitando más versos.
Pizcas de resentimientos variados.	Espolvoree cuidadosamente los resentimientos variados.
	Alce la llama y haga que la mezcolanza de ingredientes hierva por segunda vez. Deje al caldero burbujear; deje al *Sonajero Ético* sonar ruidosamente, que suene hasta que reviente.
Sonajero Ético	Pesque y saque las piezas del *Sonajero Ético* del caldero y deséchelas en la basura. Ya no tienen mayor utilidad.
Presentación	Sirva generosamente y muy caliente sobre la carne roja.
Alcohol u otras bebidas combustibles.	Añada el alcohol y utilice el soplete para flambearlo todo.
Porciones.	Asegúrese de que haya más porciones para todos porque querrán llevar para compartir con sus amigos y familia. Agregue tanto Caldo de PNDJs como haga falta.
Aderezo de copos de nieve.	Para darle un toque especial a nuevas porciones añada copos de nieve a la salsa *Verschwörung*.

Capítulo II: Salsas.

Arte de
Jose Rafael Páez: *Evolución Zombi* (2023)
Representación de personajes y lugares para relato gráfico.
Marcadores de color, tinta y guache sobre papel. Tamaños varios.
Diagramación y letras, Magdalena Rangel.

XI

COPIA COPIÓN TE LO DICE SIMPLÓN

"Cuba es el mar de la felicidad. Hacia allá va Venezuela".

HUGO CHÁVEZ F.
La Habana (8 de Marzo, 2000)

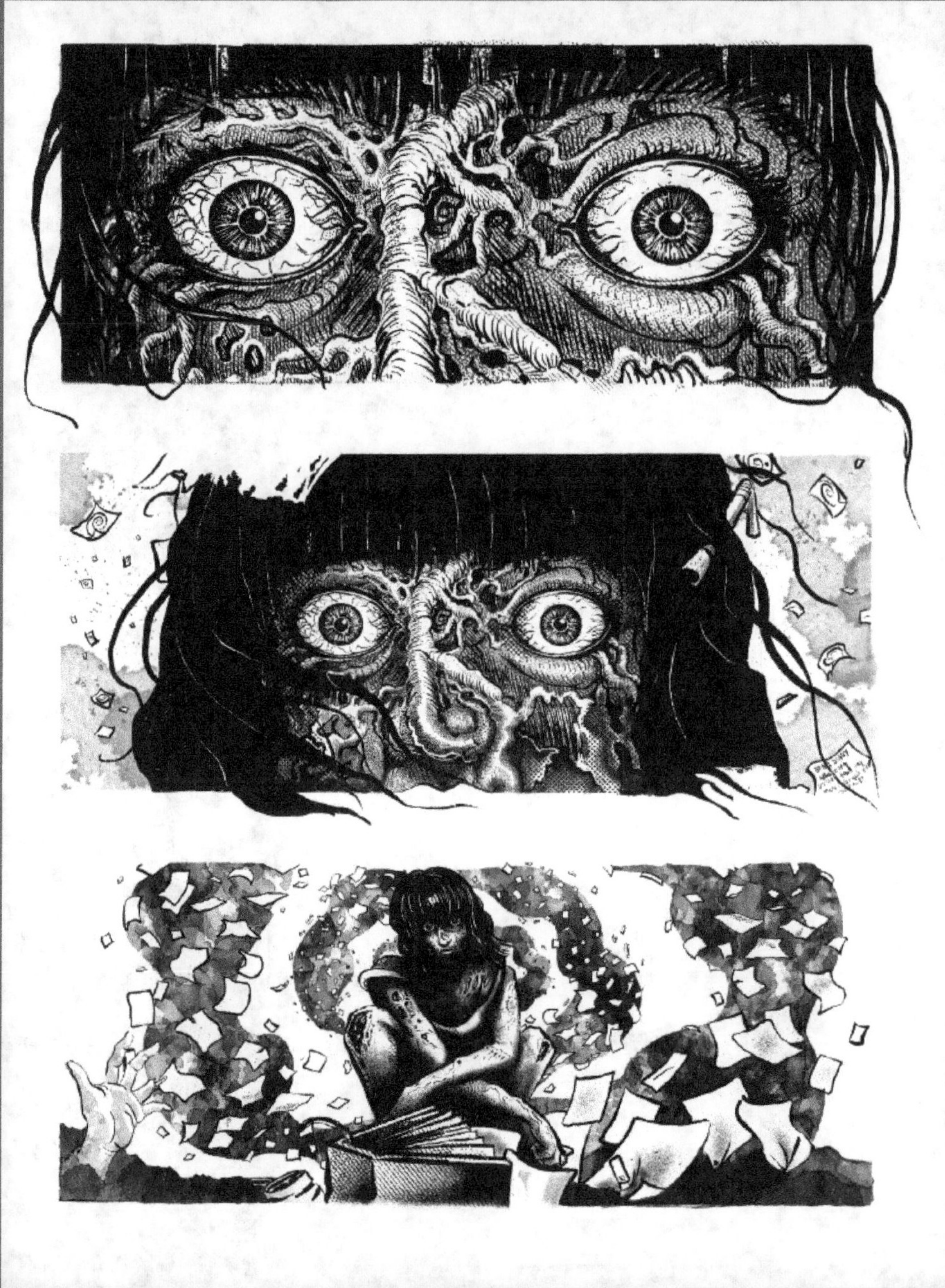

COPIA COPIÓN TE LO DICE SIMPLÓN

"Lo dice Simón..."

Día 1

en D.Onde HAy
cerEbros
dóndE eStan
cereBros
nO reCuerdO
necesitO mis
cerebRos
no tengO cerebro
3.141592653...

tOdoS nO teNemos
cerEbro MovemoS
vAmos haCemoS
siN ceRebro
tenEmoS rAbia
queRemos cereBros
SOMos nosotroS
somos toDo
naDie mas
qUeremos maS nosotrOS
sin ceRebro con
hAmbRe
de cerebRos
lo sEguImoS
son los CincuENTa de Pi.

Hambre, rabia.
No recuerdo.
No hay memoria.
¿Mi cabeza en
CÍRCULOS?
¿Por qué?
No lo sé.
Mi matemática,

COPIA COPIÓN TE LO DICE SIMPLÓN

Día 1 (luego)

Él nos dice vamos,
le seguimos.
Somos su masa, sí.
Su furia.
Su ira.
Su rabia.
Somos él.

Día 2

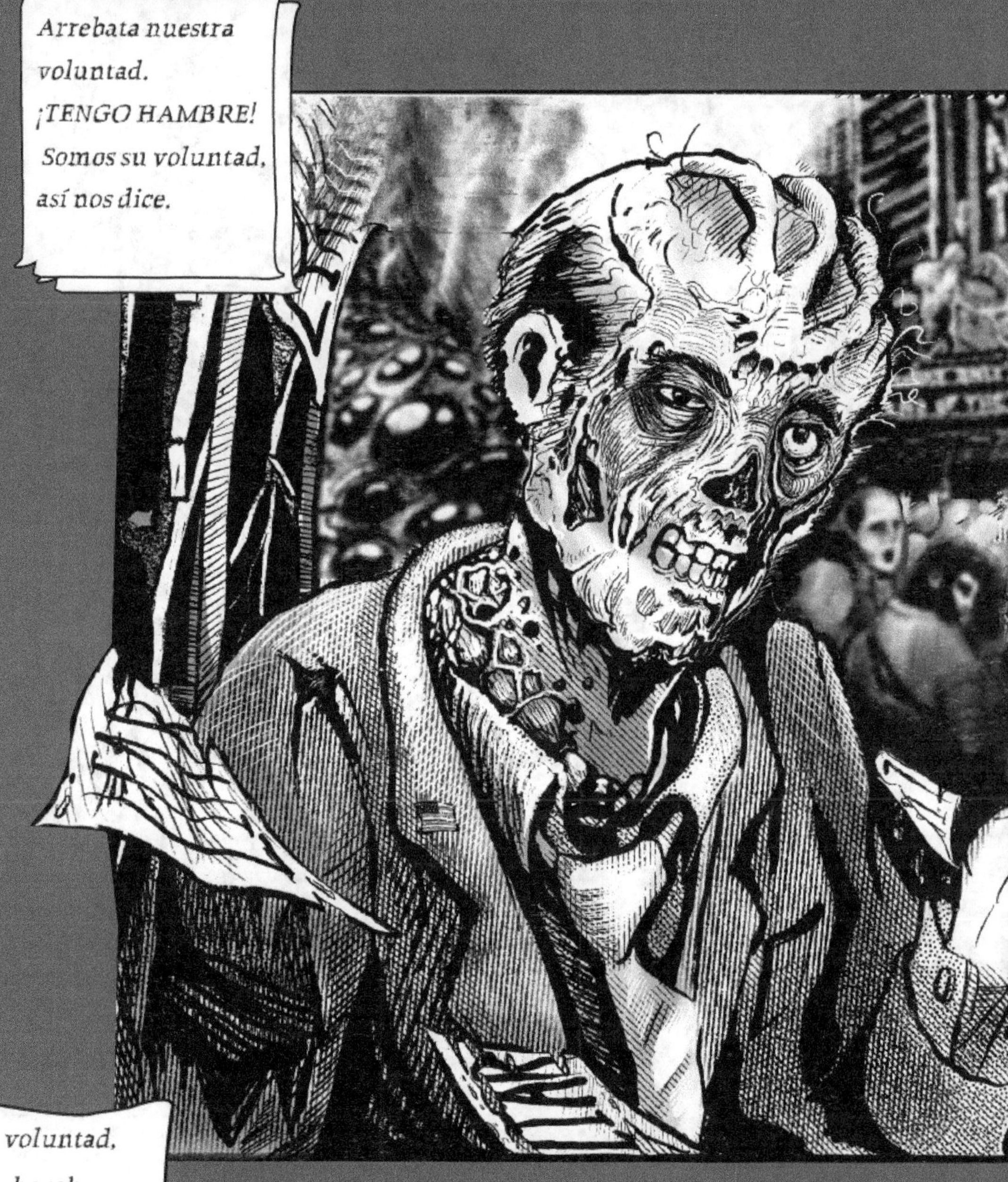
Arrebata nuestra voluntad.
¡TENGO HAMBRE!
Somos su voluntad, así nos dice.

Sin voluntad,
sólo hambre,
nos movemos,
le seguimos,
vamos.

COPIA COPIÓN TE LO DICE SIMPLÓN

Día 3

Muerta.
Estoy muerta.
Sola, solo soy
para mí
y mi líder.
Tal vez estoy viva,
para otros,
¿acaso estoy?
¿Qué es morir?
¿vivir?
¿Acaso le importa?

COPIA COPIÓN TE LO DICE SIMPLÓN

Día 5

¿Por qué no sé
si estoy viva o
si estoy muerta?
¿Qué me pasó
a **mí**?
¿Qué **es** vivir?
¿Me hace **viva**?

¿Cómo perdí vivir?
¿Dónde?
¿Cuándo?
Tengo que
caminar mejor.
Tengo que
hablar mejor.

no en grrrrruññ ñ.

¡Grrruññññ!

Lidera, lo seguimos,
Nos da un nuevo
orden, un propósito
que no sabíamos.
¡**NO** somos caos!
Vagamos, paramos,
gruñimos, cazamos cerebros.
hacemos nuevos seguidores
para nosotros, para él.
¿Acaso estaban vivos?

¿Por qué escribo
estas notas?
Cada vez que me
hago una pregunta
estoy mejor,
estoy menos muerta,
si es que puede haber algo así.

No muerta.

No viva.

Día 8

¿Cuantos somos?
Muchos sin cerebro
para él, ni vivos
ni muertos. No veas.
no escuches, no hables,
no sientas, solo al líder.
Nuestro líder,
¿Por qué es él nuestro
líder?

Nos guía, no sabemos
porqué. Allí está,
no sabemos porqué.
Gruñe sus palabras;
no escuchamos qué,
no importa.
Su ruido
ensordecedor
nos mobiliza,
abre apetitos,
le seguimos,
no sentimos,
sin cerebro,
sin aliento,
sin pulso.
No tenemos nada,
¿es esto la muerte?
¿nada que sentir?
¿Insensibles?...
¿Porqué?

¿Por qué escribo
en este diario?
¿Por qué, cuándo?

HAMBRE

COPIA COPIÓN TE LO DICE SIMPLÓN

Veo, toco, oigo;
eso es nuevo.
Escucho al líder
y esta vez oigo sus
gruñe palabras.
Él nos jala para seguirle.

Si lo seguimos morimos.
Sus gruñidos son
palabras de muerte.

Vi a alguien.
Nueva o de nuevo también.
No era comida,
era alguien.
Nos vimos la cara.
Conectamos.
¿Es que así estoy
más viva?¿Conectamos?
¿Estamos vivos
cuando conectamos
y muertos cuando no?
¡Qué es más viva?

Esta manzana roja
que tengo en mi mano,
Era parte de un árbol,
ya no.¿Está viva?
Tiene vida en su interior.
Puede seguir,
aun después
de que me la coma.
Siente la vida.
La regla dorada.
Orden en el caos que
siempre vivimos.

Este líder es... no.
No es un líder.
Ahora lo veo,
lo que es:
un líder de
cerebros muertos.
Lo que quiere es
nuestros cerebros.
¡SÓLO QUIERE
NUESTROS
CEREBROS!

Dia 8 (cont.)

Más de nosotros
en conexión.
Sentimos de nuevo:
pensamos de nuevo.
Somos de cada uno,
con cada quien.

¿Es acaso Cumbayá?
¿Y qué significa eso si acaso?
¿Es acaso la vida?
¿Y qué significa eso
verdaderamente?

Ella me gusta.
Ella es ella,
yo soy yo.
Somos amigas,
somos un nosotros.
Con los amigos
que tenemos
estamos vivos.
Teníamos familia.
Con la familia
que teníamos
estamos vivos.

Dia 13

¿HOLA?

Mi diario, otra vez.
Cinco días con sol,
nubes y lluvia:
seis noches
con estrellas.

Dije "Hola" hoy.

Podemos tocar la tierra,
sentir y ser parte de ella.
Siempre podía
y lo había olvidado.
Estaba muerta.

Viviremos para siempre
hasta que ya no más.
Algunos infinitos son
más pequeños que otros.

COPIA COPIÓN TE LO DICE SIMPLÓN

YA NO ESTOY MUERTA

XII

PUREZA

La ciudad brillante

"En mi mente, era una ciudad alta y orgullosa, construida sobre rocas más fuertes que los océanos, barrida por el viento, bendecida por Dios y rebosante de gente de todo tipo viviendo en paz y armonía; una ciudad con puertos libres que zumbaban con comercio y creatividad. Y si tenía que haber murallas alrededor de la ciudad, las murallas tenían puertas y las puertas estaban abiertas para cualquiera con la voluntad y el corazón para llegar aquí".

RONALD REAGAN
Discurso de despedida de su presidencia (1989)

Arte de
Rolando Peña: *Our Daily Dracula* (2022)
Photomatón y acrílico sobre papel 26 × 18 cm.

PUREZA

---

mina@castillod.com

>>>>> **De: Vlad** <conde_Tepes1@castillod.com>
Domingo, 23 de Febrero, 20xx, a las 6:55 AM
Para: mina@castillod.com
Asunto: Re: El recodo final

Ya es hora, el círculo a mi alrededor está completo.
Ahora saldré a mi querido jardín y veré el amanecer.
La pira está lista, yo estoy listo. Mi viejo maestro me preparó
para este momento. El fuego que encendiste y me consume
desde adentro estallará al barrer la aurora mis tinieblas.
Tu espíritu vital será parte del mío, sublimados en la ardiente
gloria de este frío amanecer. Desde la distancia nuestro
enemigo verá esas llamas purificadoras como su victoria
y creerá que ha ganado, sin verlas como lo que son, un
destello matinal pasajero. Pero tú y yo seguiremos viviendo,
más allá, unidos a pesar de su ceguera. Es nuestro destino.

Lo mejor para siempre y más,

V

>>>> **El 23 de Feb., 20xx, a las 2:15 AM,**
Mina M <mina@castillod.com> **escribió:**

Siempre mi Vlad:

Los vencedores escriben la historia y los vencidos serán
los demonios. No dejes que te destruyan. Si no sobrevives,
si tu vida no es nuestra historia, entonces nuestro amor
fue en vano. Ellos cocinarán su propio cuento. Vuelve a mí.
Escribamos nuestra verdadera historia. Regresa a nuestro
hogar. No me hagas llorar por ti, déjame quererte.
No les dejes ganar. ¡El momento para nuestra vida es ya!

Tu abrazada,

Mina

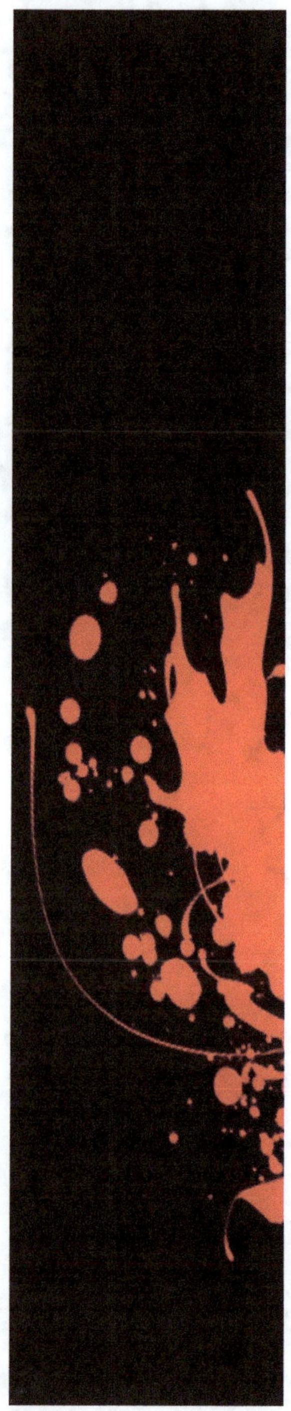

>>> El 23 de Feb., 20xx, a las 2:05 AM. Vlad
<conde_Tepes1@castillod.com>, escribió:

Perpetuamente Mina,

Hay algo que nunca te dije: la razón verdadera por la
cual fui a buscar fama y fortuna en una inhóspita tierra
distante. Tengo que decirla ahora: la razón fuiste tú.
Tú siempre has sido el propósito de mi corazón.

Tu prometido vino a nuestras tierras también buscando
fortuna propia. Llegó acá como uno de esos hombres
de negocios creídos con lengua de plata, no, de oro,
buscando aprovecharse de los mal informados y
estafarles en su buena fe por las ganancias y el poder.
Desconfié de él desde el principio. No estoy seguro de
lo que te habrá dicho de sus viajes, pero pasó mucho
tiempo con esas mujeres alegres del pueblo; su idea de
una despedida de soltero, supongo.

Cuando me mostró tu fotografía, sentí pena por tu futuro
con un hombre como ese, un evidente confabulador;
pero fue entonces que me di cuenta de que tenía que
encontrarte. Fue la chispa detrás de esos ojos y tu sonrisa
radiante revelando un alma brillante en el interior, un
alma que de alguna manera conocía, lo que me llevó a
ti. Reuní todos mis ahorros e invertí en lo que me vendió
como una mansión "reparable" en La City. Partí en un
barco de carga para finalmente llegar a ese cascarón
decrépito que conoces, un lugar quizás en un estado
más lamentable que mi hogar aquí en estas montañas.
Reparable era un eufemismo. Mentes menos generosas
hubiesen calificado de fraude lo que me hizo.
Estoy seguro de que sus colegas pensaron que fue
brillante, entre carcajadas y una buena comisión.

No me arrepiento de eso, fue una bendición haberte
encontrado. Te hallé. Todo después fue la felicidad y el
infierno al mismo tiempo. Mi piel siempre me ha hecho
el diferente. La piel hiper-fotosensitiva y mis ojos sin
pigmento me obligan a vivir en la oscuridad y pueden
ser una discapacidad paralizante. Pero a ti no te importó;
contigo, nuestras almas se iluminaban desde adentro.
Fuimos pareja desde tiempos inmemoriales,
nos encontramos antes y lo haremos otra vez,
al terminar nuestro tránsito actual.

Arte de
Rolando Peña: *Our Daily Dracula (detalle)* (2022)
Photomatón y acrílico sobre papel 26 x 18 cm.

PUREZA

>>>

-- Cuando me dejaste entrar y finalmente te abracé, encontré la vida, me llené plenamente de ti. Recuperé fuerzas, me incendiaste por dentro. Desapareció la ciudad hostil cuando te abracé, besé tus dedos, tus brazos, tu cuello...

Pero para tus cercanos, yo era demasiado diferente. No podían vernos juntos como una sola vida, eres demasiado especial para ellos. Te he ocultado aquella fantasía de horror que idearon acerca de mí; ya la escucharás a su tiempo, pero quiero que sepas desde ahora que es una falsedad ocultando su propia naturaleza malvada. Es una quimera fantástica ideada para separarnos porque, para ellos, es abominable que pertenezcamos juntos: su preciada joya familiar seducida por un horrible monstruo extranjero.

Cuando vi que enfrentabas verdadero peligro ante el frenesí enloquecido de tu celoso prometido y sus gamberros, me fui. Me fui para protegerte. En cualquier momento te encontrarían culpable de algún pecado mortal; enfilarían contra ti sus sermones santurrones, sus estacas afiladas, sus cruces en llamas. Tuve que desviar su mirada, dirigirlos solo hacia mí. Lograron separarnos en esta vida, pero viviremos de nuevo y juntos una vez más.

Comenzaré el ritual ahora: afeitarme la cabeza y vestir la túnica naranja. Pronto todo terminará. Nuestras almas se hallarán nuevamente en un mejor lugar, en un mejor momento, una vez llegadas al océano todas nuestras lágrimas derramadas.

Por siempre tuyo,

V.

>> El 23 de Feb., 20xx, a las 12:10 AM,
Mina M <mina@castillod.com> escribió:

Querido Vlad,

Nunca me perdiste. He extrañado tanto tu voz y tus palabras. Me alegré tanto al recibir tu mensaje, pero no tanto cuando lo leí. Desde que te fuiste, me "protegen" hombres que dicen ser amigos, pero lo que hacen es mantenerme callada, encerrada, sin dejarme que yo sea yo. ¿Amigos de quién? ¿Por qué se dicen dueños de la verdad? ¿Quién les dio este poder sobre mi para encerrarme en este corral, como si fuese solo carne sin cerebro?

Estoy tan aliviada de que me dieras esta dirección de email, la que no conocen. Siempre sueño contigo, esperando que vengas, sentir tu abrazo nuevamente, compartir nuestro amor. Pero me asustas cuando dices que Jonathan llevó un grupo armado para cazarte en venganza. Temo por ti, sobre todo porque escribes que ellos están cerca. Por favor, protégete.

>>

-- Sé lo que sientes y lo que estás pensando cuando
hablas de nuestro futuro juntos y por siempre pero,
para mí, creer que la felicidad existió en un pasado
fantasioso y que regresará en un futuro imaginario
solo nos ciega a nuestro presente posible, aquí y
ahora. Quiero apreciar cada buen momento que
tenemos cuando lo tenemos, porque sé que no
durará.

No sé si será cierto que fuimos almas puras y
benditas en algún pasado. No me importa ese
cuento; debemos vivir nuestros hoys. ¡Muchos hoys!
El destino es lo que hacemos de él. Hazme a _mí_
tu objetivo, tu destino: haz que sea sobrevivir y
regresara mí, no defender nobles principios desde
una elevada plataforma moral. Hazme tu propósito,
ven a casa, donde te amaré ahora y por siempre.
No todos los para siempres son iguales.

Siempre tuya,

Mina

> El 22 de Feb., 20xx, a las 11:27 PM,
Vla <conde_Tepes1@castillod.com> escribió:

Queridísima Mina:

Este es mi último mensaje para ti. El final está cerca.
El odio ha recorrido su curso. He perdido. Te he
perdido. Pero, conozco el camino para reencontrarte.

Que yo dejara La City no fue suficiente para aquellos
que odian lo que soy y lo que represento. Han
venido hasta acá, a perseguir y darme caza en mi
propia tierra, para asegurarse de que tú y yo nunca
volvamos a estar juntos. Para asegurarse de que se
aprenda una lección y que todos la sepan: que
personas como nosotros nunca más, nunca más...
en nombre de la pureza.

Mi región es pobre y remota, no una rica metrópolis
como la tuya. Después de la ruina traté de hacer
fortuna en tierra extranjera, la tuya, pero eso no l
legaría a ser. Tus paisanos y pares me miraban
desconfiados a causa de mi piel, incluso ¡hasta de
mi nariz! Mi acento extranjero, ininteligible para
sus mentes cerradas, desencadenaba siempre esa
pregunta de clivaje que reafirma su pertenencia y mi
condición entre ellos: "_¿De dónde eres?_", asegurándose así de que sepa cuál es mi lugar, no de aquí;

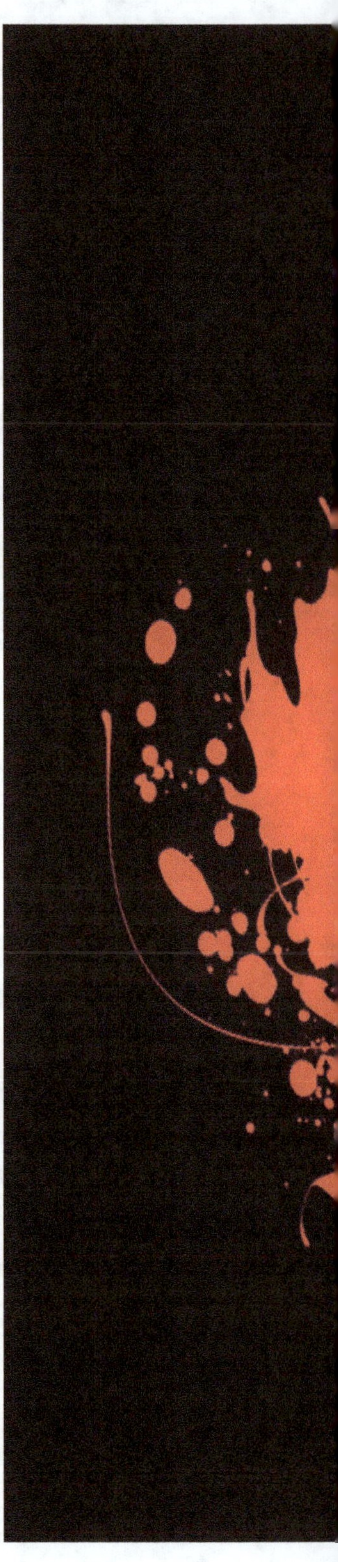

PUREZA

-- de que soy un huésped temporal con cortesía temporal
en su pequeña burbuja; un huésped, eso sí, hasta el
momento en que creen que extranjeros feos y llenos de
enfermedades han venido a violar a sus mujeres, a robarles
sus empleos y dinero; hasta que se sienten amenazados
por los diferentes, por la impureza.

El propósito de mi mente al dejar mi país era enviar dinero
de vuelta. Enviar ganancias a los míos, que languidecen
con expectativas de que sea yo quien les rescate de sus
miserias, simplemente porque vivo en un castillo en los altos
de esta montaña. Sin embargo, yo también estaba
arruinado, no tengo sirvientes y este lugar está que se
desmorona. Mi esperanza era crear fortuna en La City,
con gran comercio entre nuestros países. Pero el miedo a mi
presencia y a mi gente ha creado barreras que ahora nos
separan aún más.

Desde tiempos inmemoriales mi familia ha protegido esta
provincia. Era mi turno ahora. Quería que dejáramos de ser
una región remota y olvidada; quería ser parte del mundo.
He fracasado. Sólo he traído conquistadores a nuestro
entorno, con Harker a la cabeza, buscando destruirme.
Fuiste tú lo único ganado, y ahora también te he perdido.

Mi fin llegará pronto, de una manera u otra. Sólo me
queda elegir la manera. Nuestro viaje juntos por este mundo
ha llegado a su recodo final. Mi condición física me obligó
a perseguir la reflexión y la vida interior, y un viejo maestro
del antiguo oriente me enseñó las vias de la sabiduría y los
senderos del destino. Me enseñó el rito de purificación que
concede la paz y el tránsito a una vida renovada cuando
ya todo está perdido. Estoy listo para seguir sus pasos.
Es mi único camino para reencontrarme contigo, el único
que veo por delante. Mi despedida es solo un hasta luego.
Decido, no con desespero sino con esperanza.

Tuyo, por siempre

V.

Arte de
Rolando Peña: *Our Daily Dracula (detalle)* (2022)
Photomatón y acrílico sobre papel 26 × 18 cm.

XIII

ÉRASE UNA VEZ...

"Pero me gustan las inconveniencias... Pero no quiero comodidad... Quiero a Dios, quiero poesía, quiero peligro verdadero, quiero libertad, quiero bondad. Quiero pecado...

Si es así, entonces reclamo el derecho a ser infeliz. Sin mencionar el derecho a envejecer y volverme feo e impotente; el derecho a tener sífilis y cáncer; el derecho a tener poco que comer; el derecho a ser repugnante; el derecho a vivir en constante aprehensión por lo que pueda pasar mañana; el derecho a contagiarme de tifus; el derecho a ser torturado por dolores indecibles de todo tipo... Los reclamo todos".

ALDOUS HUXLEY
Un Mundo Feliz (1932)

Arte de
Annika Connor: *Because Of You* (2022)
Óleo sobre lienzo. 41 × 51 cm.

ÉRASE UNA VEZ...

El Sueño de Cindy

El nudo en su estómago aprieta mientras Cindy se pregunta, "¡cómo pude haber sido tan estúpida! ¿Por qué se lo dije a Anna?"

Escucha a Anna riéndose, casi cacareando desde la cocina. Fuerte y burlona, la voz de Anna le dice a Drina: "Érase una vez tres hermanas... ¡pero no lo eran! ¡La más pequeña era una hermanastra! ¡Ese fue su sueño! Y al final se casa con un príncipe que se la lleva con un baile y una canción a un lejano palacio. ¡Por favor!"

Anna se ríe de nuevo, fuerte y ruidosa, como solo ella puede hacerlo al divertirse. Una explosiva mezcla de burla, felicidad y bravuconería que tantos muchachos encuentran atractiva, como polillas a la llama, condenados por ese brillo con fingida dulzura. Tal vez moscas en una trampa de miel sea mejor imagen. ¿O acaso esa sería Drina? Siempre buscan a los muchachos; y los muchachos siempre las buscan a ellas, acabando petrificados por su inteligencia, ingenio y encanto. ¡Idiotas!

Cindy sacude el polvo del estante donde posan las fotos de la boda de su padre. Él junto a ELLA. Las tres niñas en finos vestidos de princesa... Nunca debió contárselo a Anna; pero... pero un sueño tan bonito... hasta musical. No pudo contenerse. Sabe que fue solo un sueño, pero...

Érase una vez un viudo rico con una hermosa bebé llamada Cindy que vivían felices en una casa grande con muchas criadas y asistentes. Cindy tenía toda la atención y todo el amor que pudiera desear. Entonces su papá se casó con una viuda para que lo ayudara a criar a su pequeña hija. La viuda tenía dos hijas a las que no les gustaba Cindy. Su papá murió y la mujer, ahora dos veces viuda, se gastó toda la fortuna. Todas las criadas y los ayudantes tuvieron que ser despedidos y Cindy quedó al servicio de la viuda y sus dos hermanastras. Mientras Cindy vive esta vida de miseria, un ser mágico se le aparece y la ayuda a encontrar un Príncipe que la sacará de su infortunio. Ella y el Príncipe se enamoran a primera vista, pero las hermanastras intentan evitar que Cindy se vaya, engañando al Príncipe para que ame a una de ellas. El amor verdadero prevalece al final, se revela el malvado engaño, y el Príncipe se lleva a Cindy para vivir felices para siempre, dejando a su madrastra y hermanastras para que limpien su propio asco y se mueran solas.

Y, ¿qué tiene eso de malo? ¿Por qué le pareció tan chistoso a Anna? Hubo una vez, piensa Cindy, en la que tuvo una vida mejor. ¿Por qué tuvo que casarse otra vez su papá? Estaban perfectamente bien sin nadie más. Recuerda poco de aquella época, tal vez su imaginación la recuerda algo mejor de lo que realmente fue, pero para ella, ese era el Paraíso. Sin maldad, sólo amor; sin sufrimientos, sólo alegría; sin privaciones, solo abundancia. Era un tiempo mejor, de seguro, no como esta vida de ahora. No esta pelea constante y rivalidad entre todas nosotras.

Cindy no se da cuenta cuando lo dice en voz alta: "Qué tiene de malo querer a un salvador? ¿Qué hay de malo en la esperanza de que alguien me lleve a una nueva vida, a un nuevo paraíso, sacarme de este, este... valle de lágrimas sin esperanzas?"

"Pero, mírame esas palabrotas tan elegantes. Siempre pensándote tan especial, tan mejor que nosotras", dice Drina, sacudiendo a Cindy de su ensueño. "¿Que qué tiene de malo, dices? Por el amor de dios, niña, no es como que vivamos aquí en un basurero. Es verdad, el apartamento es pequeño, si, pero para tí es como que si fuera el peor lugar del mundo. ¡Mamá trabaja muy duro para llegar a cada fin de mes y todos tenemos que poner de nuestra parte, incluso tú!"

Cindy callada, siempre timorata. Drina parece estar más furiosa que su normal mientras fustiga más a su hermanastra.

"Escúchame ya, niñita, no hay príncipe, solo nosotras. Nosotras somos las que tenemos que hacer lo que sea mejor para nosotras. Si encontramos a un tipo que nos gusta, okey, es cosa nuestra, no magia. ¡Despierta, por-a-favor! Tienes rollo, hablemos. No te vas soñando con encontrar un príncipe que desaparezca tu familia, muertos para tí por no querer compartir. ¿Eso es lo que quieres? ¿Ese es tu deseo? ¿En serio?"

Cindy trata de contestar, pero Drina descarga: "Esperar a un tipo por ahí, un 'príncipe' cualquiera por ahí para quitarte tu poder, niña, tu voluntad y, sí, tu voz también, a cambio de su 'Castillo de la Felicidad' donde él es tu comandante sobre todo mientras ¿nosotras, tus hermanas? Convenientemente invisibles y olvidadas. Y créeme esto cuando te lo digo, sí: tu comandante siempre va a quererlo todo y más. ¡Solo migajas para ti! ¿Es eso lo que de verdad quieres? Serás entonces, niña, verdaderamente, efectivamente, otra carne ambulante sin cerebro como zombi."

Se miran, tal vez en desafío. La confusión hierve en Cindy. Finalmente, saca "pero Drina, ustedes siempre me lo complican todo cuando solo lo que quiero es una vida sencilla, sin complicaciones. Siempre se amontonan en mi contra, siempre me ganan entre las dos. ¡Siempre soy minoría!"

"Eso no significa que no puedas hablar, niñita, que no tengas tu voz propia ¿o no? No hay tal cosa como una vida simple. Sipa, a veces te escuchamos a tí, y a veces deberías escucharnos a nos. Ajá, tienes razón, una familia de nosotras es mucho más complicada que simplemente un tipo diciéndote qué hacer y que te calles, pero la verdad es que, juntas, nadie nos para; somos un nosotras que puede hacer lo que sea; te lo digo, peleando entre nosotras, somos el afiche que anuncia el desorden, la definición del caos en la enciclopedia, dulces desastres en su punto".

ÉRASE UNA VEZ...

Desde la cocina, suena la voz de Anna: "dile, dile, dile duro". Entra en la habitación con tres Coca-colas colgando de su anillo plástico de seis. Fastidia a Cindy ofreciendo y quitando la que le trajo, hasta que finalmente se la deja agarrar.

Anna abre su lata, psssst. "Nuestra hermana te lo canta claro, 'niñita': somos familia. A lo mejor pensamos distinto, o lo decimos distinto... pero todas deberíamos querer lo mismo, seguir unidas y hacerlo bien. A lo mejor no es exactamente como yo quisiera, o como tú quieras... pero la idea es seguir juntas para que cada una haga lo que cada una quiere hacer y así estar bien todas. ¡Déjame echarte el cuento de mí sueño!".

Érase una vez, el padre bondadoso de una linda bebé halló alivio del dolor de perder a su primera esposa al encontrar y casarse con otra buena mujer, la cual, a su vez, era viuda. Esta mujer tenía dos hijas y todos hicieron vida de familia juntos durante un tiempo. El luto los visitó de nuevo con la muerte prematura del padre. Llegaron tiempos difíciles y la madre trató de ganarse la vida en un mundo cruel, abusivo de su débil situación. La madre se esforzó por hacer lo mejor que pudo para sus tres hijas, asegurándose de que todas recibieran una educación y crecieran fuertes e independientes, no como ella. Pero la más joven recordaba un pasado inexistente y anhelaba un futuro imaginario, rescatada de sus obligaciones diarias por un salvador mágicamente aparecido en un poderoso corcel. Mientras esperaba el día de su redención, languidecía alrededor de la casa extrañando a su querido padre muerto, sin superar, sin avanzar, o como sea que se diga...

Cindy protesta: "¡Eso es fácil para tí decir, pero era mi papá!" Drina y Anna: "¡Era nuestro papá también!" El silencio entre todas crece incómodo. Diría una abuela que pasó un ángel.

Las fotos de la boda erguidas en su estante silenciosamente contemplan a las tres hermanas. Drina contiene una lágrima y le hace señas a Anna para que termine su cuento.

Arte de
Annika Connor: *Because Of You (detalle)* (2022)
Óleo sobre lienzo. 41 × 51 cm.

ÉRASE UNA VEZ...

...Todas las niñitas finalmente crecieron y se convirtieron en una empoderada fuerza de cambio en su mundo, encontraron amor en la pareja que querían, o no, y vivieron la vida que todos esperamos vivir: trabajar todos los días por la búsqueda de la felicidad en un mundo lleno de oportunidades. Sabiendo muy bien que cada día vivido es un día más cercano al día de nuestra muerte – sin para siempres. Fin.

Otro silencio incómodo... de repente, Anna explota con su risa contagiosa.

Cindy se ríe, toma un sorbo de su refresco y, tras un momento dice, algo burlonamente: "Supongo que ese es un sueño mejor. Pero sigue siendo otro cuento de hadas ".

FIN

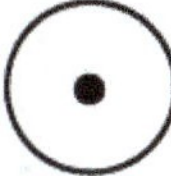

EPÍLOGO

> "Dices que quieres una revolución.
> Bueno, ya sabes,
> Todos queremos cambiar al mundo.
> Me dices que es una evolución,
> Bueno, ya sabes,
> Todos queremos cambiar al mundo...".

JOHN LENNON
Revolution (1968)

Arte por
Marc Lafia: *Loren Eisely #20* (2023)
Pintura digital. 106 × 145 cm.

EPÍLOGO

El ejercicio de la democracia es relativamente reciente en la historia de la humanidad. Aun cuando hubo intentos de institucionalizar repúblicas democráticas en la Grecia y Roma antiguas, el destape del potencial de innovación y creatividad mediante este experimento en gobernabilidad no será completamente realizado sino hasta la revolución liberal del S. XVIII. Fue entonces cuando la idea de renovación institucional, combinada con la idea de renovación económica, el capitalismo, sacudirá al mundo.

Este sacudón estructural resultará en una profunda transformación social, económica y política, y la noción de democracia tal como la cono-cemos hoy día. Conducirá a una era de prosperidad abarcando a lo sumo apenas unos doscientos cincuenta años de los seis mil años de historia de la civilización; una era que ha creado y distribuido más riqueza y bienestar que todo el tiempo anterior, incluso a naciones que no practican la democracia por su efecto de difusión colateral. Dado el tiempo que abarca la democracia moderna, no es de extrañar que las leyendas heroicas, mitos, fábulas y todos los elementos históricos de nuestra cultura muestren un mayor sesgo hacia lo que podemos considerar como iliberalismo — el orden autoritario centrado en lealtades tribales.[1] Pero el liberalismo no surgió de la nada. Sus raíces, y algunos demonios, se hallan en esos mismos mitos, leyendas y fábulas que han formado nuestras mentes durante milenios.

● ACERCA DE LAS IDEAS

Hace un tiempo fui invitado a participar en un equipo de consultoría política trabajando a favor de un candidato presidencial en un país latinoamericano. Como sucede frecuentemente en la región, un amplio espectro de organizaciones de tendencia demócrata liberal se enfrentaba a un amplio espectro de organizaciones populistas cada una calificándose (o acusando a sus rivales) de "nacionalistas", "socialistas" o alguna otra etiqueta similar, dependiendo de la base política a la cual querían persuadir. Resultaba claro, nuevamente, que mientras que los populistas fundamentan su relato normativo en una narrativa fácilmente transmitida de "hechos" con raíces profundas en la emotividad y una ligeramente espolvoreada racionalidad, los liberales (en la acepción del S. XVIII) típicamente hacen esfuerzos para transmitir ideas complejas con raíces profundas en la racionalidad y una ligeramente espolvoreada emotividad.

Esto no ocurre únicamente en America Latina. Es una tendencia humana natural la de preferir al control y el orden simple que la incertidumbre y el desorden complicado. Hombres fuertes (no siempre hombres) pueden utilizar las instituciones democráticas para lograr y mantener el poder político con la promesa de restaurar el orden y acabar con la incertidumbre.

---

[1] El mando autoritario se asocia con el instinto tribal de "sangre y tierra", el cual tanto la llamada derecha e izquierda pueden apropiar en cualquier momento con distintas variantes. Hugo Chávez, invocando a Bolívar para luchar contra el imperialismo yanqui, evoca el mismo instinto que Viktor Orbán protegiendo la pureza húngara de (inexistentes) hordas migratorias ("la xenofobia es peligrosa, pero el patriotismo es bueno" – V. Orbán). Líderes de la retórica nacionalista en todo el espectro político tales como Maduro, Ortega, Xi, Putin, Orbán, o Erdoğan, por mencionar unos, personeros de la Derecha Alternativa en los EE. UU., y candidatos como Le Pen, Meloni u otros, frecuentemente usan el oportunismo para hacer causa común con el nacionalismo autoritario en contraposición a principios libertarios.

Durante los últimos veinte años hemos visto una gran ola de antiliberalismo barrer el globo, una posible reacción a esa fuente de incertidumbre y desorden que es la democracia liberal y que tuvo su pico a principios de la década de los 90 – el "Fin de la Historia" de Francis Fukuyama.

Fué así, nuevamente ante las rivalidades y péndulos entre orden y desorden, que aquel contrato de consultoría me condujo de vuelta a un proyecto de libro que había apartado; un proyecto que busca identificar y entender arquetipos subyacentes en nuestros relatos populares comunes, e interpretados dentro de una narrativa de democracia liberal.

En un libro previo escribí un segmento sobre el poder del populismo con su narrativa emocional seductora: la promesa de satisfacer una heterogeneidad de agravios, cobijados bajo un manto de malestar general, con ideas simples, lemas contagiosos, y símbolos, colores y hasta ropaje distintivo, casi icónicos.[2] Como contra narrativa, era mi argumento, las promesas racionales del liberalismo pueden ser muy atractivas cuando se articulan: dignidad individual, trato igual y justo bajo la ley, igualdad de oportunidad, y protección de la propiedad privada — promesas que de una u otra manera frecuentemente hacen todos los candidatos durante campañas electorales democráticas (por ser las elecciones, a fin de cuentas, una idea básicamente liberal) mientras disfrutan comida local, besan bebés y declaran su amor por mamá, papá y el país.

En aquel mismo libro propongo definir la libertad como la condición bajo la cual un ser umano tiene la oportunidad de desarrollar plenamente su potencial como tal. La libertad está en la esencia del libre albedrío; es el centro ideológico de la democracia liberal. En el presente libro, yuxtapongo este paradigma de gobernabilidad con su rival, el mandato autoritario. Este último se puede definir como la condición bajo la cual seres humanos sobreviven y prosperan dependiendo de los caprichos oportunistas de un régimen cuyo centro ideológico es el derecho legítimo de concentrar el máximo poder en su líder.

---

[2] "Populismo, o la ceguera colectiva que conduce los pueblos al abismo", Rangel, C. J. en *La Venezuela Imposible: Crónicas y reflexiones sobre democracia y libertad.* Alexandria Publishing House, Miami, FL, 2017.

EPÍLOGO

Las promesas de la democracia liberal son invariablemente rotas bajo un régimen populista, lo cual conducirá al autoritarismo. No importa si el régimen se tilda de derecha o de izquierda: la igualdad de oportunidad y de amparo ante la ley están condenadas a desaparecer y la injusticia a prevalecer. Tanto en la política como en la vida, surgirán monstruos de la dicotomía razón/emoción cuando duerma la razón.

Si las (atractivas) promesas y reglas de un sistema liberal democrático se mantienen, inevitablemente estas conducirán a la rotación de cualquier líder populista cuasi-autoritario y posibles enfrentamientos violentos entre ambos sistemas y sus seguidores. La auto-preservación, un instinto básico en la política, se enfrenta al principio básico de la democracia: la renovación de ideas, líderes e instituciones, sin importar lo que vino antes. Esto se enuncia frecuentemente como "fuera lo viejo, bienvenido lo nuevo", o el más común: "¡Saquen a los zánganos!" (dicho aquí de manera decente). Este aspecto de renovación institucional periódica de la democracia es el tema subyacente en la primera viñeta: RENOVADO.

Los viejos mitos griegos ilustran repetidamente a la sucesión de liderazgos como una secuencia de tiranos derrocados de manera violenta, a veces por sus hijos o hijas, a veces por el héroe del momento. Esos poderosos relatos, posiblemente reflejando observaciones de la vida real, tal vez los llevó a idear la renovación institucional sistemática mediante reglas y métodos con orden y, eventualmente a la democracia. Esta idea, a pesar de sus muchas fallas, parece mejor que la sangre derramada descrita en sus leyendas, teatro y relatos. Pero como en toda bella ficción, la realidad frecuentemente choca con los mejores deseos.

Arte por
Marc Lafía: *Loren Eisely #16* (2023)
Pintura digital. 106 × 145 cm.

Las ideologías de izquierda y derecha son deliberadamente ofuscadas por sus adeptos como medio de autopreservación política. Las bases ideológicas de estas facciones opuestas y sus metas se pueden encontrar en la época de la Revolución Francesa cuando la entonces llamada izquierda era campeona de los derechos a la oportunidad, en todas sus manifestaciones posibles, mientras que la entonces llamada derecha defendía los derechos a la propiedad, nuevamente, con toda implicación posible. Un sistema de verdadera democracia liberal busca equilibrar los derechos de oportunidad y los derechos de propiedad para lograr el mejor resultado posible para toda la sociedad. En otras palabras, para que la democracia exista y prospere, también debe existir la alternancia política y el permanente agitar creativo generado por esa rivalidad entre la izquierda (oportunidad) y la derecha (propiedad). La necesidad de opuestos para construir un todo, desde ideas y comportamientos, mecanismos y sistemas, hasta la propia humanidad, está en el contenido de todos los textos de este libro y, por supuesto, trae a la mente el antiguo concepto de Ying/Yang.

Pero esta búsqueda de la máxima autopreservación política, es decir, lograr y mantener el poder sin importar el costo, conducirá a otros resultados, incluso a veces comprometiendo la seguridad de una nación y sus ciudadanos. Partidarios de izquierda y derecha podrán preferir elevar la retórica antagónica, con cada facción acusando a la otra de ser la anti-democrática (porque "democracia" es una de las palabras favoritas del discurso populista y autoritario moderno), la que va a "destruir nuestro país y nuestros valores tal y como los conocemos y amamos", con el corolario de que para proteger la esencia de nuestra nación los opositores (y disidentes) deben ser silenciados, cancelados, eliminados... Llega la polarización, el extremismo se acelera y los resultados sociales positivos disminuyen. Este es el tema subyacente de la viñeta final, ÉRASE UNA VEZ... que termina con la nota amarga acerca de las dos caras de la moneda del mismo cuento de hadas, sin 'felices para siempres', solo lucha constante. [3]

Es importante destacar que cuando un subconjunto de estas facciones se comporta de manera verdaderamente antidemocrática, usando su poder para subvertir normas e instituciones,[4] llegando incluso hasta la intimidación y violencia política, ese comportamiento a veces es resistido (en defensa heroica) en vez de colaborado (traicionando a las instituciones) por algunos miembros de la misma facción. Pero las etiquetas de traición, lealtad, cobardía y valentía dependen de los resultados y, como tales y en relación con la transformación social, son exploradas en la quinta viñeta, PETRIFICADO.

---

[3] Friedrich Hayek, en su Postdata a Fundamentos de la libertad (1960), ***"Por qué no soy conservador"***, propone que la ideología política no es un espectro lineal sino triangular, con Derecha e Izquierda en dos vértices y Liberalismo en el tercero. En los dos primeros extremos existiría autocracia, con la voluntad de unos pocos buscando imponer el control sobre muchos en nombre del bien común, sea mediante dictadura mercantilista o dictadura comunista. En este caso podemos entonces inferir (como lo han hecho algunos críticos de Hayek) que el liberalismo extremo del tercer vértice podemos asociarlo con la anarquía, un orden social donde cada individuo es responsable del control de su propio bienestar y progreso. Conceptualmente, la democracia moderna como modelo de gobierno (nuevamente) estaría hacia el centro de este triángulo, satisfaciendo a muchos, en el sentido de Herbert Simon, pero nunca suficientemente, conduciendo a esa lucha constante.

[4] Por ejemplo, por miembros del partido polaco 'Ley y Justicia' en el 2015, subvirtiendo normas constitucionales y políticas para empujar a las instituciones democráticas y a la sociedad hacia la extrema derecha, o de la coalición Morena tratando de hacer lo mismo en México hacia la extrema izquierda en 2022, como han hecho o intentado hacer otros adherentes al Foro de Sao Paulo en América Latina.

EPÍLOGO

Es así como desde la primera hasta la última viñeta, la intención del libro es intentar identificar qué es lo que hace funcionar y mantener ese desordenado mecanismo institucional que llamamos democracia, y las raíces que pueda tener en nuestros antiguos y familiares relatos perdurables.

● ACERCA DEL LIBRO

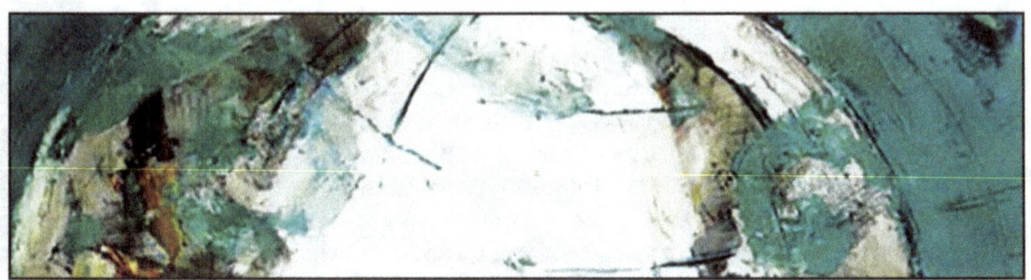

Tras un estallido inicial y afiebrado de escritura hace unos años, había dejado languidecer mis reflexiones acerca de esas raíces hasta que, nuevamente, sentí la naturaleza imperativa de plasmarlas por escrito debido a aquel contrato de consultoría. Además, me di cuenta de la necesidad de ilustraciones que acompañaran el texto cuando este se nutre de mitos y relatos, puesto que ya tenemos imágenes estampadas en nuestra mente acerca de los mismos. De esta manera, el proyecto del libro fue concebido en su totalidad.

La obra se presenta en trece "viñetas", cada una centrada sobre un mito o relato arquetípico, y cada una acompañada con ilustraciones por una constelación de artistas de alrededor del mundo quienes contribuyeron generosamente a la realización de este proyecto. La interacción con cada artista me ayudó a enfocarme sobre el tópico de cada viñeta, y de verdad agradezco esta interacción y su apoyo. Los siguientes párrafos son extraídos (con algunas paráfrasis para mayor claridad) de mis comunicaciones con ellos como intento de guía en la selección y creación de imágenes en el texto:

> ● "...Las viñetas pueden abarcar más de un tema a la vez, incluyendo democracia como renovación, tiranía, 'me too', noticias falsas, la naturaleza de la vida, belleza, demagogos, negación de la ciencia, populismo, empoderamiento del individuo, diversidad, y muchos otros. Cada viñeta está escrita para ser leída rápidamente y transmitir con su relato el tema subyacente".

> ● "...En cuanto a TIRANÍA, la viñeta se basa sobre un poderoso y tal vez olvidado mito, uno en el cual el creador de la humanidad es castigado por un dios superior por, básicamente, darles a los humanos una oportunidad contra los caprichos de los dioses... [Prometeo] tiene su recompensa (¿redención?) en que su creación, la humanidad, surge y prospera por lo que él hizo. Sin mencionar que Zeus mismo, el tirano, ha pasado a ser un dios menor. El aspecto de autosacrificio en el héroe se explora más en una viñeta posterior, PETRIFICADO".

● "…Algunas de las leyendas de Prometeo dicen que, aun cuando él fue quien creó la forma humana modelando barro a semejanza de los dioses (como ocurre en todo mito de creación), fue Atenea, la diosa de la sabiduría, quien con su aliento trajo el barro a la vida. Esta es una parte interesante e intrigante del mito porque contiene dos ideas. La primera es que Prometeo, un dios titán del viejo orden del universo, hace alianza con el nuevo orden del universo, una diosa del Olimpo, para crear a la humanidad. Me sumerjo directamente en el viejo/nuevo orden del universo (en esencia la naturaleza vs. el hombre) tres veces más en el libro, previa y directamente en RENOVADO, después en BELLEZA, e indirectamente en VIENE DE VUELTA. El segundo mensaje contenido en el mito de creación Prometeo/Atenea es que para crear a la humanidad, al igual que hizo falta lo viejo y lo nuevo, hizo falta un hombre y una mujer".

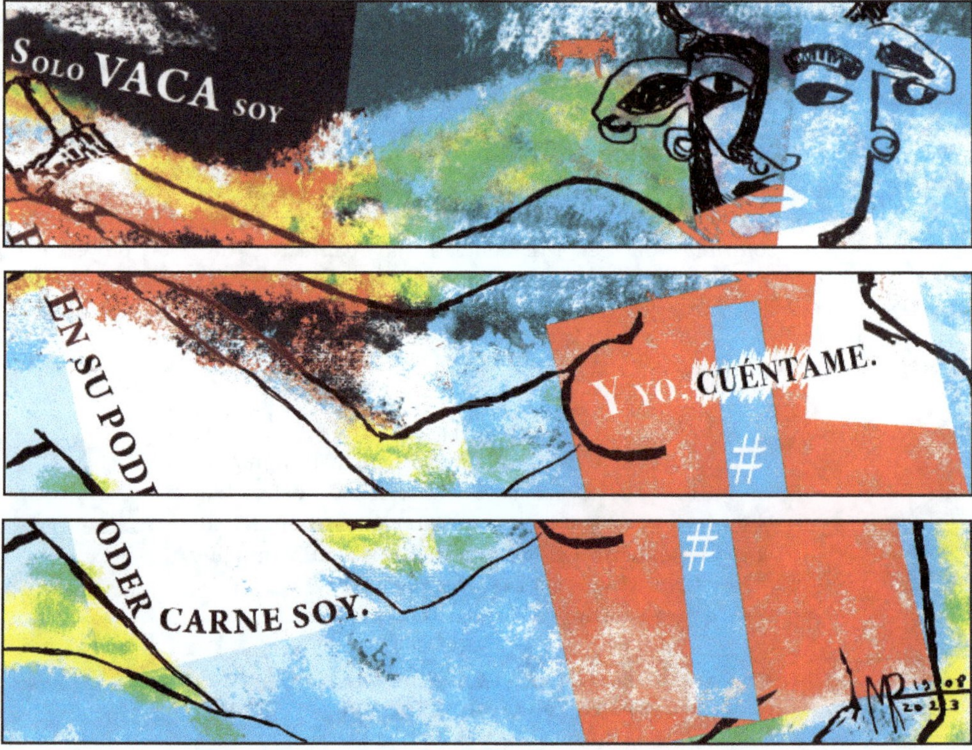

● "…[Sobre ÍO MASCULLA] debemos tener presente la capacidad de transformación que tiene el poder. Él ha sido acusado por más de 100 mujeres de abuso verbal y sexual, de tocarlas y violarlas, sintiéndose con derecho a hacerlo por su poder sobre ellas. Eso no es aceptable. Una serie destacando ese desempoderamiento de sus víctimas es un proyecto que vale la pena".

EPÍLOGO

● "…la viñeta de LA BURBUJA busca reflejar una dualidad antagónica entre la mentira y la verdad, y el peligro de que una añorada fantasía pueda esconder la peligrosa realidad que uno enfrenta".

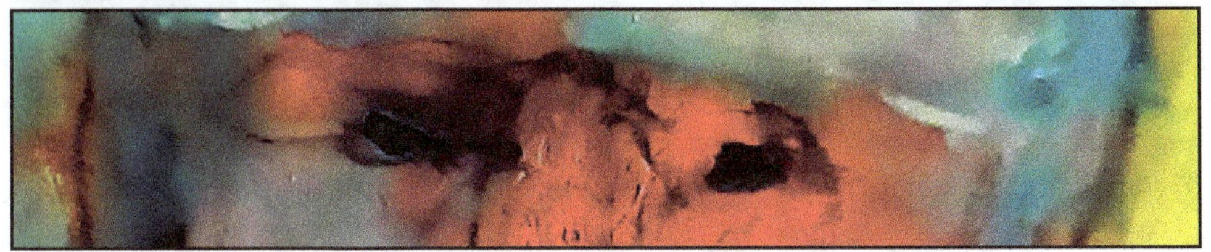

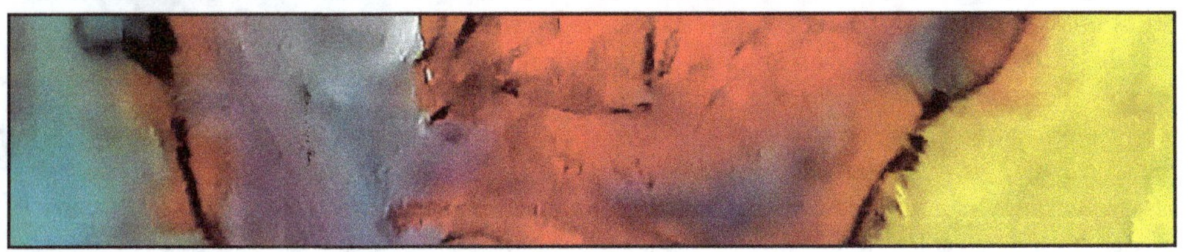

● "…al usar viejos cuentos, mitos y leyendas, uno de los propósitos del libro es arroparse con la atemporalidad de los relatos que utiliza. Hacer cualquiera de las ilustraciones demasiado relevantes al momento que vivimos disminuye el poder en el tiempo de los mensajes… [EL MONSTRUO] se aplica a cualquier aspirante a hombre fuerte, del presente o del pasado, respaldado por cualquier despistada oligarquía política y/o económica".

● "…COPIA COPIÓN TE LO DICE SIMPLÓN [ilustra] muchedumbres que pueden llegar al punto de su autodestrucción al manipularles su pensamiento mediante lemas [gruñidos] sin significado. Para escaparse de esa mentalidad de masa colectiva, los individuos tienen que reafirmar su propio ser, no importa cuán difícil. La viñeta también toca el tema de la esencia de vivir y de cómo ésta solamente se manifiesta, y estamos felices de estar vivos, a través de la conexión con lo que nos rodea y con otra gente".

● "…[PUREZA usa] los tres mensajes del Conde Tepes como una dramatización de las etapas de K-R de ira, negación, aceptación, negociación y depresión, asociadas con la certidumbre de que la muerte se aproxima…[5] Su primer mensaje, el último en el texto, hace referencia directa a la segunda viñeta del libro, la del mito de Pandora/Eva, TOCANDO FONDO. Pero volteando la relación entre esperanza y desesperación; la violencia asociada a la persecución del Conde por supuesto se relaciona con la violencia utilizada por los poderosos para mantener sus privilegios (y no ser 'RENOVADOS')…" "…La objetificación de Mina por sus 'protectores' es referencial a la tercera viñeta ÍO MASCULLA; y la interacción entre Mina y el Conde es la eterna dicotomía entre idealismo colectivo y pragmatismo individual, tema también visto en la quinta viñeta basada sobre el mito de Perseo, PETRIFICADO (y representada famosamente en la película 'Solo Ante el Peligro', con Gary Cooper y Grace Kelly)…"[6]

● "…La historia de la Cenicienta es uno de los relatos más tóxicos estampado en nuestras mentes desde la infancia. Envuelto en bello papel de caramelo y espolvoreado excesivamente con azúcar, desempodera de manera abismal a las mujeres y crea expectativas nada razonables para los hombres. El poder del relato es quese deriva de una idea que ha hecho retroceder al progreso y desarrollo de la humanidad a lo largo de la historia (y la cual mi padre refuta dentro del contexto de América Latina en su libro más famoso[7]); la idea de que la existencia tiene tres etapas: una del paraíso perdido, una de sufrimiento, y una del paraíso recuperado mediante un redentor. En la Cenicienta hubo un tiempo de abundancia, hay tiempos de sufrimiento, y hay un 'felices para siempre' guiado por un poderoso y mágico redentor. Esto, por supuesto, es el mito cristiano (entre otras variantes religiosas), pero también es el mito marxista, lo cual lo hace resonar poderosamente en tantas sociedades. El origen de este arquetipo viene de las etapas de inocencia infantil, maduración (fruta del conocimiento del mito Eva/Pandora), y racionalización del propósito de la vida (vida en el más allá o, para los marxistas, el futuro bienestar inalcanzable). Pero estos mitos terminan desempoderando al individuo y distrayendo del aquí y ahora… ".

[5] Kubler-Ross, E., *On Death and Dying.* (Routledge, 1969).

[6] La viñeta "PUREZA" está escrita como una cadena de correos electrónicos, por lo cual puede leerse como se presenta en el libro o al revés, siguiendo su hora marcada cronológicamente. En la primera lectura, el Conde Vlad le escribe/responde a Mina. Cuando se lee siguiendo la línea cronológica, son las respuestas de Mina después de leer el primer mensaje del Conde.

[7] Rangel, C., *Del buen salvaje al buen revolucionario: Mitos y realidades de América Latina.* (Monte Ávila, Caracas, 1976).

EPÍLOGO

Amigos, colaboradores y conocidos usando con gran amabilidad su tiempo para leer porciones y borradores iniciales del texto me han hecho, entre otros generosos comentarios, dos observaciones. La primera es que las breves viñetas han despertado su curiosidad para explorar algo más acerca del relato o del tema. Esa era una de mis intenciones, encender esa curiosidad. La segunda es más bien una pregunta acerca de que si pudiesen venir más relatos así en el futuro.

De entre la amplia gama de relatos en nuestra trova occidental, me reduje a éstos. Sí pensé en algunos otros, como Midas, el Minotauro, Ícaro y Dédalo, David y Goliat (al cual hago referencia en una viñeta), Caín y Abel, Caperucita Roja, Rumpelstiltskin, Moby Dick y varios más. Algunos pudiesen haber cabido dentro de mi arco narrativo, otros no, o eran demasiado obvios y trillados.[8] El relato del Emperador Desnudo, por ejemplo, está sobreexpuesto: un político con cruda ambición, sintiéndose con derechos adquiridos al poder y la riqueza, teje relatos fabulosos para sus seguidores. Sus partidarios creen que solamente un tonto no admiraría a un líder como este, que exhibe desafiantemente su impunidad y desnuda ambición, desfilando en la Gran Avenida o sentado en su trono dorado de baratijas. Ninguno de sus súbditos osa decir que el emperador está desnudo, no sea que le llamen idiota, traidor, o se le someta a un destino peor. Un relato demasiado sobre expuesto, demasiado del momento. O ¿lo es verdaderamente?

Esta aparentemente disparatada selección de relatos se usa para desarrollar un tema singular, la dualidad autocracia/democracia, desde varias facetas y dentro de una simple narrativa. Había considerado el proyecto completo con doce viñetas y sus ilustraciones cuando un amigo mío, el Dr. Nemesio Mondelo, sugirió que entre los estilos de escritura incluyese una receta de cocina. Primero descarté la idea. Ya había dedicado demasiada energía al proyecto y estimaba que estaba listo.

---

[8] Habiendo terminado el texto del libro y escrito este epílogo, tuve la oportunidad de presentar un libro distinto, una nueva traducción al italiano de ***Del buen salvaje al buen revolucionario***, ante el Instituto Bruno Leoni, Milán, en noviembre del 2023 (el texto completo de la presentación está disponible en mi blog, ***carlosjrangel.com***: ***Carlos Rangel y la democracia como el anti-mito***). En esa presentación hago referencia al cuento de El Niño y el Lobo para hablar acerca de la complacencia cívica y de los medios ante las amenazas permanentes a las democracias. Como he tratado de argumentar en este libro: la democracia siempre está asediada, interna y externamente, y las advertencias y peligros son verdaderos. El lobo acecha, siempre.

Pero tras una lectura del libro *El Ocaso de la Democracia de Anne Applebaum*, me percaté que sí me faltaba un ingrediente: elementos conspirativos, esenciales para el dominio autoritario. Escribí entonces una última viñeta, SE ESTÁ COCINANDO, una receta, completando así la docena del panadero. Uno de los artistas colaboradores, Andrés Salazar, batió rápidamente una composición fotográfica, incluyendo temor, sabiduría corrupta, e ideas nacionalistas, para acompañar el texto de manera perfecta. Si bien las recetas no son exactamente mitos, leyendas o cuentos, para algunos son parte de una deliciosa tradición familiar compartida, como el aroma de comida reconfortante emanando desde la cocina de nuestro tío borracho favorito.

Carlos J. Rangel
Junio 2023

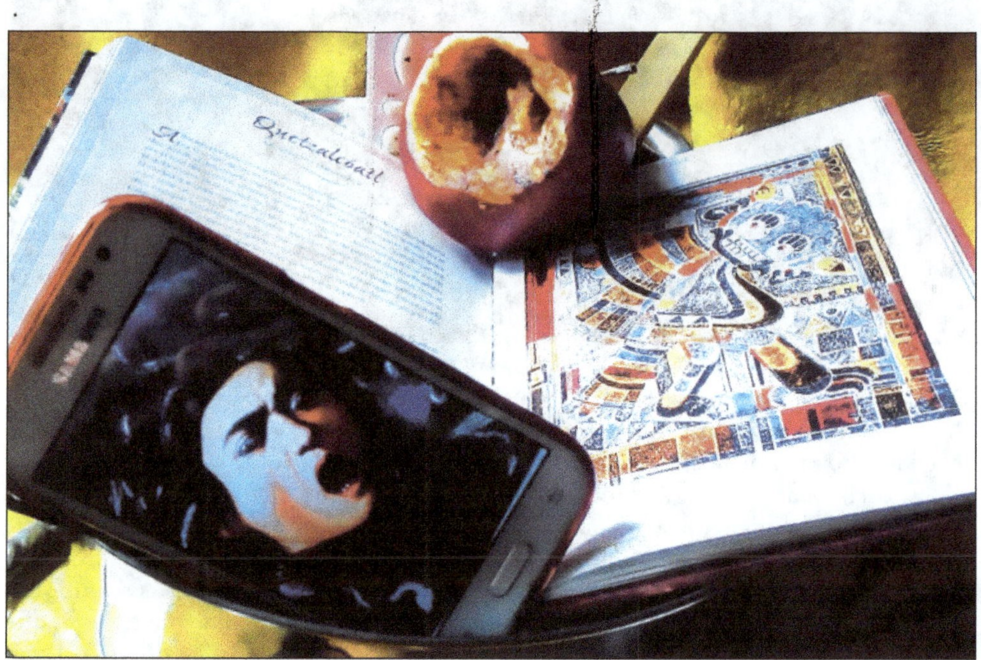

ILLUSTRACIONES EN EL EPÍLOGO SON DETALLES DE IMÁGENES PROVENIENTES DEL LIBRO:

Pág. 96:	**MARC LAFIA:** LOREN EISELY #20 (2023)
Pág. 99:	LOREN EISELY #16 (2023)
Pág. 98:	**MAGDALENA RANGEL:** PANDORA'S GIFT #3-color-4 (detalle) (2023) Véase también: Pág. 8.
Pág. 100:	**MIMI ABERS:** BACK (detalle) (2007) Véase también: Pág. 22.
Pág. 101:	**NURIA ROMÁN:** DE SUR A NORTE (detalle) (2001) Véase también: Pág. 48.
Pág. 102:	**MAGDALENA RANGEL:** IO MASCULLA ¿YO TAMBIÉN? #50. Inglés #48 (detalles) (2023) Véase también: Pág. 12.
Pág. 103:	**ITAMAR MARTÍNEZ:** HOMBRE HERIDO (detalle) (2019) Véase también: Pág. 54.
Pág. 104:	**ROLANDO PEÑA:** OUR DAILY DRACULA (detalle) (2022) Véase también: Pág. 80.
Pág. 105:	**NURIA ROMÁN:** COSER LA TIERRA: LITHICA (detalle) (2013) Véase también 17: Pág. 48.
Pág. 106:	**ANDRÉS SALAZAR:** RECETA TECNOVISUAL PARA GUISAR PATRAÑA (detalle) (2022) Véase: Pág. 60

LOS ARTISTAS

Mimi Abers

PETRIFICADO

BACK (2007)
Arcilla cocida al horno.
69 x 43 x 38 cm. Pág. 22.

BENT OVER (2008)
Arcilla cocida al horno.
58 x 36 x 33 cm. Pág. 25.

OUT OF MIND (2009)
Vidrio. 36 x 18 x 15 cm. Pág. 31.

Fotografías por Mimi Abers.

Mimi Abers se apasiona por su arte, el cual usa como su permanente interacción entre la luz, las sombras, la textura, y la oscuridad. Dice de su obra: "Recibí mi diploma de Maestría en Arte en escultura a finales de los años 70, trabajando la arcilla y el metal. Con frecuencia mezclo otros medios con la arcilla y cuando comencé a explorar el vidrio, a principios de los 90, combiné la arcilla con el vidrio y todavía lo hago. Para mi trabajo en vidrio comienzo con un molde en arcilla que lleno de vidrio para cocerlo en el horno. Mi trabajo refleja mis demonios personales: temor a la edad; sentimientos de constricción o dolor; sentimientos de incapacidad o incomodidad por mis limitaciones o algún tonto arrepentimiento. Escojo arcilla como medio primario porque estoy enamorada de su textura, y la arcilla es un material que nunca se detiene". Un artículo en *Stanford Magazine* describe a su obra como un estudio en texturas. Texturas de "vidrio raro" y arcilla, dispersas en el piso de su atelier, incorporando experiencias táctiles.

Para Abers, su exitosa carrera como Artista Compositora de Efectos Visuales Especiales (VFX) en Industrial Light & Magic (la aclamada empresa de George Lucas) era el trabajo de diario que le permitía enfocarse sobre su verdadera pasión, la escultura. Su entusiasmo por el descubrimiento la condujo a explorar orangutanes, aves exóticas y otras experiencias sensoriales de la naturaleza alrededor del mundo para inspirar su alma y su arte.

Durante casi veinte años fue miembro de una colectiva de artistas llamada **Gallery Route One**, donde participó en numerosas exposiciones, incluyendo una dedicada al múltiple uso y sensación de manos tocando. Su obra ha sido presentada en varias exposiciones calificadas por jurados en el área de la Bahía de San Francisco, donde vive. Su sitio web es ***mimiaberssculpture.com***

Una imagen parcial de la escultura de Mimi Abers "BACK" (2007)) ha sido incluida en el arte de la tapa del libro.

Annika Connor

LA BURBUJA

WOLF PACK (2022)
Acuarela sobre madera.
76 x 102 cm. Pág. 36.

ÉRASE UNA VEZ...

BECAUSE OF YOU (2022)
Óleo sobre lienzo.
30 x 130 cm. Pág. 88.

Annika Connor se describe como artista del romanticismo contemporáneo y mujer renacentista para los tiempos modernos, integrando y promoviendo su visión artística en un amplio campo de actividades e intereses. Se le conoce principalmente por sus acuarelas y óleos donde, con fuerte simbología y apasionada imaginación, ilustra su exploración de la estética femenina y el rango que abarca la imaginación encendida por la belleza. Sus herramientas son la precisión, el detalle y la alegoría, usadas como ganchos que atrapan el ojo del observador al mismo tiempo que destacan imágenes que encienden narrativas frecuentemente misteriosas.

Es defensora vehemente de la igualdad de género, utilizando sus pinturas para explorar temas que van desde lo político, hasta la belleza y la naturaleza, al mismo tiempo que plasma temas acerca de la identidad femenina. Como artista/activista, Connor está muy involucrada con su apoyo a la comunidad artística dentro de la cual crea. Es propietaria/presidente de **Active Ideas Productions**, una organización con la misión de servir a la comunidad artística facilitando la presencia y publicación de jóvenes artistas talentosos, y difundiendo al público sus obras. Sus propias obras y las de los artistas que ella patrocina se presentan en su libro, *Point Suite Contemporary Art*, disponible en Amazon. También es miembro del sindicato de actores SAG/AFTRA y guionista, una habilidad adicional utilizada para transmitir su visión artística.

Connor es dueña de **Annika's Art Shop**, una boutique en línea para ropa creativa, accesorios, artículos para el hogar y regalos, destacando el arte de Annika Connor. Todos los artículos en la tienda son producidos con fabricación ética, y hechos en los Estados Unidos y Canadá. Su sitio web es *annikaconnor.com*.

Marc Lafia

EPÍLOGO

LOREN EISELY #20 (2023)
Pintura digital. 106.5 x 145 cm. Pág. 96.

LOREN EISELY #16 (detalle) (2023)
Pintura digital. 106.5 x 145 cm. Pág. 99.

Marc Lafia es un artista y cineasta estadounidense cuyo trabajo emerge con la cultura de las redes a medida que cambia nuestra relación con el conocimiento, con nosotros mismos, con nuestros recuerdos y con nuestros cuerpos, de una relación de representación a una de presentación, y de la contemplación de nuevos modos de encarnación, produciendo nuevas subjetividades y nuevas formas de estar en el mundo.

Su obra ha sido expuesta en el Walker Art Center, la galería Tate Online, ZKM, el Centre Pompidou, Anthology Film Archives, el Festival Internacional de Cine de Rotterdam, el Museo Minsheng, Shanghai, y la 8ª Bienal de Escultura de Shenzhen. Fue aclamado por su exposición interactiva en el Whitney Museum of American Art titulada **PROGRAMADO: REGLAS, CÓDIGOS Y COREOGRAFÍAS EN EL ARTE, 1965–2018** y, más recientemente en la Trienal de Guangzhou, 2023.

El trabajo de instalación y performance más reciente del Sr. Lafia, **EVERYTHING IS EVERYTHING AND THERE IS NOTHING ELSE**, compuesto a lo largo de 5 años, consta de cinco poemas largos en prosa hablados y musicalizados. Este logro ha sido llamado una obra maestra por su caos delicadamente equilibrado y su intento de mostrar la belleza desordenada del "todo" de la vida.

Ha sido docente en la Universidad de Stanford, el Instituto de Arte de San Francisco, el Art Center College of Design de Pasadena, el Pratt Institute, y la Universidad de Columbia. Es autor de *Image Photograph* (2015), *Everyday Cinema* (2017) y *The Event of Art* (2020), todos publicados por **Punctum Books**.
Su página web es *cargocollective.com/marclafia*.

Itamar Martínez

RENOVADO

UNTITLED (CRONOS DEVORA A SUS HIJOS)
(2022) Carbón y Acuarela sobre papel.
38 x 25 cm. Pág. 2.

UNTITLED (ZEUS, HIJO DE CRONOS Y REA)
(2022) Carbón y Acuarela sobre papel.
38 x 25 cm. Pág. 4.

UNTITLED (RETRATO DE PHEME)
(2022) Carbón y Acuarela sobre papel.
38 x 25 cm. Pág. 5.

EL MONSTRUO

HOMBRE HERIDO (2019)
Óleo sobre madera.
38 x 25 cm. Pág. 54.

UNTITLED (2022)
Tinta y acrílico sobre papel.
 38 x 25 cm. Pág.

Itamar Martínez es un artista plástico cuya experimentación artística temprana incluye videos, poesía visual, arte de correo, así como arte conceptual y de performance. Desde 1980 se ha dedicado exclusivamente a la pintura como medio para su visión artística. Ha realizado múltiples montajes individuales en Caracas y Londres, y participado en exhibiciones colectivas curadas en Londres, Berlín, Tokio, París, Río de Janeiro, Copenhague, Madrid, México y Nueva York. IKEA ha incluido obras de Itamar como parte de sus gráficas a la venta con más de 350,000 vendidas. Su obra está incluida en la colección permanente del Museo de Arte Moderno en Nueva York y del Palacio de Bellas Artes, en Santo Domingo.

Sus estudios desde temprana edad incluyen prestigiosas escuelas de arte en su país natal, historia del arte en la Universidad Central de Venezuela (UCV), dirección de cine en el Instituto Jean Lukas Caragiale de Cine y Teatro de la Universidad de Bucarest, para la cual los gobiernos de Rumania y de Venezuela le otorgaron una beca, y artes visuales en el Royal College of Art, en Londres, Inglaterra. Fue jefe del Departamento de Educación y asistente del jefe de coordinación de exhibiciones de bellas artes en el Museo de Bellas Artes en Caracas, Venezuela.

Un prolífico productor de arte, Itamar dice: "La vida es un laberinto de obras, solo por ellas me conocerás". Itamar administra su atelier y espacio para exhibiciones, **The Yellow Chair Gallery** en Reading, Reino Unido, donde reside.

José Rafael Páez

COPIA, COPIÓN, TE LO DICE SIMPLÓN

EVOLUCIÓN ZOMBI (2023)

Representación de personajes
y lugares para relato gráfico.
Marcadores de color, tinta y guache
sobre papel. Tamaños varios.
Págs. 64-77.

José Rafael Páez dedica su experticia profesional y naturaleza creativa al diseño de experiencias que aumentan la facilidad de uso y captación de productos e ideas, logrando su puesto en el mundo corporativo de los EE.UU. con la facilitación de estrategias de diseño visual. Combina sus antecedentes académicos y de negocios con su estudio de varios campos y formas artísticas, utilizando todos los medios, desde la pintura, el boceto, la poesía, el vitral, y la carpintería hasta el dibujo digital para explorar los sentidos y la percepción, desde la presencia física tangible hasta la imagen conceptual efímera.

José tiene título de *Masters in Design Management* de la Savannah College of Art and Design, y es egresado en negocios internacionales y administración de la Florida International University. Para destacarse en el rápido mundo corporativo del país, busca fusionar su carrera profesional con su profunda pasión por la creación visual. Para lograrlo, usa su habilidad en la creación de obras que trascienden el límite de lo convencional, explorando áreas en amalgamas del surrealismo y el pop-art, para aterrizar sus visiones imaginativas en la vida práctica.

El talento y las pasiones de José han hallado su lugar dentro del mundo empresarial, pero su compromiso firme en el apoyo de sus compañeros creativos se mantiene como el centro de su trayectoria artística. Desde su cargo en una importante empresa informática agrega capas visuales con su arte para destacar a nuevos escritores resaltados en la revista cultural de la empresa. Con cineastas locales en Austin, Texas, donde reside, ha colaborado en tormentas de ideas sobre bocetos de escenas para ayudarlos a plasmar sus visiones. Su dedicación y contribución desinteresada a la gran comunidad artística no solo nutre los sueños de aspirantes al arte, sino que añade un toque de creatividad vibrante al mundo que lo rodea.

Rolando Peña

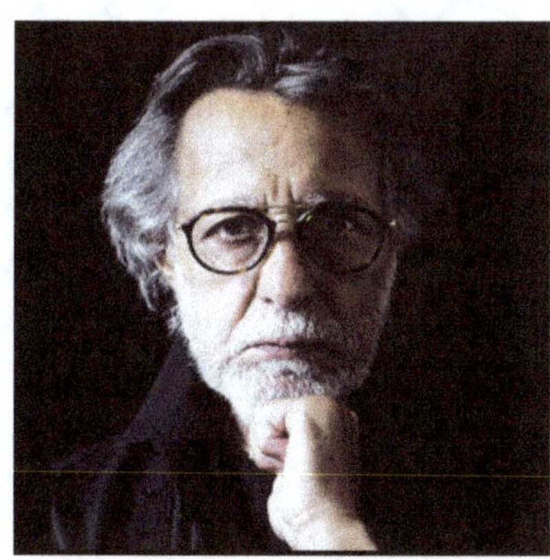

PUREZA

OUR DAILY DRACULA (2022)
Photomatón/multimedia.
19 x 27 cm. Pág. 80.

Rolando Peña es uno de los artistas latinoamericanos más destacados de los siglos XX y XXI. Su larga e ininterrumpida carrera internacional se ha caracterizado por buscar la innovación, el diálogo con conceptos fundamentales de nuestro tiempo, y como pionero en el uso de la tecnología en el arte.

Su rica carrera artística lo ha llevado a participar en importantes olas universales de creatividad a lo largo de su vida. Comenzó su carrera combinando su formación en danza y arquitectura con "happenings" en la escena Avant Garde de Nueva York en los años 60. En aquel momento colaboró con figuras como Allen Ginsberg, Timothy Leary y Andy Warhol, en **The Factory**.

A partir de 1980 inicia el desarrollo de su obra densa, continua y crítica sobre el tema del petróleo en sus diferentes manifestaciones como factor de ilusión económica y de poder. A través de esta línea de trabajo, abarcando dibujos, grabados, fotografías, películas, videos, performances y esculturas en el espacio público, estableció una posición político-ecológica de primer orden, pionera en los desafíos de este siglo. Su trabajo en esta área le valió una beca Guggenheim en 2009. Más recientemente es destacado en el libro *Material Refinado* por Sean Nesselrode Moncada (2023), el cual explora la integración entre la industria petrolera global y la ascendencia en las artes de la abstracción geométrica, el arte cinético, y la arquitectura moderna de la segunda mitad del S. XX en Venezuela.

Su búsqueda de vínculos entre el arte, la ciencia y la tecnología lo han llevado a experimentar con las ideas más vanguardistas de la física. Dice que su legado en el arte es convertir la vida en el poema del infinito. Rolando Peña ha presentado su obra desde 1963 en múltiples museos y galerías de USA, España, Francia, Alemania y Venezuela, y participó en la Bienal de Venecia de 2008. Una nueva antología de su obra, *Bienvenidos a mi mundo del arte*, fue publicada en 2022 y está disponible a través de Amazon. Reside en Madrid, España.

Su serie PHOTOMATONS, la cual comenzó en 1960 y de la cual forma parte su ilustración en este libro, continúa hasta el día de hoy. Su página web es *rolandoart.work*.

Magdalena Rangel

TOCANDO FONDO

EL REGALO DE PANDORA #3-COLOR-04
(2022) Pintura Digital con iPad Pro.
25.4 X 17.78 cm. Pág. 8.

ÍO MASCULLA

IO MASCULLA, ¿YO TAMBIÉN? #50
(2022) Pintura Digital con iPad Pro.
25.4 X 35.56 cm. Págs. 12, 13.

Diseño y diagramación del presente libro y su portada.

Magdalena Rangel durante décadas ha sido creadora de imágenes artísticas generadas con asistencia de computadoras. En las artes, sus intereses se han centrado en la exploración de la naturaleza dinámica de la vida. Su profesión la ha llevado a participar en numerosos proyectos, incluyendo créditos animados para películas y diseños gráficos en el mundo de cine y aeroespacial de Los Ángeles, con clientes como Paramount, Touchstone Pictures, Polygram Pictures, Propaganda Films, CSI, Virgin Records, Hughes Aircraft, JPL, Northrop y muchos más. Fue miembro del colectivo de cine independiente **Oasis**.

En Seattle fue asesora de arte para Starwave (una empresa tecnológica establecida por Paul Allen, el co-fundador the Microsoft, con misión de desarrollar banda ancha durante su incepción). Proyectos incluyeron una adventura interactiva en música y arte, llamada *EVE*, con el músico Peter Gabriel. El projecto fue galardonado con el Milla D'Or Grand Prix, en Cannes. Anteriormente, Magdalena recibió el premio para el mejor cine animado experimental en el festival de cine de Montpallier, en Francia, y en el Festival International de Cine de Houston por su película *House Taken Over (Casa tomada)*, basada en un cuento de Julio Cortázar.

Magdalena cursó estudios en la Escuela de Artes Visuales the Nueva York, La Academia de Arte y Diseño Otis-Parsons (BA en Dibujo & Pintura) y la Escuela de Cine de la Universidad de California, Los Angeles (MA en Artes Cinemáticas, UCLA). Fue profesora de Animación en la Escuela de Cine de UCLA, y en la Extensión Profesional de UCLA. Montó talleres de animación para niños en LACMA (Museo de Arte del Condado de Los Ángeles).

Desde su estudio, **JumpAngel dEsign**, en Santa Cruz, California, Magdalena desarrolla su actividad creativa diseñando sitios web, haciendo ilustraciones y generando animaciones, entre otros proyectos. En 2022 publicó su libro *Young Heart Menagerie (Bestiario de un corazón joven)* bajo su propia editorial JumpAngel Press. Recientemente lanzó su nuevo sello editorial llamado **Relatos de Tierra Firme** (*relatosdetierrafirme.com*) con la missión de desarrollar y publicar obras creativas entrelasadas con las historias de la América de Sur. Anteriormente colaboró con Carlos J. Rangel en el diseño de la portada e ilustraciones para su libro de 2017, *La Venezuela imposible: Crónicas y reflexiones sobre democracia y libertad.* El sitio web de Magdalena Rangel es *jumpangelcom*.

Una imagen parcial de la pintura digital de Magdalena Rangel "EL LAMENTO DE ÍO #50" (2023) ha sido incluida en el arte de la tapa del libro.

Nuria Román

VIENE DE VUELTA

DE SUR A NORTE (2001)
Materiales mixtos sobre madera.
130 x130 cm. Pág. 48.

COSER LA TIERRA: LITHICA (2013)
Arte Conceptual. Cuerda sobre piedra.
Altura: 30 mts. Pág. 50.

*Materiales donados por la comunidad. Véase
el proyecto en COSIR LA TERRA Latitud 40° –
(vimeo.com/49245006).*

Mediante su arte, **Nuria Román** explora diversos temas tales como la relación de la mujer con el mundo; la búsqueda de nuevas soluciones a los problemas que aquejan al mundo; la relación norte-sur; la tierra como lugar de acogida y como espacio roto; la necesidad de crear puentes y de "coser la tierra".

Su obra ha sido expuesta en París, Nueva York y varias ciudades de España. También ha curado varias muestras colectivas, entre ellas la destacada **ON SON LES GIFTS? LA ILLUSIÓ** en el Museo de Menorca, 2015, un análisis de cómo los artistas masculinos han representado a las mujeres a lo largo de la historia.

LITHICA es parte del proyecto **LATITUD 40° - COSER LA TIERRA. L40°** es un proyecto artístico ideado por Román que propone restaurar las fracturas que el hombre ha generado a lo largo del tiempo, al unir con instalaciones artísticas diferentes puntos por los cuales el paralelo 40° N. le da la vuelta al mundo. Ha promocionado, presentado y desplegado este proyecto en varios lugares a nivel internacional con trabajos y colaboraciones en España, Italia y Estados Unidos.

Desde el año 2016 dirige la galería de arte **LOCAL-Nuria Román**, en Maó, la cual describe como un lugar para el encuentro y presencia de artistas locales en Menorca. Su sitio web es *nuriaroman.com*.

Andrés Salazar

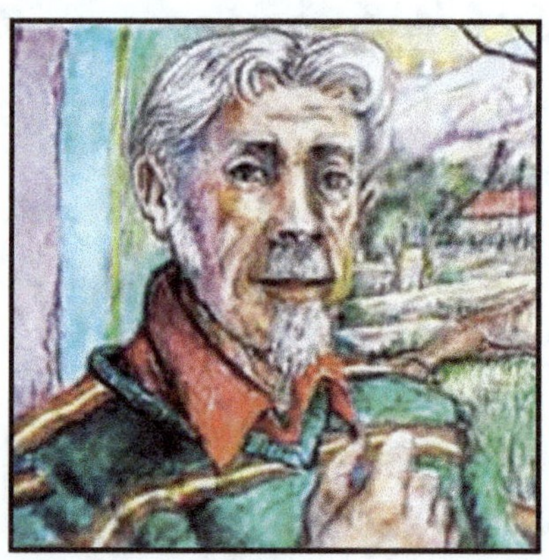

LA BURBUJA

ESCALAS, SUBES Y BAJAS DE LO INCONMENSURABLE (2022)
Acrílico sobre papiro soñador.
32 x 24 cm. Pág. 34.

SE ESTÁ COCINANDO

RECETA TECNOVISUAL PARA GUISO DE PATRAÑA (2022)
Nature mort. Fotografía Digital.
27 x 18 cm. Pág. 60.

"No pocas veces nuestra mente juega a sorprendernos, ocurre en duermevelas y sueños. Para visibilizar esos estados casi mágicos, necesitamos recurrir al collage, fotográfico o pictórico, como en esta pieza que bordea la patafísica." Andrés Salazar.

Andrés Salazar inició su trayectoria artística autodidacta desde temprana edad, absorbiendo de su entorno la gran vocación. Es por esa razón que se adentra con pasión en múltiples campos de su quehacer con notable éxito, incluyendo la pintura, el diseño gráfico, la publicidad, la escenografía, el diseño de murales, la escultura y la fotografía. Por su amplio rango artístico, fue seleccionado como miembro fundador del Taller de Arte Experimental del INCIBA, Instituto Nacional de Cultura y Bellas Artes, la más alta institución de su tipo a nivel nacional en Venezuela.

Su enfoque ecléctico le lleva a ser exitoso en el campo del diseño gráfico, diseñando logotipos y marcas para productos de amplia difusión en su país, incluyendo comestibles, sellos disqueros, farmacéuticos, etc., y como ilustrador de libros infantiles por renombrados autores nacionales. Tras ser invitado a gran cantidad de Salones de Arte Nacionales fue incluido en la colección permanente del MACCSI, el Museo de Arte Contemporáneo de Caracas Sofía Imber, que en su tiempo fuera uno de los más prestigiosos de Latinoamérica. Su trayectoria artística se destaca en el libro *La búsqueda infinita*, por Agatha de la Fuente y Rubén Monasterios.

Reseñas críticas de Salazar incluyen: "Digamos que en Salazar [sus] lenguajes se interconectan y toman una suerte de todo segmentado donde cada fragmento tiene un valor simbólico independiente, que a la vez puede estar en rotación permanente por las diferentes fases del tramado plástico"; "...[en Salazar encontramos] la firme voluntad de transformar una cantidad considerable de elementos, donde se advierte la presencia de técnicas, recursos, formas y texturas en expresiones propias de su gran versatilidad y pasión creadora".

Authorizaciones
DE MUSEOS Y GALERÍAS:

PREFACIO Págs. XVI, XVIII:

FRANCISCO DE GOYA Y LUCIENTES: *EL SUEÑO DE LA RAZÓN PRODUCE MONSTRUOS, CAPRICHOS #43* (1797-1799) Aguafuerte, aguatinta sobre papel verjurado, 306 x 201 mm / lámina 213 x 151 mm (Cat. G2131). © Archivo Fotográfico Museo Nacional del Prado. Reproducción e imagen usadas con autorización del Museo Nacional del Prado, Madrid.

TIRANÍA Págs. 16, 18:

PEDRO PABLO RUBENS y FRANS SNYDERS: *PROMETEO ENCADENADO* (1611-12, 1618) Óleo sobre lienzo, 242,6 x 209,6 cm. Adquirido por el MAF mediante el fondo W.P. Wilstatch, 1950. (Acc. W1950-3-1). Fotografía por Alberto Otero Herranz, cortesía del Museo del Prado, 2015. La reproducción e imágenes se usan con autorización del Museo de Arte de Filadelfia.

PETRIFICADO Pág. 30:

CARAVAGGIO: *ESCUDO CON LA CABEZA DE MEDUSA* (1597) Óleo sobre tela montado sobre madera, 60 x 55 cm. (Inv. 1890 n. 1351). Reproducción usada con permiso de las Gallerie degli Uffizi, Florencia, Ministerio de la Cultura.

BELLEZA Págs. 40, 42, 44:

SANDRO BOTTICELLI: *EL NACIMIENTO DE VENUS* (C. 1485) Témpera sobre tela, 172.5 x 278.5 cm. (Inv. 1890 n. 878). La reproducción e imágenes se usan con autorización del Museo de las Gallerie degli Uffizi, Florencia, Ministerio de la Cultura.

SE ESTÁ COCINANDO Págs. 60, 62:

CARAVAGGIO: *ESCUDO CON LA CABEZA DE MEDUSA* (1597) Óleo sobre tela montado sobre madera, 60 x 55 cm. (Inv. 1890 n. 1351). Imagen usada con permiso de las Gallerie degli Uffizi, Florencia, Ministerio de la Cultura. La imagen de Quetzalcóatl es del libro *Enciclopedia de la Mitología,* Editorial Libsa, 2015.

Carlos J. Rangel

Foto: © Wenceslao Cruz Blanco.

LIBROS PREVIOS:

***CAMPAIGN JOURNAL 2008:** A Chronicle Of Vision, Hope, And Glory* (2009)
Transaction Publishers, New Brunswick.

***LA VENEZUELA IMPOSIBLE:** Crónicas y reflexiones sobre democracia y libertad* (2017)
Alexandria Library, Miami.

Este es el tercer libro de **Carlos J. Rangel.** El primero, *Campaign Journal 2008: A Chronicle of Vision, Hope, and Glory.* (Transaction Publishers, New Brunswick, 2009), es acerca de la insurgente y exitosa campaña presidencial de Barack Obama. El libro fue caracterizado por el Chairman y Director de la casa editorial de la Universidad Rutgers, en New Jersey, Dr. Irving Horowitz, como muchísimo mejor que los otros dos reseñados por el New York Times en su momento sobre el mismo tema. Entre los muchos comentarios favorables recibidos acerca de este libro, uno fue por el expresidente Jimmy Carter: "....un bienvenido aporte a mi colección y con aprecio por recordarme de manera tan ponderada".

Su segundo libro se titula La Venezuela imposible: Crónicas y reflexiones sobre democracia y libertad. (Alexandria Library, Miami, 2017). Este libro explora en dos secciones los eventos y la situación en Venezuela al momento de ser escrito, 2012-2017, (pero incluyendo correspodencia y un ensayo editorial publicado en 1992 para establecer contexto), y el entramado estructural que creó esa situación; un entramado político y cultural que afecta el país hasta el día de hoy.

Cuando fue publicado, La Venezuela imposible, estuvo entre los títulos más vendidos dentro de su categoría temática en Amazon y mantiene sus ventas al día de hoy. Resalta entre los comentarios recibidos uno por el destacado intelectual Carlos Alberto Montaner, que lo describe "valioso, escrito con claridad y sin pasiones estériles".

Como analista político y estratégico colaboró en un papel de trabajo titulado: *Que caiga el martillo: desde los bandidos en la ruta de la seda hasta los estados irregulares, el surgimiento del Crimen Transnacional Organizado (CTO) y lo que el mundo puede hacer al respecto* (conjuntamente con Beatrice Rangel y Mateo Haydar), para el **Interamerican Institute for Democracy (IID),** un *think tank* de democracia liberal basado en Miami.

Carlos J. Rangel fue editor de las nuevas ediciones en-linea publicadas por **CEDICE Libertad** de los tres libros más importantes de su padre, el analista político Carlos Rangel. CEDICE Libertad es un centro de estudios enfocado sobre temas de democracia liberal y basado en Caracas, Venezuela. Rangel también ha sido instrumental en la publicación de nuevas ediciones de estos libros en Brasil, Italia y Chile.

Rangel se graduó de arquitecto del Pratt Institute en Nueva York, y de la Universidad Central de Venezuela, UCV, en Caracas, donde ejerció su profesión durante muchos años. Obtuvo su Master en Administración del Instituto de Estudios Superiores de Administración, IESA, en programa conjunto con la Escuela Andersen de Negocios de la Universidad de California en Los Ángeles, UCLA, y tiene Certificado Profesional en el Programa de Planificación Estratégica en la Industria de Entretenimiento, también de UCLA.

Un enlace para el presente libro, incluyendo donde comprarlo se puede encontrar en el Blogspot de Rangel: *mythsofourhumanity.com*

X-Twitter: @CarlosJRangel1   Threads: cjrangel712   www.carlosjrangel.com